A HAVEN
FOR THE
WANDERER

Praise for Jenny Frame

Longing for You

"Jenny Frame knocks it out of the park once again with this fantastic sequel to *Hunger For You*. She can keep the pages turning with a delicious mix of intrigue and romance."—*Rainbow Literary Society*

Hunger for You

"I loved this book. Paranormal stuff like vampires and werewolves are my go-to sins. This book had literally everything I needed: chemistry between the leads, hot love scenes (phew), drama, angst, romance (oh my, the romance) and strong supporting characters."—*The Reading Doc*

The Duchess and the Dreamer

"We thoroughly enjoyed the whole romance-the-disbelieving-duchess with gallantry, unwavering care, and grand gestures. Since this is very firmly in the butch-femme zone, it appealed to that part of our traditionally-conditioned-typecasting mindset that all the wooing and work is done by Evan without throwing even a small fit at any point. We liked the fact that Clementine has layers and depth. She has her own personal and personality hurdles that make her behaviour understandable and create the right opportunities for Evan to play the romantic knight convincingly…We definitely recommend this one to anyone looking for a feel-good mushy romance."—*Best Lesfic Reviews*

"There are a whole range of things I like about Jenny Frame's aristocratic heroines: they have plausible histories to account for them holding titles in their own right; they're in touch with reality and not necessarily super-rich, certainly not through inheritance; and they find themselves paired with perfectly contrasting co-heroines…Clementine and Evan are excellently depicted, and I love the butch:femme dynamic they have going on, as well as their individual abilities to stick to their principles but also to compromise with each other when necessary."
—*The Good, The Bad and The Unread*

Still Not Over You

"*Still Not Over You* is a wonderful second-chance romance anthology that makes you believe in love again. And you would certainly be missing out if you have not read *My Forever Girl*, because it truly is everything."—*SymRoute*

Someone to Love

"One of the author's best works to date—both Trent and Wendy were so well developed they came alive. I could really picture them and they jumped off the pages. They had fantastic chemistry, and their sexual dynamic was deliciously well written. The supporting characters and the storyline about Alice's trauma was also sensitively written and well handled."—*Melina Bickard, Librarian, Waterloo Library (UK)*

Wooing the Farmer

"The chemistry between the two MCs had us hooked right away. We also absolutely loved the seemingly ditzy femme with an ambition of steel but really a vulnerable girl. The sex scenes are great. Definitely recommended."—*Reviewer@large*

"This is the book we Axedale fanatics have been waiting for…Jenny Frame writes the most amazing characters and this whole series is a masterpiece. But where she excels is in writing butch lesbians. Every time I read a Jenny Frame book I think it's the best ever, but time and again she surprises me. She has surpassed herself with *Wooing the Farmer*."—*Kitty Kat's Book Review Blog*

Royal Court

"The author creates two very relatable characters…Quincy's quietude and mental torture are offset by Holly's openness and lust for life. Holly's determination and tenacity in trying to reach Quincy are total wish-fulfilment of a person like that. The chemistry and attraction is excellently built."—*Best Lesbian Erotica*

"[A] butch/femme romance that packs a punch."—*Les Rêveur*

"There were unbelievably hot sex scenes as I have come to expect and look forward to in Jenny Frame's books. Passions slowly rise until you feel the characters may burst!…Royal Court is wonderful and I highly recommend it."—*Kitty Kat's Book Review Blog*

Royal Court "was a fun, light-hearted book with a very endearing romance."—*Leanne Chew, Librarian, Parnell Library (Auckland, NZ)*

Charming the Vicar

"Chances are, you've never read or become captivated by a romance like *Charming the Vicar*. While books featuring people of the cloth aren't unusual, Bridget is no ordinary vicar—a lesbian with a history of kink...Surrounded by mostly supportive villagers, Bridget and Finn balance love and faith in a story that affirms both can exist for anyone, regardless of sexual identity."—*RT Book Reviews*

"The sex scenes were some of the sexiest, most intimate and quite frankly, sensual I have read in a while. Jenny Frame had me hooked and I reread a few scenes because I felt like I needed to experience the intense intimacy between Finn and Bridget again. The devotion they showed to one another during these sex scenes but also in the intimate moments was gripping and for lack of a better word, carnal."—*Les Rêveur*

"The sexual chemistry between [Finn and Bridge] is unbelievably hot. It is sexy, lustful and with more than a hint of kink. The scenes between them are highly erotic—and not just the sex scenes. The tension is ramped up so well that I felt the characters would explode if they did not get relief!...An excellent book set in the most wonderful village—a place I hope to return to very soon!"—*Kitty Kat's Book Reviews*

"This is Frame's best character work to date. They are layered and flawed and yet relatable...Frame really pushed herself with *Charming the Vicar* and it totally paid off...I also appreciate that even though she regularly writes butch/femme characters, no two pairings are the same."—*The Lesbian Review*

Unexpected

"If you enjoy contemporary romances, *Unexpected* is a great choice. The character work is excellent, the plotting and pacing are well done, and it's just a sweet, warm read...Definitely pick this book up when you're looking for your next comfort read, because it's sure to put a smile on your face by the time you get to that happy ending."—*Curve*

"*Unexpected* by Jenny Frame is a charming butch/femme romance that is perfect for anyone who wants to feel the magic of overcoming adversity and finding true love. I love the way Jenny Frame writes.

I have yet to discover an author who writes like her. Her voice is strong and unique and gives a freshness to the lesbian fiction sector."
—*The Lesbian Review*

Royal Rebel

"Frame's stories are easy to follow and really engaging. She stands head and shoulders above a number of the romance authors and it's easy to see why she is quickly making a name for herself in lesfic romance."—*The Lesbian Review*

Courting the Countess

"I love Frame's romances. They are well paced, filled with beautiful character moments and a wonderful set of side characters who ultimately end up winning your heart...I love Jenny Frame's butch/femme dynamic; she gets it so right for a romance."—*The Lesbian Review*

"I loved, loved, loved this book. I didn't expect to get so involved in the story but I couldn't help but fall in love with Annie and Harry...The love scenes were beautifully written and very sexy. I found the whole book romantic and ultimately joyful and I had a lump in my throat on more than one occasion. A wonderful book that certainly stirred my emotions."—*Kitty Kat's Book Reviews*

"*Courting The Countess* has an historical feel in a present day world, a thought provoking tale filled with raw emotions throughout. [Frame] has a magical way of pulling you in, making you feel every emotion her characters experience."—*Lunar Rainbow Reviewz*

"I didn't want to put the book down and I didn't. Harry and Annie are two amazingly written characters that bring life to the pages as they find love and adventures in Harry's home. This is a great read, and you will enjoy it immensely if you give it a try!"—*Fantastic Book Reviews*

A Royal Romance

"*A Royal Romance* was a guilty pleasure read for me. It was just fun to see the relationship develop between George and Bea, to see George's life as queen and Bea's as a commoner. It was also refreshing to see that both of their families were encouraging, even when Bea doubted that things could work between them because of their class differences...*A Royal Romance* left me wanting a sequel, and romances don't usually do that to me."—*Leeanna.ME Mostly a Book Blog*

By the Author

A Royal Romance

Courting the Countess

Dapper

Royal Rebel

Unexpected

Charming the Vicar

Royal Court

Wooing the Farmer

Someone to Love

The Duchess and the Dreamer

Royal Family

Home Is Where the Heart Is

Sweet Surprise

Royal Exposé

A Haven for the Wanderer

Wild for You

Hunger for You

Longing for You

Dying for You

Wolfgang County Series

Heart of the Pack

Soul of the Pack

Blood of the Pack

Visit us at www.boldstrokesbooks.com

A HAVEN
FOR THE
WANDERER

by

Jenny Frame

2022

ISBN 13: 978-1-63679-291-0

This Trade Paperback Original Is Published By
Bold Strokes Books, Inc.
P.O. Box 249
Valley Falls, NY 12185

First Edition: December 2022

CREDITS
EDITOR: RUTH STERNGLANTZ
PRODUCTION DESIGN: STACIA SEAMAN
COVER DESIGN BY TAMMY SEIDICK

Acknowledgments

Big thanks to Ruth for all of your help and patience. Thanks to all those at BSB who work hard to make our books the best they can be.

To Lou and Barney.
You are my safe haven.xx

Chapter One

"Thanks, mate."

Griffin Harris jumped off the bus that brought her within a mile of Rosebrook village. She lifted her large rucksack onto her back and started the walk to the edge of the village. Griffin could have stayed on to the next stop, but she wanted to draw out the time before she got to Rosebrook. She wanted some more time to be on her own.

Ahead of her stretched the open country roads of Dorset, in the southwest of England. If she followed her heart, Griffin would just keep walking, wandering along the coastline, ending up who knew where.

But she had an obligation to fulfil to a good friend, so Rosebrook was where she would be staying, for a while at least.

It was a cold October day. There was a white frost over the hedgerows and grass verges. Dorset's weather was generally mild compared to many parts of the country, but this year the weather experts said it might be unusually cold. Griffin's friend, ardent environmentalist Evan Fox, would say it's another sign that the climate was way out of whack.

She walked on slowly, trying to draw out the time before she met the high road that led down into the village. When Griffin arrived at the top of the high road, she stopped.

Griffin looked down to her left into Rosebrook, and then to the right back along the coastal road, where she could wander until maybe her head and heart could make sense of the world again.

But she couldn't let her friend down and so turned left and started the walk down the road which eventually led to the village. On the right hand side of the road the trees started to thicken into a forested area.

This was one of her favourite places to go when village life got a bit restrictive.

Before Griffin knew it, her legs were carrying her over there. There was time for extra solitude before the world wanted her again. She made her way through the trees and eventually found her little clearing.

It still had the remnants of the stone circle she used to enclose a fire, and the area marked out with string where she had intended to build a tiny cabin. When she had intended to stay in Rosebrook for some time, she'd needed to find an outlet for the need for freedom that only the outdoors could bring. Clementine—the Duchess of Rosebrook—and Evan gave her permission to use this area of the woods as a camp, and a place to build a tiny cabin or shelter.

She had just started marking out the area and taking delivery of the wood and supplies to build her new project when she got the call that her mum had a heart attack. Griffin had dropped everything and gone to her. Little had Griffin known that the time she spent caring for her mum would open up some old wounds that would tear them apart.

Griffin put her bag on the ground beside the stone circle and sat on the log she had placed beside it when she first came here. She took a breath and closed her eyes, tried to quieten out the noise of her mind.

Even under normal circumstances, city life got too much for Griffin before long, but this time had been even harder. Griffin and her mother had a complicated relationship at the best of times, but two months of rehab had brought out new revelations that Griffin didn't know how to process.

As her mind started to dwell on them again, she decided to make a fire and stay out here for a while. The making of a fire and sitting by one always soothed Griffin's mind.

Bronte de Lacey zipped up her holdall and laid it by the front door of her flat.

"Bronte, listen to me."

She was followed around her flat by her mother, the fierce matriarch of the de Lacey family, Matilda de Lacey, Baroness Lawton.

Bronte carried on with her final bits and pieces of packing in the living room to her flat. "I'm not listening because I've already heard what you've said, and I said no."

"But Bronte—" Her mother looked out of the living room window for what seemed like the fiftieth time since she'd arrived.

Bronte looked up. "I'm quite sure your Mercedes is safe, Mother."

"This isn't a good area. A de Lacey shouldn't be living here."

Bronte let out a big sigh. She was sick of this kind of comment. She sat on her couch and began to check that she had everything in her last rucksack.

"Mother, if the family is as broke as you say we are, then this is exactly where a de Lacey should be."

Her flat wasn't even in a bad neighbourhood, but it was beneath the snobbish Matilda de Lacey's dignity. The flat was Bronte's, and she was proud that it was bought outright, but as far as her mother knew it was rented.

Bronte's flat and Jeep parked outside were bought from a little pot of money her mother knew nothing about, a small inheritance left to her by a beloved uncle. Knowing Matilda de Lacey and the way she leapt on any money and ploughed it into the family seat, his lawyer arranged for it to be dealt with complete secrecy, and so Bronte did the same.

"De Laceys are never broke, Bronte. We are simply going through some fiscal difficulties, although how you managed to buy that hideous car outside, I'll never know. Those fiscal difficulties would be solved if you'd do what you were told once in your life and meet up with Antonia Carey."

Bronte gave a rueful laugh. "She's even more snobbish than you, Mother."

"I'm not snobbish—I simply know my position in life," her mother said.

"Above others."

"Of course. That's how the world works, Bronte. You have just never accepted it. Listen, just meet Antonia once. Her mother says she's had a crush on you since school, although God knows why."

Bronte rolled her eyes. "Thank you, Mother." She picked up her tie-dye headscarf and fixed her hair from falling in her face.

"I mean, look at your beautiful face, and your strawberry-blond hair. You have everything, and yet you insist on being knee deep in mud rescuing an injured wombat or something."

"Wombat? I think you have the wrong continent, Mother."

Bronte had been an animal lover all her life, and after university she trained as an animal rehabilitator. She worked at animal shelters and at wildlife sanctuaries all over the world, like the Serengeti National Park, plus spent many weekends protesting fox hunting parties in the English countryside.

"Well, whatever. Dicky Melville said you were on his land last month, disrupting a perfectly legal trail hunt."

"Yes, I was. You and I both know Dicky Melville does not trail hunt. It's a smokescreen for hunting foxes illegally," Bronte said.

"You see? This is why you don't get a husband or a wife."

Bronte shook her head in frustration. "*You see*, Mother, this is what gets to me. You weren't the nicest person to me when I came out. In fact you wanted me to marry a man for money and status, and told me to have a female lover on the side if I must."

"A sensible arrangement that has always been used by the aristocracy. Marriage is about what each person can bring to the relationship, so that they both become stronger as a family and more powerful."

Bronte wasn't even going to go down that road. They had argued about these issues most of her life.

"My point, Mother, is that when a few of your friends started having gay sons or daughters coming out, you saw the potential of an even greater marriage market and have been trying to set me up with women ever since."

"You said you were a lesbian, and I found well-bred or rich, or both, lesbians for you, and you haven't taken me up on one. Harry Knight, for example."

The Dowager Countess of Axedale, Harry Knight's mother, was in her mother's social circle, and she'd tried to match Bronte with her.

"Mother, Harry Knight had to fall deeply in love to ever settle down," Bronte said as she zipped up her bag.

"Love?"

"I know that's a foreign concept to you, Mother. But some of us—" Bronte corrected herself. "Some people do look for love."

Her mother crossed her arms defensively. "I suppose that's a dig at me?"

"No, Mother," Bronte said, but it was. Her mother had ruined her chance at long-lasting love, but today wasn't the time to go down that old road again. "I'm just pointing out that everyone isn't like you."

"No, they wouldn't have my luck. Marry a multimillionaire to fill the family coffers and have him lose it with one bad investment after another," her mother said with disdain.

Bronte hated to hear her mother talk about her dad that way. He was a sensitive man who had been swept away with love, only to find it lasted as far as his money did. This was another reason Bronte had to get away. The arguments that she could and did get into with her mother, over the years, were exhausting and only hurt Bronte. She had to get away, and this was her chance. A chance of a lifetime.

"I'm going, Mother, and I'm not going to meet with Antonia."

Bronte's heart still beat fast when she had to stand up to her mother. It hadn't come to her naturally, but she had learned over the years that to get the life she wanted, she had to force herself to be strong, or Matilda de Lacey would run right over her.

Her mother got up and started to pace in frustration. "We could lose Lawton House. Is that what you want? You're my oldest child, my heir. It's your duty to keep Lawton House going for the next generation."

"What I want is to live the life I want to live. I may be the oldest, but my sister has conformed. Jo Jo has the husband and kids to continue the line."

"And look where that has got us. Jocasta's husband was about as reliable as your father. I will not be the de Lacey who loses our ancestral home. Don't you want your own child to be baroness after you?"

Lawton House was one of the oldest mansions in London, and her mother was very proud of the fact. A former nunnery, taken off the order by Henry the VIII, it sat on the banks of the River Thames, was a beautiful place to grow up. When Bronte met new people and described her home, they rarely believed that such a green and pleasant estate existed in London, not far from Richmond train station.

As beautiful as it was, all Bronte ever saw in it was wasted money, hurt, arguments, and repression. Her mother was Captain Ahab and the house her own Moby Dick.

"Mother, I doubt I'm going to be in that kind of relationship in my life."

Love and broken hearts weren't something she was going to get into again. Maybe at one time she would have liked a partner and family, but now she knew her life was going to be dedicated to the animals she cared for.

"We've all tried to tell you the answer, Mother. Sell the house and grounds to the National Trust. They'll repair it to its former glory and let you and Dad stay for your lifetime."

Her mother gave her the steely, hard gaze, the one that, as a child, had frightened her into complying. "I will not be the de Lacey who loses our ancestral home to the National Trust so that old ladies and men can wander through and have a cup of tea and a cake in *my* summer house."

There was no reasoning with her. This new project had come to her at exactly the right time.

"For the last time, Mother, I'm going to Rosebrook village. Evan Fox has given me the chance of a lifetime, and I intend to take it."

"Evan Fox," her mother said, "yet another rich lesbian you should have tried to bag. If my two daughters can't make the hard choices, maybe I will have to."

"What is that supposed to mean?"

"Just as it sounds. I will need to rely on myself, it seems."

Bronte had heard enough. She grasped her last bag and walked to the door, and what she thought would be a new life.

CHAPTER TWO

Clementine Fitzroy grasped her handbag beside her as her Range Rover pulled up at the front of Fox Toys. All the cars in Evan Fox's fleet were electric, and this was no different.

"Thanks, Jared," Clementine said.

"No problem, Duchess."

Clementine had tried to get him and Fox's other staff to call her by her first name, but they found it hard. Jared was sweet. In his East End London accent, he made *Duchess* sound like a cool nickname.

"I'll take the car down to the charging point in the garage. Get her juiced up."

There was a large parking garage below the Fox Toys building that served as a parking area and charging point for the Fox Toys staff.

"I don't know how long we'll be, Jared."

"No problem. I'll be ready and waiting whenever you are."

Jared got out and opened the door for her. How much her life had changed since meeting Fox.

Before the love of her life came bouncing into her life like Tigger, Clementine was working as a freelance architect, trying to make ends meet while looking after her mother, the dowager duchess, and while her former ancestral home was being sold to yet another buyer. Her life had been falling apart around her. Then Fox came to Rosebrook and bought her former home, restoring it to its former glory and being annoyingly determined that Clementine should fall in love with her. Fall in love she did, and life went from dull grey to Technicolor in an instant. Clementine had been wary at first but was soon charmed by Fox's excitable nature.

She was greeted by the doorman at the entrance of Fox Toys. Johnny wasn't your average stiff, formal city doorman. Although he had served in the Queen's Guard, Johnny was zany, fun, and suited the Fox Toys mentality down to the ground.

He wore the colours of Fox Toys, a deep claret suit and waistcoat, with a white shirt plus a bow tie with amber coloured foxes on it. You could tell Evan Fox had designed this uniform.

"Hello, Your Grace," Johnny said with a big smile.

He might have been not your average stiff doorman, but his military background gave him his respect for titles.

"Good afternoon, Johnny. How's the world with you?"

"Beautiful. Just like your good self, ma'am," Johnny said as he opened the door for her.

Clementine smiled and felt the warmth of the welcome she got when she visited Fox at her office building. Fox had this unique knack of drawing the right kind of people to work with her, and it tended to create a happy staff.

She walked into the huge reception area and took a deep breath. For an office building it was so calm and tranquil. There was glass and natural light everywhere, plus trees, greenery, tropical plants, and you could hear the splash and gurgle made by the large fountain.

Clementine already had the security codes, so she just smiled and waved as she passed the young woman at reception and headed to the lift. As it took her up to Fox's office floor, Clementine mentally ticked off all that she had wanted to achieve in London today. October had come upon them quickly, and she had spent her time pre-ordering what she would need for Christmas. Now that Lucy was with them, Fox wanted to make Christmas extra special, and make her feel loved and wanted.

But to be honest Clementine knew Fox wanted it just as much. Fox had asked her to give them the old-fashioned kind of Christmas that would have been celebrated at Rosebrook House.

Fox had already made a start by ordering some eco-friendly real alpine Christmas trees. Not only had she found the trees with the least carbon footprint, she had a special plan for their disposal. She'd found out zoos gladly accepted real Christmas trees for their elephants to eat, so the elephants at London Zoo were in for a treat come January.

Clementine had ordered Christmas hampers at Fortnum &

Mason's for everyone in the village as a thank you for all their hard work making Rosebrook the best it could be this year. She also ordered their own Christmas food and one or two presents to make a start—she would still have the majority left to buy.

Clementine had asked Lucy to make a list, but she wasn't a demanding young woman, so she probably wouldn't ask for much.

Lucy, her cousin Peter's daughter, was her god-daughter, and heir to the Dukedom of Rosebrook. When Peter died, Clementine was the only family member left to take care of her. But she adored Lucy and would have fought to give her a home anyway. Peter had not been a loving father, and so Lucy had become a new girl when moving in with them. Clementine loved her like her own daughter as did Fox, but Fox's unending positivity had made the fifteen-year-old come out of her shell.

The lift doors opened on Fox's floor, and she was greeted by Violet, Fox's PA. She always seemed to know Clementine was on her way up. She suspected Gayle at reception phoned when she passed.

"Good afternoon, Your Grace."

Violet was another one who insisted on formality. "Hello, Violet. How are my two charges?"

"Evan took her into an *important* board meeting."

Clementine chuckled at Violet's use of her fingers for inverted commas. Fox's use of the word *important* was mostly violently different from Violet's or her own use.

"Thanks, Violet."

She walked to the boardroom doors and walked in. She found Fox sitting back in her chair, feet up on the boardroom table, whilst holding her iPad. Lucy was in a similar position. On a large screen in front of the table was an ongoing Zoom call.

Fox turned around and gave her the brightest of smiles. "Your Duchess-ship, you finished with your ordering at the shops?"

"Some of it. I see you're busy playing games."

"Playing? No, this is a planning meeting for *The Woodlanders*. Tell her, Lucy."

"Yes, the game is going to be available on the app store now. We're adding some extra characters."

"Lucy is an avid player, and she is part of the age group we are hoping to attract."

"Oh well, don't mind me. Carry on."

Fox winked at her. "Okay, Daniel, carry on."

"We came up with a range of new female characters for your approval, and we'd love any comments."

Lucy looked up at Fox for approval, and of course she was encouraged.

"I think," Lucy said, "that most of these new female characters conform to gender stereotypes."

"That's my girl," Fox said.

Clementine chuckled inside. Fox's mum Cassia was certainly influencing her. Since Lucy came to stay with them, Fox and her parents had taken her as their own. Now she had two loving grandparents, and it couldn't have made Clementine happier. Cassia was a lifelong campaigner for women's rights, and Lucy was learning to never just accept male standards.

"So, team, I think Luce and I would like you to go back to the drawing board and come up with more enlightened ideas. We'll reconvene in a few weeks."

Once Fox ended the call, she came over and gave Clementine a kiss. "Did you get some Christmas things ordered?"

"Yes, but could you please ask Lucy to make a Christmas list?"

"Luce, make a Christmas list. Your aunt Clem and I want you to have a lovely Christmas."

"It will be an amazing Christmas just being with you both."

"Isn't she the sweetest?" Fox clapped her hands together. "Now why don't we have dinner here before heading back to Rosebrook?"

"Oh, can we go to that Japanese place where the chefs with the big knives make the food in front of you?" Lucy said.

Fox snapped her fingers. "Yes, great choice."

Clementine, ever the voice of reason, said, "We'll never get in there at this short notice. It's booked out months in advance."

Fox rolled her eyes. "This is me you're talking about." She pressed a button on the desk. "Violet, can you get me Emille Gossard, please."

"No problem. Ringing now."

"Gossard here."

"Emille? Evan Fox here. I believe your group owns the little Japanese place in Soho."

"Yes, we do, and before you say it, it's booked out for months."

"Come now, Emille. Who makes sure your two girls get

Christmas's must-have toys each year? Or do you want to explain that Santa Claus ran out?"

Fox laughed silently, but exaggerated it for Lucy's sake. Lucy giggled along with her.

Emille sighed. "Fine, how many for?"

"Three, for an hour's time. Oh, and the best seats next to the chef's station."

"You don't want much, do you? Santa better be generous this year, Fox," Emille said.

"Oh, he will." Fox hung up and snapped her fingers. "No problem."

Clementine could only shake her head.

Bronte zoomed along the coastal road towards Rosebrook in her shiny forest-green Jeep. Such a weight had been lifted from her since she left the outskirts of London and her mother behind.

Even though it was a cold and frosty day, Bronte had her window down and was singing along to her music like it was the middle of summer. The release she felt at being away from London and her overbearing mother was enormous.

She came to the sign for Rosebrook and her excitement doubled. When she turned the corner into Rosebrook, Bronte was starting a new chapter in her life. There weren't many opportunities like this for animal rehabilitators. The Rosebrook Trust was providing her with premises, a budget, and a prime location to start an animal rescue. Rosebrook was connected by road to a wide network of towns and villages in a rural area. It was a great base to start her work of not only saving animals but educating in local schools and tourist areas.

She drove down past a large wooded area that she couldn't wait to explore. The first thing she would have to do would be a survey of the local flora and fauna, just to get an idea of what she might face here.

Bronte slowed as she saw smoke billowing from the forested area. Unattended fires were not a good thing to see in the woods. She quickly stopped, got out of her Jeep, and walked over to the edge of the woods.

She couldn't see much but heard chopping and then sawing of wood. Bronte had to satisfy her curiosity and picked her way through the undergrowth. Everything was covered in a frost, which made her journey noisy as she crunched the leaves and twigs underfoot. It was so strange to have frost in October in the south of England. It looked like it was going to be a hard winter.

As she got closer, Bronte could make out a tall, lanky but athletic figure, wearing a baseball cap back to front. She couldn't tell if it was a man or a woman at this point given they had their back turned on her.

They had a pile of wood on the one side, which they were sawing, and a bag of tools to the other. As she got close enough to see better, her quarry started to take off their camouflage jacket. They must be freezing in this weather.

When the jacket was removed, she saw a pair of long sinewy arms revealed by a sleeveless T-shirt, which looked as if they could envelop every part of you. Bronte's eyes were drawn up to her quarry's strong shoulders.

Bronte had forgotten to breathe, and a heat seeped into her that was certainly not coming from the weather around them. It filled her body so quickly that, depending on the identity of the person in front of her, she might be questioning her sexuality.

A twig cracked underfoot, and her quarry turned round quickly. "Hello? Hello? Can I help?"

Bronte was on her toes and ran back to her Jeep. She didn't want to be caught spying on who she now knew was a woman. What had been a quest to find out if the fire in the woods was supervised had resulted in warming her own body on this cold morning.

Bronte followed the directions of her satnav until she came to a cottage, just outside the centre of the village. Fox had shown her around the place about a month ago. It was perfect. The cottage fronted a large parcel of land. Lady Clementine explained it had been a small holding at one time, with goats, chickens, pigs, and a couple of cows. Plenty of room to begin her dream and hopefully make her new home.

Griffin dropped her bags off at her cottage and was on her way to the brewing factory. She needed to see Fox as soon as possible but felt the need to check in with Patrick.

Patrick Doyle had come to make a fresh start in Rosebrook after being kicked out by his mum and dad and living on the streets of

London. Fox asked Griffin to take him under her wing as an apprentice. She did, and they'd become great friends. They were making great strides in setting up the brewery and had even taken on a few members of staff from the surrounding villages. They were doing well together before Griffin dropped everything to go to Mother.

This was the original factory that Clementine's grandmother had built for the original beer factory in Rosebrook, making it an old-fashioned design. Griffin liked it, though. She went in through the side entrance, where stairs took her straight up to the office, without going through the main factory. Patrick wasn't in the office, so he must be on the floor somewhere. The office was up two flights of metal stairs from the floor and was surrounded in glass, so it made you feel close to the workers on the floor.

Griffin walked up to the window and got a good view of the staff going about their work, among the big copper vats where the brew process happened. She pressed a button to open an intercom to the floor.

"Hey, guys." Pete, Winston, and Carol looked up from the floor and waved. "Just to let you know I'm back. Is Paddy about?"

She saw Winston shout to the other side of the factory, and then he gave her a thumbs-up.

A couple of minutes later Paddy came striding into the office. "Hi, Griff. We weren't expecting you back so soon." He gave her a hug.

"It was kind of a last minute decision. I just came in to let you know I was back and see if there were any problems."

"No, everything's been going okay. I've been working on my own brew, and we're getting the Christmas orders made up."

"Good, good." Griff was delighted everything was going well. It meant she wouldn't have to feel as guilty when she left. As long as Fox got someone in to help Patrick, the beer factory would be fine. "I'll leave you to it then. I'm just going to the Trust office to see if Fox is there."

Patrick gave her a worried look. "Are you sure you're okay, Griff?"

Griffin patted Patrick on the shoulder. "Just tired, mate. I'll see you soon."

Chapter Three

Bronte drove to the Trust office. She saw the cars lined up beside electric charging ports and remembered that Evan Fox had offered her an electric vehicle, as all Trust employees got. She ran her hands over her steering wheel. Bronte didn't want to give up her pride and joy. She would have to investigate the prices for converting it when she could afford it.

Bronte got out of the car and was hit with the sound of Christmas music. It was only the beginning of October. A tad too early for the Christmas spirit, although for Bronte there was never any Christmas spirit.

Her mother choreographed Christmas for the benefit of her social circle. The de Laceys went to the right parties and mixed with the right families, since she was a little girl. There was never any magic in it.

Putting those miserable thoughts out of her mind, Bronte walked up to the door and opened it slowly. The scene she saw was quite comical. Evan Fox was tottering on a set of ladders, trying to put up Christmas lights, while singing Christmas songs at the top of her lungs. The young girl she had met at the pitch she had given for the plot of land was handing Evan the Christmas lights up, and was as happy and smiling as Evan. The other staff, two women and a man, were busy putting up one of five Christmas trees, the others leaning against the wall.

There was only one person who appeared not to be enjoying the early festivities. Steff Archer, whom she had met once at the pitch meeting, was sitting at her desk, holding her head in her hands, massaging her temples.

Bronte walked up to her desk and said, "Steff Archer?"

She looked up and recognition spread across her face. "Ms. de Lacey. Call me Archie." Archie stood up and extended her hand.

"Please call me Bronte."

"You are very welcome." She indicated to Evan and the others. "I'm sorry about all this. I've been dealing with it all morning."

Bronte laughed softly. "It's like Christmas exploded."

"I know, and it's only October. There's more to come."

"You are not a fan of all the joys of Christmas?" Bronte asked.

"Not really. It's given me a headache. Although my wife is, and she's trying to change my opinion."

"I'm with you, Archie. Especially since it's not even December yet," Bronte said.

"Bronte!"

"Uh-oh. You've been spotted." Archie indicated over to Evan.

Bronte turned and saw Evan climb down a few steps of the ladder before jumping the rest and almost bouncing over to her. Bronte wasn't a lethargic person by nature, but next to Evan Fox she felt as slow as a snail.

"Lucy? Look, Bronte has arrived." Lucy came to Evan's side, and Evan draped her arm over Lucy's shoulders. "We're so happy to have you here and to start another big adventure. Aren't we, Luce?"

Lucy was a shy kind of girl but very sweet and had a strong passion for animal welfare. When Bronte first met Evan to propose opening an animal rescue, Evan had asked if Lucy could get involved and work part time with her.

Of course this could have been awkward. Hiring the boss's wife's little cousin might cause problems. But from the brief talk she'd had with Lucy, she could tell she loved animals and was keen to learn from her.

"Yeah, hi, Bronte."

"Let me introduce you to our motley crew. You know Luce, Archie, that's Rupert my PA, our admin team Zara and Emma. Archie's wife Ash is normally here, but she's with the duchess at the moment. Everyone? This is the Right Honourable Bronte de Lacey."

"Hi, everyone. Bronte is fine."

"Bronte is coming to run the animal rescue in the village, and we're extremely exited to have her." Fox ushered her over to her desk. "Sit down, sit down. Tea, coffee, bottle of juice, water, smoothie?"

"A bottle of water would be lovely, thanks."

Lucy jumped up. "I'll get it for you, Bronte."

Once she was away, Fox said, "Thanks for allowing Lucy to help at the animal sanctuary. I wouldn't have suggested it if she wasn't committed."

"She will be a great help. I'm always happy to teach people who are willing to learn."

"Fantastic. Lucy will be duchess one day. All of this land will be hers to manage, and Clementine and I think this will be a good education for her. So, to business." Fox tapped out a beat on the desk before speaking.

"My PA in London has worked with my lawyer to set up the Trust for the wildlife sanctuary. The accounts with the funds are set up in your name—it's up to you how and when you use your budget."

Lucy returned with the drinks. Bronte had to keep pinching herself. This was her dream come true. An animal sanctuary with her own yearly budget. It was like being handed the keys to the kingdom.

Fox continued, "My lawyer just needs a couple of signatures, but she'll email you."

"The equipment and supplies you asked for are at the cottage," Archie said, "or on their way. Are you sure you don't need help with putting up the enclosures?"

"I'll be fine, but first I'd like to lay out the area myself and get everything set up before I have others come in. I'm a bit of a control freak." Bronte smiled.

"I can understand that…" Fox trailed off as she started to speak. "Griff? You're back early."

Bronte heard a low languid voice say, "Yeah, I was able to come back earlier than I expected."

She turned around and saw it was her. The sexy woman in the woods sawing firewood. This move might be even more interesting than Bronte anticipated.

❖

Griff looked around. The Christmas music was playing and all the staff were getting involved in putting up Christmas decorations. Jubilant was a word she would use, and normally Griffin would be right in amongst it. But not now. The whole scene that greeted her was exactly what she didn't want.

Fox approached and said in a lower tone, "Is everything all right, Griff?"

"Could I speak to you in private?"

"Of course, but let me introduce you to our new arrival." Fox walked a few paces and said, "Bronte? Let me introduce you to our friend and brewery manager, Griffin Harris. Griff, this is Bronte, who will be opening and managing the new animal rescue centre."

"Hi, Griffin."

Griffin had instant recognition. This Bronte was the flash of strawberry-blond hair and headscarf she had seen through the trees.

"Bronte. So you were the one spying on me in the forest."

"Spying? I wasn't spying. Coming into the village I saw smoke coming from the trees. I had to check that someone had it under control, as any good conservationist would."

"Fair enough. Just make yourself known next time."

There was a long uncomfortable silence that Fox eventually filled by clapping her hands together. "Well, let's go to the conference room and have a chat. Shall we, Griff?"

Griff nodded and followed Griffin into the room.

When the door shut, Fox said, "How's your mum, Griff? We didn't expect you back here this side of Christmas."

"She's doing better—she's going to be okay. My aunty is looking after her now. They're going on a cruise over Christmas to help her relax and recuperate, so it seemed like the right time to come back."

That was, at least, the story she was comfortable telling her friends at the moment.

"I'm glad to hear she's doing well," Fox said. "You know I'm here to help in any way I can."

Griffin did know that. That's why what she had to say next was hard. "Can we sit down?" They took a seat next to each other and Griffin began. "I've had such a great time working and teaching Patrick all about the brewery business and living in this great community."

"I hear a but coming," Fox said.

"We talked about me staying indefinitely as brewery manager, but I've changed my mind. I'll stay until you have someone else lined up."

"Is it your mum? Has something changed? We'd be very sorry to lose you."

Griffin ran her fingers through her hair. "I can't really explain. I just need to be on the road again. I need to find my peace."

"Is there anything I can offer you to help you stay?" Fox asked.

"No, I need to get out on the open road again, but I'm not going to just walk away. I know it would be too difficult before Christmas, but maybe after you could find a few candidates." Griffin felt so guilty doing this.

"If that's what you want. I'll have my PA in London start the ball rolling, but we'll be so sorry to lose you."

Griffin looked up at Fox. "There is one thing. Can you please make sure that it's someone who will work well with Patrick? He's gained so much in confidence, and I've tried to help him wherever I can. He's come a long way from that boy that arrived in Rosebrook."

"Of course I will. In fact, why don't you come on the interview panel? That way you can make sure it'll be someone who is a good fit, and you're the expert in brewing."

It was a good idea, but it tied Griffin down to a time frame. The very thought made her claustrophobic—she was so desperate to get back on the open road. But she owed it to Patrick to make sure everything was right.

"Okay, I'll do that. Paddy and I have worked too hard on our recipes and branding to have someone come in and do away with it. I need to make sure Paddy will be allowed to make these drinks."

"That's settled then. Are you sure there isn't anything I can help with? A friendly ear? A hug?" Fox grinned.

Griffin squinted. "I know you would. No, just some old baggage that only the open road can help with."

"Fair enough. I better get back to our new resident. She's nice, you know."

Griffin knew she was giving her a gentle push, to tell her that she had been offhand with her. "I'm sure she is, but she should have made herself known. That wasn't the right thing to do. I could have mistaken her for a poacher. She could have been any person at my back with a shotgun." Griffin knew she was pushing it a bit, but people shouldn't just spy on people.

"We don't have many poachers, do we?"

"Some. Not in the old sense of the word, poaching to feed a family, but gangs of men do come with dogs to go rabbiting for sport or go after the badgers. I've come across them when I've been camping."

"I never knew," Fox said. "I don't want anyone like that anywhere near our wildlife in Rosebrook."

"The duchess knows. She's had some of the estate workers do a sweep for traps and any other evidence."

Fox smiled. "That's why she is the lady of the manor, I suppose. I better get back to Bronte."

Next, Griffin had to tell Patrick. He wasn't going to like it, but in the long run this would give Patrick more responsibility. Griff believed in him. Patrick just had to believe in himself.

❖

Griffin took a back road through fields behind the old Rosebrook school, so as not to go through the centre of the village. The people of Rosebrook were the kindest, most neighbourly you could meet, but she wasn't in the mood for a friendly word, joke, or welcome back.

This wasn't like her. Griffin was a people person. She had travelled with a hunger to meet new people and learn about their cultures. Now all she wanted to do was run away from everyone that knew the bright, happy-go-lucky Griff and try and sort out the new feelings and emotions she'd been saddled with.

The trauma of her mum's heart attack and the thought of losing her had been the worst thing she thought she would have to deal with, after racing home to take care of her. But as she found out to her cost, secrets and lies often had the habit of coming to the surface around family trauma. The things she had found out while searching through her mum's papers while she was in hospital changed her outlook on her own childhood. The image of a hand-drawn birthday card entered her mind.

It was a beautifully drawn teddy bear holding a little girl's hand with balloons drifting around behind them. Griffin cleared her throat and tried to dismiss the emotion that welled up in her.

The sound of a car coming from far behind Griffin interrupted her thoughts. She was well back from the road, but when she jumped the gate into Mr. Mason's field, Griffin could see in the distance a green Jeep cresting the brow of the hill on the other side of the field.

It must have been their newcomer. No one else at the office had such a distinctive car.

"The Right Honourable Bronte de Lacey," Griffin said. *Sounds as if she has more than one plum in her mouth.* Griffin thought back to their encounter in the woods. Why had she not said anything? Bronte worked with animals. Surely, she had some common sense? Out here in the woods, in the countryside? Griffin could have been a poacher, or a farmer with a gun.

Then guilt edged into her mind. She hadn't exactly been welcoming, and she did have to live here until after Christmas at least, so it wouldn't do anyone any good to have bad feelings.

Maybe she would make amends next time she saw Bronte.

CHAPTER FOUR

B ronte pulled up into the cottage driveway and parked outside the front door. Even though she had seen the cottage and land when she'd come to meet both Evan and the duchess, work had been done in her absence to make the property meet Bronte's specifications.

The first thing she noticed was the two car garage over on the other side of the driveway. During their Zoom meetings Bronte had only asked for a wooden lock-up to house the sanctuary vehicles, as she thought she'd have to purchase a large truck, through the Trust, for her work.

Instead, there was a brick double car garage with a roll-top door. She looked at the bunch of keys Fox had given her, including a fob with a button.

"I wonder…" Bronte pressed the button, and the garage door started to rise up. Inside was ample room for a car and a truck, and any equipment she might have.

"Thank you, Fox. I've landed on my feet here."

She pressed the fob to slide the garage door down again, unlocked the front door, and walked into the house. The house was beautiful. Everything was finished to a high standard. Bronte was sure she could see Clementine's hand in this.

Bronte popped her head into the living room and saw a lovely, refurbished stove-style fire, with firewood piled up at the side.

"They really have thought of everything."

What a lovely house she would have to live in. But Bronte didn't stop to admire it all very long. The outside space was what concerned her the most. She hurried through the kitchen and unlocked the back door. It opened out into an all-glass summer house room. Bronte had asked for this. Some of the animals might not be fit enough to be left alone, and Bronte needed a warm, dry place to look after them.

She then stepped out into the outside space and took a large breath of air.

Bronte was so excited. There was so much outside space and, even better, untouched space. Fox offered to have the Trust build the enclosures for her, but Bronte wanted to make sure everything was done the way she wanted it.

Directly in front of the glass extension was animal-friendly artificial grass, so that in the bad weather the place didn't become a quagmire. And it was resistant to any little animal accidents.

Bronte walked up to the former stables at the end of the grass. The stables were now indoor cubicles, where animals not quite ready for the elements could bed down. Bronte's excitement grew and grew as she walked over to a farm gate that led out to three fields. This was where she would build the pens for some of the longer staying guests.

This was truly what she had always dreamed of. There was a lot of work to do, but she couldn't wait to get started.

Bronte heard a voice shout, "Knock-knock." She turned around and saw a woman with stylish short blond hair. The woman had a big, warm smile on her face and was holding a basket.

Bronte hurried over to meet her.

"Hi, I'm Kay Dayton. I hope it's not too early to come and introduce myself, is it?"

"No, not at all. I'm Bronte de Lacey."

Kay pulled her in to kiss both cheeks. Bronte could tell right away that she and Kay were going to get along well.

"Lovely to meet you, Bronte. I brought you some homemade bread, cakes, muffins, and scones."

"That's so kind of you. Where do you live in the village?"

"We're on the outskirts, like you." Kay pointed. "Two or three fields to the left, over there. My husband Casper and I have a small holding. A few pigs, a couple of cows, some chickens, oh, and a couple of kids," Kay joked. "Two boys, Toby and Dexter."

"Lovely, well, I'm glad to have you as neighbours."

"You too. How do you like everything so far?" Kay indicated to the house and land.

Bronte lifted her arms and sighed. "It's just perfect. I can't wait to get started."

"You know everyone around here is behind you in your mission to help the wildlife or any animal around here."

"Thanks, it'll be great to be part of this fantastic community. I've never known anything like this concept village."

Kay chuckled. "It wasn't always so harmonious. When Evan Fox turned up in a old-fashioned traditional farming village, trying to sell the idea of a diverse, ecological village that would be an example to the world, it wasn't going to be an easy sell. But you've met Fox. She's—"

"Persuasive," Bronte finished.

"Exactly," Kay said.

Bronte rubbed her hands together. The cold was seeping into her bones. "Would you like a cup of tea? It's getting cold. Evan said that the duchess left some essentials for me to get started. I'm quite sure there's tea."

"Spend some more time away from two boys with too much energy? Oh yes. Dinner's cooking in the oven anyway."

They walked back to the cottage, and Kay said as she rubbed her arms, "You know it's not normally like this in Dorset. We normally get mild winters, but the weather reporters say the whole of the UK, even us, are to get the coldest winter in decades. Fox says it's global warming gone mad, but don't get her started. You'll be listening for hours."

Bronte laughed along with Kay. She was loving Rosebrook already.

❖

"That's fantastic! Tell them to make that date, and we've got a deal."

Clementine looked up at Fox as she worked on dinner at the kitchen island. Fox was striding about with the same energy as she started the day with. It never ceased to amaze Clem the energy that her partner had.

But when she slept, she slept so soundly that a freight train coming through the bedroom wouldn't wake her. It was the only time she truly switched off, although sometimes Clem wished there was such a button, and sometimes when she heard the deep breathing coming from Fox's side of the bed, she let out a sigh, and happily read her book. It was the only time Clementine truly got a moment of peace to herself.

But that was Fox. A whirlwind of optimism and passion, and Clem loved her dearly for it.

Clementine turned around to take her stir-fry off the cooker and heard Lucy laughing quietly about Fox's antics.

She turned back around and rolled her eyes and smiled to Lucy, who was doing homework on the information Bronte gave her to study. It was so good to see Lucy smiling. She fitted into their life perfectly, and Clementine got a wonderful sense of satisfaction from training her own heir about the estate and its running. Just as her father had done for her.

On top of that Lucy had the larger-than-life Fox to learn from. Not only a successful businesswoman, but a positive person who saw obstacles as merely problems. Not to mention how fun she was.

Clementine raised her eyebrows at Lucy when Fox said, while she continued pacing, "If they can meet us halfway we'll be sipping limoncello by the Trevi Fountain in two months. See ya, buddy."

Fox ended the call and rubbed her hands vigorously. "I love it when a plan comes together."

When Fox saw Lucy smiling and Clementine shaking her head she said, "What? It is limoncello, isn't it?"

"Yes, it is. But before you shoot off for drinks at the Trevi Fountain, can you sit down for dinner? It's ready."

Fox came over and sat at the table. "We've got a great Italian production company onboard for Fox Toys. I don't even like liquors. It was the first Italian drink I could think of."

"There's espresso," Lucy said.

"Yeah, then Campari—we could make a list. Alexa, tell me—"

Clementine wasn't going to let this develop or they'd never eat. "Alexa, don't listen to her, and don't encourage her, Lucy."

Both Lucy and Fox continued to laugh as she brought over the stir-fried noodle bowls. Clementine let out a sigh of contentment. She could never have imagined a life like this, when she was living in the gatehouse, trying to keep her head above water, just so she could pay her mother's nursing home fees.

The late duke, Clementine's father, had to sell Rosebrook House because of huge debts left by her grandmother, the social reformer Isadora Fitzroy. It broke her father's and mother's hearts and hers to watch the building deteriorate as buyer after buyer sold the building on.

That was until a certain Evan Fox came bouncing along like Tigger, determined to fix the house, the village, and her heart, not necessarily in that order. She did those things, and here she was serving a vegan meal to her new family, in their beautifully refurbished kitchen.

Lucy was a welcome addition to their family and fulfilled a need in Clementine that she hadn't served since her mother died.

She placed a bowl in front of them. "When you're quite finished chattering?"

Fox smiled and winked at her when she said, "Sorry, Your Graceship."

Clementine couldn't help but smile. Fox always liked to gently tease her about her title.

"Tonight we have Szechuan noodles with mixed veg and sesame seeds, accompanied by…give me a sec"—Clementine lifted a platter off the kitchen island and placed it on the table—"vegan sushi made and rolled by my very own hand."

"What a woman," Fox exclaimed.

Neither she nor Lucy had been vegan before they met Fox but were now vegetarian, and just by necessity they ate a lot of vegan meals. Clementine didn't always want to be cooking two different meals.

"Well, tuck in," Clementine said.

Fox lifted a piece of sushi and dipped it in soy sauce and wasabi before exclaiming, "This is the best sushi I've ever had."

Again, Clementine rolled her eyes. Everything she made was the best ever according to Fox. She did love Fox's loyalty, but she was the tiniest bit biased.

"Fox, you've been to the best sushi bars in London and I'm still learning to roll properly, I'm sure you've tasted better."

"I have not. It's delicious, isn't it Lucy?" Fox turned to Lucy for support.

"I love your cooking, Aunty Clem. Dad and I just used to eat packaged and freezer meals. This is so tasty."

"See?" Fox smiled in triumph.

Clementine sat down and reached over to squeeze Lucy's hand. "Thank you."

"Where's my thank-you?" Fox asked.

"In the post. Now, how is Griffin? Did she say why she was back early? Is her mother okay?"

"She said that her mother is doing much better and that her aunt is looking after her now," Fox said.

"Strange that she would come back so early. Griffin told me how close she was with her mother."

Fox slurped a mouthful of noodles then said, "She didn't seem herself, to be honest, and she was sharp with Bronte when she came in the office."

"Oh, why?"

"Something to do with seeing her in the forest and not announcing herself." Fox stopped midchew on her latest piece of sushi. "By the way, did you know we have poachers?"

"Yes, we have them occasionally. Back to Griff."

"You never told me. Anyway, Griff said she could have taken her as a poacher, blah blah. She was in a bad mood."

Lucy said, "Griff's always so happy."

Clementine nodded. "I don't think I've seen her in a bad mood."

"That's not the worst of it," Fox said dramatically. "She asked to see me alone and told me that she's leaving us. I mean, I know Griff always said she'd stay until the brewery was self-sufficient and Paddy was trained, but I mean now, well, after Christmas."

"Why?" Clementine said.

"Something about wanting to get back onto the open road and travel again."

"There must be a reason. Didn't you ask why?"

"I took her word that the open road was calling her again," Fox said.

"You're hopeless. Something must have happened at her mother's to make that big a change in her plans."

Lucy sighed. "I love Griff. She was going to teach me how to windsurf in the spring."

"I'll teach you, Luce."

"Do you know how to surf?" Clem asked.

"No, but we'll work it out together, eh, Luce."

Fox held her hand up to fist-bump Luce, and she reciprocated with laughter. Evan Fox was the perfect antidote for a mixed-up teenager who had just lost her only parent.

Clementine gazed at Fox, who met her eyes with love shining from them.

"Aunty Clem? You're looking again."

Clementine broke her gaze from Fox. They tended to do that. "Sorry, Luce."

Fox winked at Clementine. She could look in those eyes of hers for days.

"Luce, tell Aunty Clem about what Bronte gave you," Fox said.

Lucy held up her iPad and whizzed through all sorts of web pages and PDFs. "She sent me all this information on rescuing animals, the care they need, the kinds of pens to keep them safe. She says I can go tomorrow and help her mark out where the pens are going to go."

It was so good to see Lucy excited about life again after losing the only home she had ever known and her dad, even though he wasn't the most caring towards her.

"That's fantastic, isn't it, Clem?" Fox said.

"You'll be great, and I can't wait to see Bronte again. I'll walk you down there and then I'll do my Sunday rounds."

Clementine made it a point to visit the elders of the village and anyone that needed any help or support.

My perfect duchess, Fox thought.

"Aunty Clem, is Bronte Lady Bronte or…"

"No, her mother is Baroness Lawton. The heir to a baroness is known as The Right Honourable such and such."

"A few rungs down the pole from you, Duchess of Rosebrook." Fox joked.

Clementine took a sip of wine and said, "That's not how she'd see it, from what I've heard."

"Have you met her, Aunty Clem?"

"No, but from what I hear, she is a bit of a dragon. It's amazing she produced such a nice daughter in Bronte. Matilda de Lacey is her own name. I think Lawton was a small village in Shropshire where they had the countryside retreat many moons ago, but now they only have Lawton House in London. It is one of the oldest houses in London. Very historical."

"You don't know much then." Fox smiled.

"No, not much. Now finish your food. I've got a special vegan dessert for us."

"You're sharing?" Fox said.

"Apparently." Clementine sighed dramatically.

Maybe now was the right time to try to negotiate two subjects that had caused contention in their household.

After a minute of quiet while they all ate their meals, Fox cleared her throat and said, "Clem, can I?"

"No," Clementine said firmly.

"You don't even know what I'm going to ask yet."

"I do. I said Christmas decorations in your office and in the village, but it's too early for the house."

Fox turned to Lucy. "Luce? You're up next."

Lucy cleared her throat nervously and played with her food for a few seconds. "Fox and I thought it might be nice to have a big, long Christmas since we both love it and I haven't really had a good one before."

"Of course, Luce. We'll make it special." Clementine stroked the side of her cheek.

Fox gave a look of mock indignation. "So not for me after continued begging, but Luce just has to ask once?"

Clementine gave her the sweetest smile. "Yes, that's the way it goes. I can't give in to you too early, Foxy."

That sentence did all sorts of crazy things to her body that went right over Lucy's head.

"I suppose that's true. Maybe I'll have more luck the second time. This is to you both."

Fox pointed a chopstick at each of them.

"Oh no, here it comes, Luce."

"Give me a chance, Your Graceship. How about, after Christmas we have a clean slate and you two do Veganuary? It'll be great fun."

"We mostly eat vegan anyway. Apart from some ice cream and chocolate Netflix nights Luce and I have."

"Just try for a month. I'll get you the finest vegan chocolate and ice cream. You won't miss it. I promise," Fox pleaded.

Clementine turned to Lucy. "It's up to you, Luce. I'll go with whatever you feel. No pressure."

"I think we should try, Aunty Clem. We need to eat less meat to save the planet."

"You've been working on poor Luce behind my back, haven't you?" Clementine accused Fox.

Fox held her hand to her chest. "Would I?"

"Oh yes."

Lucy and Clementine burst out laughing, and as she always did, Fox reminded herself how much she loved having a family.

❖

Later that evening, Griff was in bed, but her body was refusing to sleep, and every time she shut her eyes she could see the moment she'd confronted her mum with the evidence she had found about her father.

But Griff didn't want to think about it. She couldn't handle what it meant and how it had shattered her trust in her mum. She grabbed the bag that her iPad was in and pulled it out. As she did an envelope fluttered out.

It was one of the cards she had found that her mum had hidden in her files. Griffin couldn't stop herself from taking the card out of the envelope. It was a hand-drawn Easter card with two chicks hatching from a couple of eggs, and an Easter bunny with a goofy looking face, holding a basket of chocolate eggs.

It made her smile every time she looked at it. But it was a different story when she opened it up. There was a cheque stapled to the inside of the card as there had been with every card and letter she found.

Most of them were for between three and five thousand at a time. But each cheque remained stapled to the card unclaimed, untouched. Griffin put back the card and went over to the window.

She opened it and leaned against the windowsill, and took a deep breath of cold, calming air. The temperature was below freezing, and the grass and stone in the garden were glistening and sparkling white.

As Griffin had travelled the world with only her backpack and the open road, she had seen many freezing days and nights. The residents of Rosebrook, however, were used to much milder winters, being on the south coast. October frosts were unheard of.

It was such a clear night. The moon and stars were bright. It truly was beautiful, but all she could think about was running. Running from the pain and confusion she was feeling.

Life and the family she loved had always been simple. She had her mum and her, unless her aunt came to visit. For as long as she could remember, she and her mum had been a team, and they needed to be, because they had nothing.

They lived on a tough council housing estate, her mum worked two jobs for very little money, and that grinding poverty built up an anger towards the man who'd abandoned them, or so she thought.

Gyles, as he was called, had an extremely short relationship with her mum and was gone as soon as he knew her mum was pregnant. At the time Griffin's hatred for the man grew as she saw her mum struggle to pay the bills and put food on the table. It was a hatred and a hurt that she dragged around wherever she went, and it only got more intense when his lawyers turned up at their door when she was eighteen.

Gyles had died, and she could be his heir if she took a DNA test. There were a lot of cousins and other family members who were hoping she wasn't.

The bogeyman in her mind now had a name and family history. The Right Honourable Gyles Beaufort, who owned an estate and land in Hampshire. His wealth only made her hatred grow and grow.

When the DNA confirmed Griffin was his child, their lives changed overnight. The bulk of the money was held in the trust until she was twenty-one, but she got a healthy allowance from it every six months. Both Griffin and her mum resented the money and estate, but Griffin's opinion was to get the last laugh on her so-called father, have a good life, and donate to charities and such, and so Griffin did.

Her mum never quite accepted it the way Griffin did, and despite the fact they had a comfortable home and life now, it affected their relationship. Arguments became more frequent. Griffin loved her mum more than anything, but she hadn't asked for this, and it was only what her mum deserved after being left destitute by Gyles.

Griffin remembered one of the last disagreements she'd had with her mum. *"He was a cold-hearted bastard who never wanted you, didn't care if you starved or survived."* So Griffin packed her rucksack, her hate and resentment for her father, and began travelling the world.

A wind blew the cold air into her face, and it reminded her of those carefree days travelling, when helping build schools and health care centres and paying for water sources to be installed in dirt-poor villages gave her a sense of purpose. She was doing the right thing with her wealth, but she still pulled the heavy weight of hatred around, every step she took.

Griffin's relationship with her mum grew stronger again as time passed, and she associated the money with Griffin. But neither of them mentioned the estate in Hampshire, and Griffin never wanted to go there. Her lawyers dealt with anything related to it.

Griffin then thought of the card she had just read and every certainty she'd held was gone.

She put her hands on her face and leaned further into the sill. "Mum, why did you do this?"

The man she had hated sent letters and cards all through her childhood, all with money, all with messages to her, messages to her mum, begging her to accept the money and begging her to let him see Griffin.

The worst of it was that the man she'd hated for abandoning her signed off every letter: *Love, Daddy.*

Griffin slammed her fist down. Every time she read that phrase it kicked her in the gut. Her mum's lies, her dad's apparent attempt at love—it was just too much.

How could she sort this out in her head?

If she couldn't run for the moment, then she'd have to walk.

She quickly pulled on her fatigue cargo trousers and her boots, then ran downstairs to take her puffy quilted jacket from the coat hook. In minutes she was dressed and outside the door.

Griffin didn't know where she was going. She just walked. She wanted the cold to numb her mind, to press pause on all these new emotions she was going to have to process. If she could just push them down deep, she wouldn't have to deal with them.

She found herself walking the road along by the woods. He mind probably took her there because that's where she was the most comfortable. There was peace and contentment in chopping wood, building a fire, and making tea over the fire. It was almost meditative.

Her thoughts were soon disturbed by loud bangs in the woods.

"That's shotguns."

Griffin knew she was right when she heard dogs barking, and then men's voices coming closer. She jumped over the stone wall across the road from the forest and crouched down.

Her breath billowed out like smoke, it was so cold.

Poachers, for sure.

She peeked over the edge and saw the light of torches shining through the trees. She had to tell Clem and Fox this was getting worse, and their new resident Right Honourable Animal Rehabilitator. She was bound to want to check on the animals.

Griffin planned to go around first thing. Although she wouldn't likely be welcomed, she hadn't exactly been welcoming herself.

Maybe it was time to build some bridges.

CHAPTER FIVE

The next morning, after her usual hot water and lemon, and a brief look through the morning news, Bronte decided to take a walk down through the village to the shop for bread and plant milk.

She didn't really need it. Clementine had left her quite well stocked, but it was an opportunity to meet some of the villagers. Fox had been right about a welcoming experience so far, apart from the bad-tempered Griffin.

Yesterday in the Trust office, Fox tried to make excuses for her. She'd had a rough time with an illness in the family, but that was for her to show—Bronte wasn't going to seek her attention.

Bronte lifted her basket up onto the counter. The woman at the till smiled broadly.

"Are you our new arrival? The animal rescue woman?"

"Yes, yes, I am. Bronte de Lacey." She offered her hand and the woman shook it warmly.

"It's lovely to meet you. I'm Erica Strickland and…" She turned to the man packing goods onto the shelves behind the counter. "I told you, Jay. It is her. Come and meet Bronte."

He was over in a heartbeat and taking her hand. "So nice to meet you, Bronte. I'm Jay."

"Nice to meet you too, Jay. You have a wonderful shop here."

"Thank you. We love it here," Jay said. He looked down at her basket and, indicating the almond milk, said, "Are you vegan?"

"Vegetarian. I was admiring your vegan section over there."

"Fox wants a good selection for the vegans and vegetarians in the community. It's very popular, isn't it Jay," Erica said.

"Yes, it is. Even those of us who still eat meat try to follow Fox's local campaign to change up one or two meals a week, for the environment."

"I bet the local farmers aren't best pleased," Bronte said.

"At first, no," Jay said.

Erica continued for him, "But when Fox showed them she wasn't trying to impose anything on the local community, just helped by giving them more environmentally friendly feed, they started to warm up. Then there was the Great Storm."

"The great storm?"

"Tell her, Jay," Erica said.

"Oh, it was just about two years ago—we had the hottest summer and then the greatest storm anyone can remember. The whole village was flooded. The houses and cottages were ruined."

Erica added, "We had to get dinghies from Mr. O'Rourke, he owns the boat shed down at the pier, and save our oldest residents from their cottages."

"That must have been very dramatic and traumatizing."

"It was. We even had water in here," Jay said. "It came up to knee height. It caused hundreds of thousands of pounds' worth in damage, but to her credit, Fox fixed everything."

Erica looped her arm through Jay's. "After that shock, our resident farmers, Mr. Mason and the Murdochs, had to admit climate change is here, it's real, and they had to make a change like the rest of us."

"There's nothing like a practical demonstration to change your mind," Bronte said.

"And we're having one right now. It's to be the coldest winter on record down here on the south coast."

"I arrived at the right time then?" Bronte joked.

"In some ways you have." Erica pointed to a poster behind the counter with a big Christmas tree on it. "It's the big Christmas switch-on, next Friday. We haven't had Christmas lights in Rosebrook in generations, so I'm told."

She'd seen men up on cherry pickers stringing lights between lampposts and houses. "Oh yeah, I saw them going up as I walked down here."

"There'll be hot chestnuts, mulled wine, and our lovely local beers and lagers." Jay pointed to a display over in the corner of the shop. The beers and ales were sitting on a wooden display case, and the lagers were inside a fridge. A sign above said *Rosebrook Brewery*.

The brewery run by the bad tempered woodswoman, Bronte thought. Griffin had shoulders and arms that she could watch sawing and chopping wood all day, but a bad personality was a huge turn-off.

"Sounds great. I'll be there."

Christmas had never been a happy time, but it would be good for Bronte to get out and make some friends in the village. She'd already made two.

Erica rang up her purchases, and Bronte paid before bidding the husband and wife goodbye. As she stepped outside, she heard her name being called. She turned around and saw an older gentleman, dressed immaculately in a tweed suit with a grouse bucket hat to match, yellow waistcoat and tie, and a green wax jacket. His pure white beard was equally immaculate, and he held a wooden country walking stick with a mallard duck shaped handle.

"Are you our new animal lady?"

Bronte smiled brightly. "I am indeed."

She held her hand out and the elderly gentlemen took her hand and kissed her knuckles.

"Wonderful to meet you, my dear. I'm Fergus."

Bronte couldn't help but smile at this true gentleman. "Nice to meet you, Mr. Fergus."

"Fergus, everyone calls me Fergus. What a delightful young woman you are. You're sure to add some sparkle to our Christmas celebrations this year."

What a lovely gentleman. He was flamboyant in his words and actions and pinging her gaydar majorly.

"I'm looking forward to getting to know everyone," Bronte said.

"Well, you have a friend in me, my dear. Anything you need help with, you come and find Fergus."

"Thank you. Are you a recent resident?" Bronte asked.

"Oh no, I'm in with the bricks, my dear. My partner and I sold our antiques shop in London and bought our cottage in oh…in 1982? Forty years ago, anyway."

"What's your partner's name?"

Bronte saw a sadness come across Fergus's face. "Ian, but he's no longer with us."

What did I ask that for? "I'm so sorry Fergus, I shouldn't have asked."

"No, no. I like to talk about Ian. It keeps him alive in my mind. He died a year and a half after we arrived, but it was exactly what we wanted. A beautiful tranquil place to just be together." Fergus took out his handkerchief and quickly dabbed his eye. "How goes your animal rescue? Any new residents yet?"

What a sweet old man. "No, we're a while off that yet. I still need to build the pens and animal houses."

"Anything you need, just ask. We're a helpful bunch around here."

"So I'm finding out." Bronte smiled.

"I'll let you get on, my dear. You must be busy," Fergus said.

"It was lovely to meet you. See you soon, Fergus."

When Fergus walked into the shop, Bronte checked her watch. Seven o'clock. Ideally, she would have been back home by now and starting her morning yoga routine, but she had planned on a walk along the beach. She was desperate to see it. Meeting her new neighbours had been too nice to rush.

If she hurried, Bronte could run over to where the steps took you down and at least take a quick look. She wasn't far from the beach. She ran over and found there was a lookout with a coin operated telescope to look out to sea.

Bronte hadn't any change with her, but even from this distance she could see how spectacular Rosebrook beach was. It was an isolated cove rounded by stark cliffs. There were walkways down at each end and a wheelchair lift. Everything about this place was traditional mixed with the modern. On the freezing cold morning, the sea was choppy, and amazingly the sand was dusted with sparkling frost. Bronte hadn't seen anything like it before.

She quickly took out her phone and snapped a picture of the scene, then quickly attached it to a text to her sister. *The view from Rosebrook village. It's so beautiful.*

When Bronte looked up from her phone, she saw a runner dressed in black shorts and T-shirt. Were they unhinged? It was freezing! Mind you, she was going to practice her yoga in the back garden—she liked the cold to concentrate her mind, but she had never done it in this cold. Bronte might be back in the house in five minutes.

Then the runner did something she wasn't expecting. They pulled off their trainers and slowly walked into the sea. They flapped their arms about and made all kinds of silly movements like they were trying to bear the cold, then ran back out.

Bronte laughed. It was too funny as she watched the same feat two or three times more. Eventually the runner came out and pulled their trainers on again.

Whoever you are, you're bonkers.

Bronte looked at her watch again and said, "I'd better run, myself."

Chapter Six

Sunday was generally a day of rest for Rosebrook, but Griffin wasn't sleeping well these days, so she was up early as usual. She wanted to go and see Ms. de Lacey first thing, but she didn't want to wake her, so she made coffee and looked over today's news on TV, but her thoughts kept turning back to last night.

What she'd seen had disturbed her. Griffin was in those woods camping all the time. She had even started to build a wooden forest shelter there before her mother's heart attack. Griffin had seen evidence of poaching before, small-time poaching, but what she saw last night was organized, and it had numbers of men involved. That was not good news for the local wildlife.

Griffin couldn't wait any longer, so she made her way over to the new animal rescue. It was extremely frosty on the hedgerows and the roads were icy, so much so that she had to watch her footing.

I could be backpacking through some warm tropical weather right now.

But Griffin couldn't let Fox and Patrick down, and so here she was, walking up to the door of some plummy London socialite with a social conscience, supported by Mummy and Daddy, no doubt.

She pressed the doorbell and waited and waited. Was the Right Honourable Bronte de Lacey still in bed?

Before Griffin abandoned her visit, she decided to walk down the path at the side of the cottage and check the garden. When she walked out past the side of the house, she stopped breathing.

Bronte was on the grass at the back in a yoga pose, facing away from her. It looked like some kind of advanced side plank, from what she could remember of yoga. But Griffin couldn't think—all she could see was the pink tinge to Bronte's skin.

She had tattoos on her arm and her shoulder blades. Browns and greens of stylized forest, trees, flowers, and vines twisted around her arm, but she couldn't see the front. On either side of her upper spine she had two artistic butterfly wings. The play of her muscles in her shoulders and back as she held herself still and in position was so feminine, but so strong, and the tumble of her hair as it draped over one shoulder made Griffin want to run her fingers through it.

Griffin felt the heavy beat of sexual attraction come upon her in a crashing wave. That was something she hadn't felt since before her life and world came crashing down.

In an instant Bronte turned her head back and said, "Griffin?"

Griffin took a panicked step forward, and the next thing she knew, she came crashing to the ground, and all the wind was knocked from her body. "Fuck!"

Bronte's face was over hers in a few seconds, and her hands were cupping her cheeks.

"Are you all right?"

Griffin had lost the power of words from the shock of her predicament and being lost in the blue-grey eyes above her.

"Griffin, are you hurt?"

Griffin came back to her senses quickly and felt the hot sting of embarrassment on her cheeks. "I'm fine, I'm fine. Let me up," Griffin said in a tone harsher than she meant. She struggled to her feet, half slipping on ice again, but she finally got there.

Bronte looked at her with annoyance. "Nothing hurt but your pride then?"

Griffin brushed herself down. "Why are you doing yoga outside in this temperature, with no jumper or jacket on at least?"

Bronte walked back to her original position and took a sip of water. "Not that it was any of your business, but I was inspired by a runner down at the beach. They only had shorts and a T-shirt on and went paddling in the sea. It looked really refreshing. I've only been out fifteen minutes anyway."

Griffin's embarrassment was still making her tense and defensive. "You should get warmed up soon."

"You shouldn't have come trespassing around to my garden, and you wouldn't have fallen like a stack of bricks."

Griffin had to change the subject. "Was that a side plank you were doing?"

"You know yoga?"

"I learned some from an Indian master when I was travelling."

Bronte gave her a mischievous smile. "Can you hold a plank?"

"Of course I can. Let's do one now."

"Are you sure you can manage?" Bronte said.

That sounded like a challenge to Griffin and a chance to restore her butch pride.

"I can manage and then some." Griffin took off her jacket and jumper, leaving her in just a white T-shirt. "I think I'm more likely to be able to hold that position than you." Griffin indicated to her body.

Bronte laughed. She actually laughed. "You think because you're bigger, taller, and more powerful than me you can hold a plank longer than me?"

"Let's do it then."

All thought of why she had come here was forgotten for the moment. She had pride to restore. They both got down on their knees.

"Ready?" Bronte said.

Griffin hoped she could remember how to do this. It was like riding a bike, surely? Once done, never forgotten.

She got into the position at the same time as Bronte. Immediately she felt the strain.

"You're too slack—tighten up your form," Bronte said sternly.

"Just leave me to it, would you?"

Griffin's arms and shoulders were already starting to shake, not to mention how her stomach muscles were feeling. This couldn't be happening. She was stronger than Bronte. Griffin started to grit her teeth, struggling even more, second by second. She turned to look at Bronte. She was perfectly still, in perfect form, and had an infuriating smile upon her face.

Griffin pushed and pushed her body, but she couldn't stop it crashing to the grass below. She'd made a fool of herself. Griffin fumed inside but jumped back onto her feet and saw that Bronte was still holding position. "It's a long time since I've done any yoga. I'm into weights, and I kind of hurt my shoulder the other week."

Bronte got up slowly and calmly. "Don't feel bad, Griffin. The world record holder is a woman with a build much like mine. It's not just about strength, it's about a state of mind. Come on, let's go inside, and I'll make you a cup of tea."

❖

Fox burst into the bedroom shivering. Clementine had just finished dressing and rushed over to her side.

"Foxy, you've got to stop running in this weather. It's not a normal winter." Clementine pulled a blanket from the bed and threw it around Fox's body.

Fox's speech was stammering as her teeth were chattering. "It's just when my body cools down."

"You could at least put on lots of clothes."

"That's part of the fun. It's endurance—it pushes and destresses your mind."

Clementine sighed. "I'll go and put the shower on for you."

She'd had to accept when loving and marrying Fox that Fox would always push the boundaries. It was just who she was, this great force that bounded through life trying to drink every last drop of life. But sometimes when Fox got too high, she had to bring her down. Clementine was the kind pessimistic soul in their relationship, the safe pair of hands who brought balance to their marriage.

When she came back into the bedroom, Fox looked up and said, "I went in up to my knees this morning."

Clementine threw her head back in exasperation before saying, "If you get hypothermia and die"—Clementine pointed her finger at her partner—"I'll kill you myself."

Fox looked quizzically at her. "But…I'd already be dead."

Clementine ignored her. "This new fad of yours could be dangerous."

Fox had fads or special interests all the time. She would get into them intensively until the next one came along. This time it was cold water therapy and open cold water swimming.

"It's not dangerous, if done properly. It helps with pain, recovery, and sharpness of the mind. In fact, it gave me an idea."

"Oh God. Here we go."

Fox got up and walked over to her, her blanket wrapped around her shoulders still. "No, no. It's nothing bad. It's an idea for the village."

"What then?" Fox opened up her blanket and Clementine stepped into Fox's arms. "Tell me."

"You know coastal towns and villages often have Christmas Eve or Christmas Day swims for charity? You've seen them on the news."

"You can't ask the villagers to do that."

"Why? Lots of towns do. It's just a quick plunge and then out. It's fun. Come on, admit you've seen it on the news."

"Okay, okay, but it isn't in years where we're having an abnormally cold winter."

Fox pulled her closer and gave her puppy dog eyes. "Please, Your Graceship?"

Clementine could feel herself weakening. She could never say no to Fox's puppy dog eyes.

Fox started to kiss her neck while saying, "Please, please, pretty please, my beautiful duchess."

"Oh, all right, but I don't want to hear one word about you encouraging Lucy to do it, because she's not."

Fox grinned widely, knowing that she had won. "You've got it."

Bronte had a smug spring in her step since her little contest with Griffin outside. It was so funny and kind of sweet to see her feathers ruffled a bit. Now at least, Griffin knew to take her seriously.

"Milk? Sugar?"

"No, just as it comes."

When she turned back around, Bronte saw Griffin looking at a picture on her kitchen wall. She had a similar one on her bedroom wall too. "Tea's ready."

Griffin looked back and then came to join her at the kitchen table. "That's a lovely picture."

The picture showed a laughing Bronte, doing a yoga pose with a red fox on her back.

"Thank you. That's my first love, my boy," Bronte said.

"Did you help save him?" Griffin asked.

Bronte nodded. "I was involved in a group of hunt saboteurs—still am, I suppose. We found a mother fox dying, and hiding behind a tree was her pup. The mother couldn't be saved, but I took him back to the animal sanctuary I was working in at the time, training to be an animal rehabilitator. Sox, as I called him, had a deformity to his leg, which was probably why he couldn't run away with his littermates when the hunters came. I hand-reared him."

Griffin smiled. Bronte liked her smile. It was open and warm, very different from the miserable face she had when Bronte met her.

"He looks really cute. Did you keep him at the animal sanctuary?"

"Yes, he wouldn't have survived in the wild with his deformity. Sox was my baby and became as tame as a dog, with me at least— no one else could control him. He was cheeky, full of fun, and really lightened up my life. Let me show you," Bronte unzipped her fleece and pulled out her left arm. "I got this artwork for him."

It was a half-sleeve tattoo of a forest scene, and further round was a red fox, with a back leg that was raised and deformed.

"It's beautiful," Griffin said. "I saw it from afar when you were doing your yoga outside. All your tattoos are beautiful."

That was a sweet thing to say. Maybe Griffin wasn't that bad, like the others had said. Maybe their first encounter had been a bad day for Griffin after all. Maybe.

"What happened to him?"

Bronte's emotions caught her off guard as her eyes welled. She looked down at the table and drew imaginary circles, trying to distract from showing her emotion. "Sox passed away at three years old. I found him in his den one morning. A heart defect, the vet thought. You probably think I'm a fool, don't you."

"Why would I think that?" Griffin replied.

"No one understood my connection with Sox, even some of the animal shelter staff, even the ones closest to me. We just had a bond, an understanding that not many have with a wild animal, I suppose."

Griffin leaned forward and said softly, "I believe it. I've travelled around the world and learned from many cultures. Most of them have stories about our deep connection to the planet and our fellow animals."

Why had this got so deep so quick? Bronte never showed her deepest feelings to someone she'd hardly met. She had to get this conversation on much firmer ground.

She lifted her mug of tea and said, "You wanted to see me about something before you fell on your behind and I outplanked you."

Griffin drew back. "Thanks for that reminder. Yes, I did. It was about poaching and hunting on Rosebrook land. It's always been, as long as I've been here, small scale. The duchess says the same thing, but something happened last night…"

"What happened?" Bronte was intrigued now.

"I couldn't sleep last night, so I went out for a walk. Walking and wandering helps clear my head."

What did the confident and changeable Griffin have on her mind, she wondered? "Yes?"

"I was walking along the road across from the bottom entrance to the forest. I heard lots of shotgun fire, then dogs barking and getting closer. Then men's voices caught up with them. I hid behind the wall across the road. Eventually some trucks came by, and the men got in them and drove away. This is much bigger than we're used to, and I wanted your advice before I go to Fox and the duchess."

"I was going to do a survey of the area tomorrow anyway. If you can show me roughly where they were, I'll check for injured animals. Once we know the general wildlife that's using that area—badger setts, fox dens—then we'll know what's been disturbed the next time," Bronte said as she got up and poured her tea down the sink.

"What then?" Griffin asked.

"Assuming they don't have the landowner's consent to be there—"

"No way would Fox and the duchess want them on their land," Griffin said angrily.

"I know that, but everything has to be done by the book. Then the landowner must make the complaint to the police. If it continues, then we'd need hard evidence. Getting them on camera would be best. We take our evidence to the police and demand they do something. There can be a lot of resistance in rural areas to hunting bans. They think it's their right. Especially foxes, who they see as vermin."

"Not in my eyes. Okay, that sounds like a plan," Griffin said.

"If you could just show me where you saw them, I can get on with the survey and you can get back to your day," Bronte said.

Griffin got up and poured her tea down the sink. "I'm going to help."

Bronte held up her hand. "Honestly, it's fine. I work better on my own."

"I love that forest, and I want to help. So if you want to find where I saw them, I'm coming too."

Bronte sighed. That's all she needed. A butch with a big ego following her around.

"Fine. Let's get going. I need to get back here by one o'clock. Lucy is coming over to help me lay out the animal pens."

"No problem."

Fox drank her smoothie while helping Clementine clean up the kitchen after breakfast.

"Did Lucy say where she was going after she got dressed?" Clementine asked.

"Into the library to study some of the information Bronte gave her."

Clementine turned off the tap and dried her hands. "Do you think she's happy? I mean, she's quite isolated out here."

Fox leaned against the kitchen island and crossed her arms. "She's made a couple of friends at school."

That was true—a girl and a boy had bonded with her over being the kids from a small village at the large town high school, and they did come over to visit.

"It's just the image of her sitting up in the library alone, or in her room. I know we spend most of our family time down here in the kitchen, well, apart from you two in your silly trampoline room."

Fox gave her a cheesy smile. "Luce loves the trampoline, and her friends did too."

"It's a big old house to live in. I just remember being a child and feeling a kind of loneliness."

"You don't think she's lonely?" Fox said with worry. "I spend as much time with her as I can. We go out on walks together, play computer games, watch TV, and you do—stuff."

Clementine laughed as Fox struggled to put together a word for what she did. "Boring stuff. Teach her about the estate, make sure she has everything for school, take care of her when she's ill, organize Christmas, birthdays—"

Fox walked around the kitchen island and took her hands. "You mother her. You're her mother to all intents and purposes, and I think her birth mother would be so happy, looking down over her, to see how well you are doing. I might do the big, flashy, exciting stuff, but you are the one she goes to when she needs taking care of."

"I hope her mother would think that. I couldn't love her more. I never really expected to be a mother, with the way my life was going, but I love having Lucy to take care of and helping her to learn about being the Duchess of Rosebrook. I want her to be happy, comfortable, and secure. When I was young, I had a dog. I thought, maybe a pet?"

Fox clicked her fingers. "Perfect! Let's go and ask."

Fox had Clementine up the stairs before she knew it. She guided Clementine through the grand art deco entrance hall at a fast pace.

"Foxy, maybe we should think about it and not just act on impulse. A pet is a big undertaking."

They stopped outside the library doors. "Impulse is my middle name."

Clementine rolled her eyes. "Oh, I know that. But sometimes impulses can lead you down the wrong road, Foxy."

Just as Clementine finished her sentence, the library doors opened and Lucy was there.

"Is there something wrong?" Lucy asked.

"No, we just wanted to ask you a question, Luce," Fox said.

There was no going back now, Clementine thought. "Let's go back into the library and we'll have a little chat," Clementine said.

They walked in, and Lucy led them over to the coffee table and chairs near the fireplace. Across the room there was a long high set of desks, with stools, where you could study the books. It wasn't huge compared to libraries in other stately homes but had been packed with some of the best books.

Isadora, Clementine's grandmother, and her father spent a lot of time in this library. Unfortunately, when it became time to sell off Rosebrook, when her father died, there wasn't enough room at the gatehouse to store all the books. Clementine and her mother picked those that had a lot of sentimental value and sold the rest.

Since marrying Fox and getting back to being the lady of the house, Clementine's mission had been to restock it and had an antiquarian book dealer working from Isadora's records to refill it. They had done well so far, but waiting for antique books to come on the market could be a long process.

Lucy looked worried when they sat down. "Is there something wrong?"

"No, no, nothing wrong." Clementine forgot just how close to panic Lucy could be sometimes. She had lost so much in her life. "We wanted to ask if you—"

"Would you like a pet?" Fox finished her sentence.

Lucy's eyes went wide. "What, really?"

"Yeah, something to keep you company in this big house," Clementine said.

Lucy answered immediately and excitedly. "I'd love a cat."

That caught both of them by surprise. Fox said, "I thought you'd say a dog."

"No, I've always loved cats. My dad would never let me get one. Look."

Lucy lifted her iPad and opened her Pinterest app. She had an album dedicated to cats, and when she opened the album, it was full of the cutest pictures.

A cat would certainly be easier than a puppy.

"Can we go to a shelter? I think we should rescue them," Lucy said.

"Of course we will," Fox said, then turned to Clementine. "Is there one nearby?"

"There's bound to be lots in town. Lucy, you do the research, and we'll go and look together, okay?"

Lucy nodded vigorously and then got up and hugged them both. "Thank you. I love you both so much."

Clementine hugged her tightly. It made her feel so good to put a smile on Lucy's face.

"Oh, I was going to ask," Lucy said, "is it okay if Jules and Mark come to the Christmas light switch-on?"

"The more the merrier." Fox smiled.

Maybe it was good to act on impulse sometimes, Clementine thought. The impulse had made a young girl extremely happy.

❖

Griffin slowed her walk and let Bronte catch up. She forgot sometimes that she had a much longer stride than average.

"Honestly," Bronte said, "you lope along what looks like so slowly, but those legs of yours cover vast distances with each step. How tall are you anyway?"

Griffin allowed Bronte to get a few strides ahead. "Six foot five."

"My God, you must have played basketball at school," Bronte said.

"I did, I love playing it."

Bronte looked back at her. "Are all the people in your family giants?"

"No, my mum's five foot two. Small woman."

"What about your dad?" Bronte asked.

Griffin stopped and gulped. She didn't want to answer that question, one of the reasons being that she didn't know. Luckily they'd arrived at the area of the forest where she'd seen the hunters.

"It was just here, Bronte."

"Was it? Okay, just give me a minute to open a new survey sheet on my iPad." It was a different iPad than the one she had at home. This one was bigger and had a military toughened case on it. On her other shoulder was an expensive looking camera, but it had kept slipping off her shoulder as they walked.

"Bronte? Let me carry your camera for you. Let me do something to help."

"Okay, thank you. Just be careful. It's a specialist camera and lens."

Griffin shook her head. That was a little condescending. "I think I can handle a camera."

"I'm just asking you to be careful—there's a lot invested in it."

"Did Mummy and Daddy buy it?" That sounded more like an insult than she intended it to be.

Bronte looked at her scathingly. Bronte could certainly give a frightening look. "Everything I have, I've worked hard to get. *Mummy and Daddy* helped me with nothing."

Griffin was put completely in her place. "I didn't mean—"

Bronte cut her off abruptly. "Forget it. I have a job to do, and if you insist on coming with me, then keep absolutely quiet. You follow my signals and follow my lead. Do you understand?"

Griffin saluted Bronte instead of replying verbally, and that seemed to annoy Bronte more.

"Follow me."

As they started to slowly pick their way through the trees, Griffin watched carefully for any signals from Bronte. She didn't want to make her any madder at her, which she had seemed to do since they first met. But Griffin had to admit she was surprised at Bronte's character. Perhaps she had jumped to conclusions going by her name and title and allowed her own complicated family history with those who were titled to colour her judgement.

Talking to Bronte had shown Griffin that she was fiercely independent, brave, and not your typical aristocratic socialite from London. She was also an extremely caring person who loved animals. The way Bronte described her relationship with Sox the fox had touched Griffin. There was clearly a long story about where she was today and how she got there. It would be interesting to find out.

The one thing that meeting Bronte had done was to take her mind off the problems and emotions that had been plaguing her, and that was just in one day. Maybe if she could manage not to piss off Bronte as much as she had been, they could be friendly.

Bronte slowed and held up her hand as she crouched down. Griffin got close to her.

"What is it?" Griffin whispered.

Bronte kept her voice low. "You see the big tree straight across from us?"

Griffin nodded.

"Just at the base, there's three flat oval holes. That's a badger's sett."

"Is it occupied?" Griffin asked.

"Without getting up close, I'd say yes. You see the fresh mounds of earth outside? That means Mr. or Ms. Badger has been active recently."

"Do you think the hunters were after them or got them?"

Bronte shook her head. "It's more likely they were after something else. Fox or deer. Otherwise the entrances to the sett would be torn up by the digging of the dogs. I'll log this sett and we can move on."

"You know your stuff, don't you."

Bronte looked back and narrowed her eyes. "You sound surprised. Did you perhaps judge me by my name before you met me?"

Just as Griffin was about to reply, Bronte moved off, leaving her smart reply frustratingly unsaid. The frustration was making Griffin angry. *I could just turn back and leave her where she is. I mean, she didn't want me here in the first place.*

But despite her frustrated thoughts, she began following Bronte again.

They arrived at the area in the woods where Bronte first came across Griffin. It was a clearing in the middle of the trees with a partially built wooden structure, some piles of wood, and a round circle of stones that marked out a campfire.

"Is this where you play at making dens?" Bronte said cheekily.

"Oh, I'm allowed to speak at normal volumes now?"

It was quite fun annoying Griffin. At least she was entertaining. She'd had more fun with Griffin or at Griffin's expense than she'd had for a long time. "You can speak normally now, yes. There's no animal activity in your"—Bronte used air quotes—"den."

"It's not a den," Griffin said.

"What is it then?"

"It's my outdoor living room. Somewhere I come to think, to talk and have a beer with my friends—"

"A den." Bronte walked over to the fire circle, and Griffin followed her. It was fun baiting her.

Griffin got so close to her she could see the deep ocean blue of her eyes. "And somewhere to stop me wandering off into the night, which is what I'd like to do."

Bronte saw hurt in Griffin's eyes, and anger. She was displaying these emotions like a wounded animal, trying to scare her off. Luckily she was an expert with wounded animals.

"What do you mean *wander*?"

There were inches of cold air and silence between them, until Griffin looked briefly down at her lips and then quickly walked off towards her piles of wood that were waiting to be used.

"I mean wander, to go travelling. That's what I do, and what I want to be doing now."

"You do look like the perennial gap year student," Bronte joked to ease the tension. "What age are you anyway?"

"Thirty-four."

"Bit old for a gap year," Bronte said.

"Where I come from we didn't have gap years—we had to get a job at sixteen just to help put food on the table. We didn't have the luxury of going to university or having a gap year like the de Laceys of this world."

That comment did sting. Even though the de Laceys thought they were poor in aristocratic terms when she was growing up, it was nothing like the kind of poverty Griffin was clearly talking about. Bronte did go to university, and she did have a gap year.

"So why don't you leave then. What's holding you back?"

"I gave my word to Fox that I would stay until the beer factory was up and running and I had trained my assistant, Patrick."

"And when will it be up and running?" Bronte asked.

"Probably another year. We are making a few beers and lagers and selling them in local shops, but our aim is to get into supermarkets, so that the factory could offer more jobs. That's what Fox wants, but the day I met you, I told Fox I had to leave after Christmas."

Bronte felt disappointed. "Oh? What about your promise?"

"My circumstances have changed. I need to get back on the road, but I promised I'd help Fox interview a new brewery manager before I go."

Bronte was desperate to ask why her circumstances had changed, but she hardly knew the woman. She could feel there was cause for Griffin to be wounded, so it wouldn't be polite, and besides it didn't sound like she wanted to talk about it.

"Let's check the site for any evidence," Bronte said.

"Fucking bastards," Bronte heard Griffin shout.

She hurried over to the shelter structure where Griffin was standing. "What is it?"

"They've kicked in one of the side panels, and there are beer cans everywhere," Griffin said angrily. Griffin pulled at the wood that was splintered. "I'm going to have to replace this whole side now."

"Is this the beer and lager you brew?"

Bronte was holding one of the discarded cans and kneeling by the bag of cans she kept in her wooden shelter. It could easily look like she was an alcoholic stashing beer out here and drinking on her own.

"This isn't what it looks like. I kept the bag out here because it would be freezing cold, and my friends often come out here and sit by the fire with me, enjoy one or two cans."

"You don't have to explain yourself to me, Griffin," Bronte said.

"I know, but I just wanted you to know. I only have a few over the weekend. I'm in the factory all week, tasting and checking the product. It wouldn't do me good to be getting drunk on it most nights."

"How do you taste-test without getting sozzled? Is it like wine tasting?"

"Exactly right. You've got to be like a chef, always taste-testing their food," Griffin explained.

"We better clear up these cans, so they don't hurt the animals. Do you want to keep these unopened ones out here?" Bronte asked.

"No, I'll take them. They're only an attractive nuisance for those idiots, and I don't want them to hurt any animals."

Bronte looked at her watch. "I better get back to the cottage. Lucy will be there soon. I'll finish my survey tomorrow."

"So we've found nothing," Griffin said as they started to walk back through the woods.

"Nothing that can help us at the moment, other than we know they were there from the beer cans and the two shotgun shells you found."

"It's frustrating. I want to catch these fuckers before they hurt the animals."

"We must be patient. They'll make a mistake, and we'll get the evidence as long as I keep checking on the welfare of the animals."

"I'll keep looking too. I'll be out repairing my shelter."

When they were clear of the forest, they walked down the road to the cottage. When they stopped outside, Bronte said, "Why are you going ahead with building your den when you're leaving after Christmas?"

That was a good question, and one Griffin hadn't really thought about. "It gives me something to do in my spare time, out in the woods. I like being outdoors, and when I'm gone, my friends can use it. And it's a *shelter*."

Bronte pursed her lips and nodded. She seemed to accept that explanation. "Thanks for your assistance today. Hopefully they won't come back in those numbers again."

"Yeah, I'll keep looking too, but you're sure the animals were okay?"

Bronte nodded. "The fox burrows and badger setts looked fine. Maybe they were too drunk to cause any problems."

There was a long silence, and Griffin was desperate to say something. "Come down to the beer factory anytime, and I'll give you a tour."

"Thank you, and if you want to practice any more yoga poses, you know where to come."

Griffin laughed. "Yeah, I do. I'll see you later then, Bronte. Have a good day."

She started to walk down into the village. That was an experience, and even through Bronte was apparently good at pushing her buttons, Griffin had enjoyed every minute she'd spent with her.

As Griffin walked towards the pub, darker thoughts started to filter back into her mind. They'd been gone all morning and now all the emotions that she wanted to forget were building. Maybe she would go back for some yoga lessons.

Chapter Seven

H ello?" Clementine said.
Clementine and Lucy came around the back of Bronte's cottage to see her carrying some grey plastic animal houses, but she couldn't immediately see what kind.

"Hi." Bronte put them down and came over to them. "Hi, Lucy, and nice to see you, Your Grace."

"You don't have to worry about formalities with me, Bronte."

"My mother would kill me if she heard me calling you by your first name, but if you insist...hi, Clementine." Bronte smiled.

"Baroness Lawton likes her formalities then?"

Bronte laughed and said sarcastically, "Just a bit. She's obsessed with aristocracy and her position in it. So as you can imagine, it's nice to get away."

Clementine laughed.

Bronte pulled off her gloves and said, "Good to have you, Lucy. There's a lot of work to do."

"I can't wait."

Clementine put her arm around Lucy. "She's been so excited and studying all the information you gave her."

"Excellent. We're going to save a lot of animals. But there's work to do before that."

Lucy pointed over to the grey plastic items Bronte had been carrying. "Are they hedgehog houses?"

"They are. We're likely to have some hedgehogs, given the rural location."

"Ah," Clementine said, "I was wondering what they were. What's your plan? Are you going to advertise for some staff now or wait?"

"I will need help once we start getting the animals in, but I think it would be a waste of the Trust's money at the moment to take on any staff. I've got contacts at my previous jobs that can give me names if I need them."

"Can I go look around?" Lucy said.

"Sure, on you go," Bronte answered.

Once Lucy walked off, Bronte said, "Griffin came to me this morning to say she'd heard a whole gang of hunters out last night in the woods. She was taking a late night walk and heard the gun, dogs, and voices."

Clementine was immediately angry. "How dare they do that on Rosebrook land. That sounds much more serious than one or two men poaching."

"It is. Griffin wanted my advice on what to do next and was going to come and see you today. We went out and surveyed the woods for any injured animals, and any evidence that they had disturbed the badger setts, or fox and rabbit holes, but everything looked undisturbed. Going by the litter they left, they were more interested in getting drunk."

Clementine folded her arms and shook her head. "I'm not having this. I'll make a report to the police."

"If you take my advice, I'd wait until we get some evidence, or your complaint will be quietly shelved. In rural places like this area, the police are sympathetic to hunters. I belonged to a group trying to stop illegal hunting, and I'll tell you it's hard. Even with video footage we took and witness statements, more often than not nothing was done."

"What do you suggest we do?" Clementine asked.

"I'll keep checking on the woods and the animals, and if it continues, I'd suggest getting cameras and recording equipment."

"Okay, we'll follow your lead. I don't often like to bring out my title, but if the police are not helpful, then it won't be Clementine Fitzroy that goes to the police station, it'll be the Duchess of Rosebrook, Countess of Thistleburn, and Baroness Portford who turns up at the station."

Bronte laughed. "That might be just what we need."

"I heard you got off to a bad start with Griffin—how was she this morning?"

Bronte had a flash of them doing yoga together, having a heartfelt conversation about Sox her first fox, and then being inches away from her lips. She had felt drawn towards them like magnetism, but then Griffin pulled away.

"It was…she was…okay."

"I'm glad," Clementine said. "Griffin is the nicest of people, but she has a lot on her mind recently."

A wounded animal.

"No, we were okay."

"Good. I better go. I'm doing my rounds. I usually visit all the villagers I can, see if anyone needs any help."

"I'll keep Lucy busy for you."

Clementine shouted, "Luce, I'll come and get you later. Have a good time."

"Bye, Aunty Clem," Lucy shouted.

"Oh," Clementine turned and walked backwards as she spoke, "Fox said to tell you that the sign for the sanctuary will be delivered sometime this week. Be prepared for it to be bright, loud, and in your face. It is Fox who designed it."

"Gotcha."

Once Clementine walked away, Bronte clapped her hands together. "Okay, Lucy. We have work to do."

❖

Sundays were busy for The King's Arms, Rosebrook's pub and social gathering point. It was run by Jonah, who lived in the village with Rupert, his husband. For those that didn't have families or couldn't be bothered cooking, the pub's Sunday lunch was popular.

Griffin always came in here on a Sunday to enjoy the good food and good company. She enjoyed a roast beef dinner and, on the way out of the pub, stopped to let their resident farmers Mr. Mason and Mr. Murdoch know about the hunting situation.

"If you see or hear anything while you're out and about, could you let me or the duchess know?"

"Aye, we will indeed. Bunch of thugs, I tell you," Mr. Mason said. "You don't control the animal population while drinking booze and using guns. They'll blow each other's heads off before long."

Mr. Murdoch agreed. "Very true. We'll let you know, Griffin."

"Thanks."

Griffin walked out the pub door and was hit by the cold. It was refreshing in a way, as the pub had been too warm for her taste. She couldn't face going home to an empty house. The silence only brought out her worries.

She walked down the road and headed towards the beach. She passed the Seascape cottages. Every cottage had shells and polished rocks embedded in the walls.

She spotted Patrick Doyle and Alanna Wilson, who lived next door to each other there. They were both at Alanna's house, Patrick helping push Alanna's wheelchair up the ramp at the door.

"Hey, Alanna, Paddy."

They both waved back. It was so good to see Patrick settled here. After living homeless on the streets of London, Rosebrook was the perfect place for him to feel safe and accepted.

She came to the steps overlooking the beach and started her descent. Rosebrook beach was beautiful whether the sun was splitting the trees or the sand itself was frostbitten. It took some time to walk down the steps to the beach, but when her feet hit the sand, it was all worth it.

The wind blew the icy chill and the salty smell of the briny sea into her face. It really blew away all her cobwebs. She walked down to the water's edge and watched the waves lap near her booted feet. The water looked so clear, so inviting, but the icy shock of cold wouldn't be so inviting.

It had been a strange day, one Griffin hadn't been expecting. It started with yoga and turned into hunting some hunters.

Griffin closed her eyes, and she saw herself walking around the corner at the animal sanctuary and her body coming alive at the sight of Bronte in her yoga pose. The artistic pair of black-outlined butterfly wings made Griffin long to tenderly stroke her fingers down her spine between the wings, and then replace her fingers with her lips.

She snapped her eyes open. Now her body had truly awakened. Griffin couldn't even remember the last time she had sex, probably before she left Bali to come to Rosebrook. It wasn't that she didn't have opportunities. She could have gone into town, or up to London for a weekend, but whenever she made plans, they never came to anything.

Rosebrook had an effect on her. It made her reassess her life and what she wanted. Was wandering the globe and one- or two-night stands all that there was?

Bronte had joked that she was a perennial backpacker, too old to be on a never-ending gap year, and though she didn't like to admit it, there was truth to that. The women backpackers got younger, and Griffin became less interested.

Coming to Rosebrook had given her a shot in the arm. There was good company with people of her own age, good times at the pub, good times on the beach, and on this beach there had been a nanosecond where Griffin thought she had connected with Ashling O'Rourke, but Ash's heart belonged to Archie long before they admitted it to each other.

Now Ash was Ashling Archer, and she and Archie were two of her closest friends.

She'd spent one day with the Right Honourable Bronte de Lacey, and now she'd started to think about sex again?

Griffin was trying to forget about Right Honourables. Her father was one, and now providence had brought another into her life. Bronte de Lacey did seem to have a few people in the village charmed already.

She'd had a good chat with Fergus in the pub, who was telling her all about the wonderful young woman he met this morning, and Jay and Erica were singing her praises too. How funny life was.

Voices pulled her from her thoughts. Griffin turned around and saw Archie and Ash walking along the beach.

"Hey, you two. A cold day for a walk," Griffin said.

Ash's arms were up inside her sleeves. Archie pointed to his wife. "We've just had Sunday dinner at her dad's, and this one says"—Archie put on a high pitched tone—"It'll be so romantic to have a walk on the blowy, frostbitten beach. Then she does nothing but complain about how cold she is the whole way."

Griffin laughed. This was the kind of thing she'd never had. Bickering and laughing, passion and love. She knew that her two friends had all of those things.

"It is pretty cold," Griffin said.

"Oh, for God's sake."

Archie opened up her big winter puffer jacket and said, "Get in here."

Ash giggled and scooted inside. Archie wrapped the jacket around Ash's back as if they were under a duvet together.

"Right," Archie said, "we might have less complaining and be able to hear each other better, Griff."

At first Griffin felt embarrassed to be a part of what felt like an intimate moment, but then started to feel jealous that she'd never had this easy way with a woman. Bickering one minute, being so very intimate the next. It was attractive.

"Have you heard Fox's latest madness?" Archie said.

"No, what is it?"

"Apparently we're all to go for a swim in the sea on Christmas morning."

Griffin couldn't believe her ears. She looked over at the freezing sea and pointed. "That? In there?"

Archie nodded. "I kid you not. In the worst winter to hit the south of England since the sixties."

Griffin couldn't even imagine how cold that would be, and she was used to being out in all weathers.

"To be fair," Ash said, "it is a thing that people do for charity, up and down the country. I know they do it at Sandbanks Beach in Poole. People come together, raise some money, and have fun."

"What's the charity?" Griffin asked.

"A homeless shelter in Bournemouth. Fox isn't a fool. She knows as soon as she adds that bit of information, all of us who are physically able will feel obliged."

Griffin could see Fox's logic. She already knew she'd have to do it. Homeless charities had looked after her friend Patrick while he was on the streets, so she had to. "I suppose we're doing it then."

Archie sighed. "Yes, I suppose."

"Don't worry, I'll have a warm flask of tea waiting for you," Ash said.

"What? Oh no, you're coming in too."

"I'll be too busy making Christmas dinner for you and Dad."

"I thought a second ago you were going to be here with a flask of tea?" Archie said.

The bickering was back. Griffin laughed internally.

"Look, let's talk about this later," Ash said.

"Yes," Archie replied, "let's argue about this later. Are you walking back up to the village with us, Griff?"

"Yeah, I should be getting home."

They walked away together, and Ash was complaining about the cold again, since she'd had to leave Archie's jacket.

Griffin's mind flipped back to this morning. She had argued or bickered back and forth with Bronte. That had been fun. Bronte had a challenging personality. She was confident, independent, and single-minded, and Griffin was looking forward to seeing her again.

But for now she wanted to get home to her warm fireplace and some warm food.

❖

The next day it was back to work for Griffin. She was looking forward to getting her head back in the brewing process and away from her problems. Griffin was also looking forward to seeing Bronte again, who said she would visit and have a tour of the beer factory.

Her mind had been on Bronte a lot since last night. For one thing, when Griffin closed her eyes she wasn't tormented with her bad memories as much. She thought about being terrible at yoga, and how she would enjoy trying to show Bronte she could best her, in some of the moves anyway.

She walked through the open factory doors and was hit by the smell that she loved. The smells of the brewing process weren't to everyone's taste—boiled grains, yeast, sulphur, and cleaners and sanitizers. Constant cleaning was vitally important in the process and was why two of their twelve staff were cleaning staff. They had worked hard to get their small brewery the required safety and food standards certificates, and Griffin wasn't going to let that slip.

Griffin greeted the staff as she walked by. They only had two members of staff who lived in the village full time—Tommy, a man in his fifties who had worked in the brewing industry, and a twenty-year-old apprentice, Hazel. The rest came from surrounding villages and towns.

Rosebrook Brewery was still in its infancy, but it was hoped that as the village grew at a slow pace, so would the brewery. No one was in a hurry.

Griffin bounded up the steel staircase to her office, two steps at a time. At the top of the staircase, she was hit with another aroma being blown in the back door, rotting grains. They stored it outside for Mr. Murdoch and Mr. Mason, to feed their cattle, a green carbon offset that Archie came up with. She was an expert in the greenest ways to farm both animals and arable farming.

A lot of visitors couldn't stand the smell, but Griffin was used to it. Luckily the back doors wouldn't be open for long. And since this cold snap began, Patrick said the industrial heaters had been cranked up all day.

She opened up the office door and was hit by a welcome wall of heat.

"Morning, Paddy, my man."

"Hi." Patrick was writing on the big whiteboard on the office wall. "We've got some big orders. We'll be working hard on the floor to make them."

"Who's ordered?"

"Jonah wants ten more crates on his order, plus ten boxes of the special Christmas branded packs. He says the tourists are still coming in their numbers, even though it is the winter, and they want to take Rosebrook Beers and Ales home with them."

"That's true. People seem to enjoy the windswept beach from the safety of their car at the lookout point, and a hot drink from Erica and Jay's shop."

"Then pop in for a beer at the pub, and there's the Christmas market."

"Yeah, we've got the big winter festival switch-on and the farmer's market in Kirkswell."

"We'll be ready," Paddy said proudly. The change from the browbeaten boy who'd come to Rosebrook to the young man he was now was like night and day, and Griffin was so proud of him.

Griffin took off her jacket and started to dress for the shop floor with a hairnet and white coat. "Oh, Bronte de Lacey will pop in some-time for a tour. Let me know when she arrives," Griffin said.

"Is that the animal rescue lady?"

"Yeah, that's her. I told her I'd give her a tour. I'd expect her today or tomorrow."

But today, tomorrow, and the next day went by, and still no Bronte. For those three days Griffin went to work with an excited anticipation that today would be the day, but she never came. Griffin started to become annoyed at Bronte. They had spent a good day together, making a connection, maybe a friendship, and now nothing.

Griffin so wanted to go to her cottage and see her, talk to her, but stubbornness stopped her. She was not going running to her.

This resolve lasted until Thursday.

Patrick had everything under control. The staff were cleaning in preparation to shut down the machines at five. Griffin wanted to see Bronte before the whole village got too dark, as it did in winter.

Griffin left about half past two. She strode quickly through the village, which was having more decorations added to it. She waved to Jay at the shop, where he was perched on steps applying a few garlands to his window.

Fox really was trying hard to a have a traditional British Christmas—or winter festival, as she liked to call it. They had people of many different cultures and a few different religions in the village, and Fox didn't want to leave anyone out.

So a winter festival it was, and in the private life of each home in Rosebrook, they could celebrate or not as they wished. But it was Fox's hope that the winter festival would be a village festival. Something they could all enjoy.

Griffin approached Bronte's cottage, and she couldn't but notice—or be hit in the face by—the huge sign in front of it. The sign would have been more at home in London advertising Fox Toys' flagship store. It featured the Fox Toys brand character, Mr. Fox, in his top hat and tails, next to the name of the place: *Fox Toys Animal Rescue: Trust Director Bronte de Lacey.*

Griffin laughed. The sign just had Fox all over it. Big, loud, and in your face.

Her laughter was interrupted by the clanging of metal and a few choice swear words. Griffin ran around the side of the cottage and found Bronte struggling to hold up a mesh metal fence panel, while trying to reach another one on the ground.

"Hey, stop." Griffin ran over and took the weight of the fence panel from Bronte. "Why are you doing this on your own? Are you bonkers?"

Bronte bent over double trying to get her breath back. "Are you saying I'm weak? Not capable?"

Griffin said with a hint of frustration in her voice, "No, I'm saying anyone would struggle to build this on their own."

Bronte stood up and appeared as if she was taking her own frustrations out on Griffin. "That hasn't stopped you building a shelter in the woods on your own."

"And look how far I've gotten. Not far. Why didn't you ask Fox's contractors to put it up?"

"Because they wouldn't do it right. I know how the pens should be set up. I let them put down these wood chip areas for the pens to sit on."

Griffin lowered the fence to the ground and crossed her arms. "Sounds a bit control freakish to me."

Bronte placed her hands on her hips. "Oh, does it, does it really?"

"I don't understand why you're so mad."

"I'm mad at myself for not being capable of putting up a fence, and at you for making me feel a fool," Bronte said.

"I made you feel a fool—" Griffin bit her tongue. She knew it wouldn't get her anywhere. Bronte could be a little bad-tempered, couldn't she? "All you had to do was come to me or anyone else in the village. That's what we do in Rosebrook—we are a collective, not individuals."

Bronte sighed. It was hard for her to ask for help, because asking for help meant admitting she was wrong, had taken the wrong path, proving her mother right. But it had to be.

"Griffin, would you assist me in putting up this pen, please?"

Griff grinned. "Happy to, and call me Griff. All my friends do."

Bronte watched Griffin with a keen eye as Griffin lifted up the two fence panels.

"You steady them, and I'll get the driver," Griffin said. Griffin screwed the top and bottom bolts together quickly and was ready for the next. "What's this going to be for?"

"A fox pen. I've got all the equipment I need for inside all the pens in the lockup out in the field."

Griffin was making short work of this and was nearly on the second to last panel. "I thought the foxes were going in a large fox run in the field."

"That's for a longer-term stay or if the fox can't be released back to the wild. This is for keeping a close eye on them and any injuries they have."

"I got you. Let's get the roof up for you. Have you got ladders?"

"Yes, in the workshop at the back, but before that, let me show you Fox Toys Animal Sanctuary's first guests."

"You found injured animals?"

"Don't worry. It's not too serious. Follow me." She led Griffin up to the row of purpose-built glass-walled heated indoor pens beside the workshop. "I like to call these our recovery rooms. I was out with Lucy, finishing my animal survey, when we spotted these two hedgehogs." Bronte pointed to the touchscreen computer panel on each of the pen doors. "From right to left we have Hedge and Hoggy."

Griffin laughed. "That's brilliant."

"Lucy chose the names. They're already social media stars. Look." Bronte got out her phone and opened the Twitter app. "Fox's PR team have an account for the sanctuary. I send them on any pictures I think they could use, and the team make stories or GIFs out of them. It's a great idea."

"Who's that?" Griffin pointed to the digital hedgehog character in a sharp country-gentleman's suit and tie, beside the photo of the two new guests.

"Lucy tells me that is Sir Hogsworth, a character from the computer game Fox has, *The Woodlanders*. Both he and Mr. Fox live in a woodland with other characters."

"Sweet. It'll be a good tie-up with the sanctuary. So what happened to the little hogs?"

The way Griffin described them as hogs made Bronte's tummy flip with the cuteness if it. Her first reaction was to reach out to touch Griffin's arm and say, "Aww, that's so—" She suddenly came to her senses and stopped herself before she went any further.

Bronte cleared her throat.

"They had both cut their feet on a discarded piece of barbed wire on the woodland floor."

"Poor little things. Do you think the barbed wire is from the hunters?"

"I wasn't sure. Is there normally discarded trash like that in the woodland?"

Griffin shook her head. "Fox has regular clean-up days of the woodland, the beach, the hedgerows—don't let Fox get started on the importance of hedgerows to the countryside," Bronte joked, "you'll be there for hours. So no, it's not normal."

"Our hunters might be responsible then. We'll need to keep an ever-watchful eye out there. I'll take a walk after work each night and check everything's okay."

"If you ever want company, just let me know," Griffin said.

Bronte felt her heart thud at that suggestion. *No. I'm not letting anything like that start to happen.* Griffin might be utterly gorgeous and sweet, but Bronte wasn't interested in any romance or even just a sexual experience. She wasn't interested.

Her one experience of falling in love had started as a rebellion, to annoy her mother, someone utterly unsuitable in her mother's eyes, but Bronte hadn't expected to fall in love. That had been her downfall.

Griffin would be utterly unsuitable to her mother too. Her mother only saw potential romance for Bronte when she saw pound signs above a suitor's head. That didn't seem likely with the rough and ready Griffin. Perfect for rebellion, but Bronte was too old for that, and she wouldn't use someone like Griffin.

"What did you have to do with our little friends?" Griffin asked.

"Clean out their wounds and bandage their feet. They just need a safe space with food and water to recover. They'll be back on their feet and back to the forest in no time," Bronte said.

Griffin was all smiles. She put her hand on the glass door and spoke to them. "Get well soon, little hogs."

Again, sweet. *Just ignore it.* She needed a change of subject.

"Will we get on? The ladders are in the workshop."

"Let's get to it."

It took more time than Bronte anticipated, getting the roof on and secured, but eventually it was down, and the metal pegs for the pen inserted into the ground. "That should do it."

Griffin stamped the last peg into the ground with her boot. It had gotten so dark, so quickly that Bronte had to get a torch from the workshop and keep it trained on Griffin as she worked. "I don't think we can start another pen tonight. It's too dark."

"Yes, it's going to be a slower process than I thought. I can't thank you enough for helping," Bronte said.

It went against Bronte's nature to ask or take help from anyone, but she had to admit, she couldn't have done this alone.

"I'll try to get away from the brewery as early as I can, since it's dark so early, and then at the weekend we should get it finished. Lucy will be around to help too, you said." Griffin leant the ladders against the pen and brushed herself down.

"You don't have to do this, you know," Bronte said uneasily.

"I know, but I want to help. If you ask some of the other villagers for help, we could get done even quicker."

The control freak in Bronte saw the back garden area full of people, all doing things their way.

"Let's just keep it to you and Lucy, okay?"

"Okay. If that's what you want," Griffin said.

"Do you want a drink before you go?" Bronte offered.

"No thanks, I better get something to eat and do some paperwork."

"Have I kept you from your work?"

"Don't worry. I loved doing this more than budgets and payroll."

"Well, thank you. I'll give you a free yoga lesson whenever you want," Bronte joked.

❖

"I can't watch," Clementine said putting her hands over her eyes. Ash clasped her hand. "It'll be okay."

"You don't even believe that. I can tell by your voice."

Ash sighed. "Well, if I have to, you do too."

Clementine opened her eyes to see Fox and Archie ascending two huge ladders beside the Christmas tree in the reception hall, with Lucy in support at the bottom.

Fox and Lucy had decorated every public room and Lucy's bedroom in Christmas decorations. It was only the end of October, but they wore Clementine down.

Mr. Morton, the head gardener, and his team had offered to do this, but Fox was determined to decorate the family home herself.

When it came time to put up this huge tree, Fox roped in Archie, and so this dangerous exercise went ahead. The art deco reception hall was now home to a large Christmas tree, with what would be coloured lights and childlike decorations.

They both made it to the top and Lucy filled a bag with baubles and tinsel, which Fox then pulled to the top of the ladder with a rope.

"She's thought about everything, hasn't she?" Ash said.

"It's not even November yet, Ash. I was all for the big country Christmas she wanted, but my *big* and Fox's idea of *big* are entirely different."

"It'll be nice when it's done," Ash said.

"As long as Lucy and I are not visiting Fox in hospital come Christmas day. That floor is marble, Ash. If she or Archie fell on that—"

"Don't finish that thought." Ash shouted up, "Be careful, Archie."

"I will, I will. Don't panic," Archie replied.

"Maybe I'm moaning too much," Clementine said. "It will be the best Christmas the village has had since my grandmother Isadora had the house."

"The big switch-on in the village next week is going to be spectacular," Ash said.

"It will. You, Archie, and Fox have put a lot of effort into the winter festival." Clementine squeezed Ash's hand.

"I hope the village will like it. Archie and I made sure the professionals put up all the lights and decorations, don't worry."

Fox's voice bellowed down from the ladder. "Luce? Last chance. Definitely the star for the top and not the angel or Mr. Fox?"

"The star, please," Lucy replied.

"Okay."

Fox had to go up to the second to last step to put the star on the tree. The ladder wobbled, and Clementine turned her back.

"Tell me when it's over, Ash. I'm terrified."

About twenty seconds later, Ash said, "It's all done now, Clem. She's back down to where she was."

"Phew. My hands are shaking." Clementine held them up to show Ash.

"Oh God," Ash said, "it's my turn."

Fox swung the bag of decorations, dangling on the rope, over to Archie. "You get the decs on your side now, Archie."

Clementine tried to distract her. "Are you having Christmas dinner at your house or your dad's?"

"Dad's. I feel closer to Mum that way."

Ash's mum had died of breast cancer when Ash was still in high school, and both she and her dad, James O'Rourke, never got over it.

"That sounds like a good idea." Clementine rubbed her back.

Ash gulped hard, trying to control her emotion. Then she said, "What about you?"

"Fox's mum and dad, Cassia and Donny, are coming. In fact they invited themselves. They weren't going to miss a Christmas with Lucy."

"They've bonded then?" Ash asked.

"Absolutely. When we took her to London to meet them, they just took her as one of their own. Grandma and Grandpa straight away."

"Aww," Ash said, "it's so nice how everything is going so well for her. She has a ready-made family."

"I'm lucky, Ash. It's not every partner that would have been happy taking on a teenager as soon as they got married."

"Fox isn't everyone."

"Very true. We'll have the Tucker twins, can't have them sitting alone, and between us and Kay, anyone else who's alone."

Their attention was turned to Archie's noisy descent from her ladder.

"No, no, no. I'm not doing it."

Fox climbed down quickly and jumped the last few steps. "Oh, come on. It's just a bit of fun. It's for the children. Children from all the nearby villages are coming."

"Why can't Mr. Murdoch or Mr. Mason do it? They're more the age and shape."

"They'll be looking after the horses and the horse and cart that they are lending me. I could have gotten reindeer, but I don't really agree with them being used like that, once a year. Mr. Mason's cart horses won't mind helping."

Ash turned to Clementine. "What's this about?"

"One of Fox's brainwaves that puts poor Archie on the spot."

Archie's voice brought their attention back to the argument. "I'm not doing it, Fox. You've already got me roped into swimming in the sea, on Christmas day, in the worst winter in decades. On top of that you are not making me be Santa Claus in front of the whole village."

Ash burst out laughing. "Is that what this is about?"

Clementine couldn't hide her smile. "Yes, Archie being led into the village on horse and cart as Santa Claus."

Ash rushed over to Archie. "Oh, you have to do it, Arch. It'll be so sweet, seeing you all dressed up, handing out presents to the kids."

Archie began to speak, but Fox interrupted. "I've gotten you the best suit and beard, and big padding to make you all cosy and cuddly."

Ash threw her arms around Archie. "Oh yes, do it, sweetheart, you'll be adorable."

"Fine. I'll do it," Archie said through gritted teeth.

Fox turned to Clementine and winked. Clementine shook her head. *You are just incorrigible.*

CHAPTER EIGHT

Griffin had been wrong. It took more than a week to put the pens up at the sanctuary. She had underestimated the Christmas rush at the factory and couldn't get away on time before the dark set in.

Bronte did what she could during the day, but she really needed that second pair of hands. Lucy had school, and dark set in by the time she got home too. She came around to help with the hedgehogs and learn about their care.

She could have asked Kay, but secretly she enjoyed Griffin's company and looked forward to it. There were just a couple of pens to go, and they'd be ready.

Bronte was in the workshop at the back of the outside area, making an inventory of supplies. She heard a voice shouting from the house and recognized it straight away because butterflies were floating about her stomach.

Griffin.

She hurried back into the garden and saw Griffin standing there with a small crate of beer. "Patrick did me a favour so I could get here before we lost the light."

Bronte started to jog but stopped herself quickly. *What are you doing? Running to her with a huge smile on your face?* "That's great. We can get so much more done."

"I brought you a crate of our beers and lagers to try."

Bronte smiled and took them from her. "That's really nice of you."

"Don't mention it. I'd like to hear your opinions on them. You do have a lot of opinions."

Griffin winked at her as she said that, and Bronte's stomach clenched. "I suppose I do, don't I?"

"Oh, something else." Griffin took off her military style jacket, and Bronte gulped when she saw Griffin was only wearing a white vest underneath.

"What are you doing? It's too cold with just a thin vest on," Bronte said. She must have sounded extremely flustered.

Next thing Griffin dropped to her knees. "I've been practising."

"Practising what?"

"The plank. Put the crate down and time me."

Bronte burst out laughing. Losing when they first met must have rankled her. "Okay, impress me." Bronte put the beers down and got ready with the timer on her watch. "When you're ready."

Griffin got into position and said, "Go."

"Right, ten seconds now. Keep that good form."

Bronte looked down and was mesmerized by Griffin's strong, tense shoulders. Shoulders that were used to manual labour and using an axe. Bronte thought about kissing Griffin's neck softly, barely touching, and wanting to take a big bite out of those shoulders.

"Bronte, Bronte? How long now? Are you dreaming? I'm in pain here."

"Sorry, sorry, thirty seconds."

Griffin collapsed to the ground panting. "God, that is so hard."

"You've improved so much since we first met. Well done," Bronte said.

"Hmm. I think you're humouring me."

Bronte picked up her jacket. "Not at all. Up you get."

"I suppose I need regular practice," Griffin said.

"Exactly. I couldn't swing an axe to save myself, but if I practised, I hopefully would get better."

Griffin put on her jacket. "I'll keep practising and one day surprise you."

"I'm sure. Now let me put you to work."

"I'll go get the ladders, and you can put the beers inside," Griffin said.

Bronte nodded and took the crate inside and over to the fridge. She didn't know which ones should be fridged and which not, so she put them all in.

When Bronte went back outside, she saw Griffin carrying the ladder on her shoulder, and her breath caught. How she could make carrying a ladder sexy, Bronte didn't know, but she appreciated the sight.

They got through a huge amount of work together, and although darkness had set in, Griffin suggested keeping going so they could finish off the last pen. To be honest, Griffin didn't want their time together to end.

It had been such a busy time at the factory that she hadn't gotten to see Bronte as often as she would have liked. She missed that feeling she had when she was around Bronte. She didn't think of the past or about her anger at her mum. She just felt present in the moment.

Griffin was up the ladder, securing the roof on. It wouldn't be much longer and it would be time to go. Maybe she could talk her way into having a drink together?

She drilled the last bolt into place and jumped down off the ladder. "There. I'll give the pegs a final hammer, and you will be ready for your animals."

Bronte fixed the torch on Griffin as she went around all the metal pegs.

"I can't thank you enough for what you've done, Griff."

"Don't mention it. Hey, do you want to have a couple of beers? I could show you the difference between them."

"Sounds good."

Yes! "Great. I'll just put the ladder and tools away. You go into the warm house. Won't be long."

Griffin hurried back to the house and reminded herself to ask Bronte to the winter festival. She was nervous. *Why be nervous? Just remember you are leaving after Christmas. You don't have time for any romantic entanglements.*

But she forgot about that when she went into the kitchen. Bronte had put out little bowls of crisps and nibbles. She looked up at Griffin with the most beautiful smile on her face, and her chest tightened.

"I thought I'd make a little pub atmosphere."

"Good thinking. Atmosphere does play a part. There's no denying that beer or lager poured at a pub seems a lot tastier than at home." Griffin rubbed her palms together. "Okay, where did you put the bottles?"

"In the fridge."

Griffin pursed her lips.

"Did I do wrong?" Bronte asked.

"You weren't to know. Lagers you keep chilled, beers you don't, but that's okay. I'll get them if you can get the glasses."

"How many?" Bronte asked.

Griffin thought for a moment and said, "Two. Let's not overcomplicate things."

Griffin brought the bottles back and took off her jacket. "Okay, these are our two most popular. The beer is Duchess Dream, and the lager is Lady of the Rose. Both original names from Clementine's grandmother's day."

"Interesting. Do you need a bottle opener?"

"It's okay. I've got one here." Griffin took out the tool on her keychain and used the opener on there to pop the lids off. She poured the beer, then the lager. "You can see straight away the colour is different. Beers tend to have darker colours and a richer flavour. Lagers are lighter."

"Yes, there's a big difference in colour."

Griffin picked up her glass of beer and said, "Basically beer is fermented at a warmer temperature than lager. It uses a different yeast and is brewed for a shorter amount of time. It generally has a darker flavour. Depending on what flavour the brewer is going for, you can get dark and smoky flavours, or malty and sweet. Take a sip."

Bronte lifted the glass to her lips and then screwed up her face. "Oh, I don't like that at all. I'm sorry."

Griffin chuckled. "It is more of an acquired taste. Try the lager."

"I know I like lager," Bronte said. "If I'm having lager, I usually have it with lime."

"Lager and lime is a great combination. Lager is brewed for longer and at much lower temperatures. Its flavours are crisp, clean, and fruity."

"Yes, I like this one. It makes me want to eat nuts." Bronte grabbed a handful from the bowl.

Griffin chuckled. "You eat the salty nuts and then you buy another pint. It's a good moneymaker."

There was silence for a few moments, and Griffin pushed herself to ask, "You said you'd come for a tour of the factory."

"Sorry, I was too caught up trying to get the rescue done, but I'll definitely come soon."

"Is that a promise?" Griffin asked.

"Cross my heart."

Now was the more difficult question. It was so hard making something a date but also not a date at the same time.

Griffin looked deeply into her glass of beer. "You know the big winter switch-on next week?"

Bronte nodded. "Yes, it should be fun."

"Do you want to go together? I could come here, and we'd walk down together."

Bronte smiled. "I'd like that."

Yes! "Perfect, I'll look forward to that."

Chapter Nine

It had been a good week for Bronte. Now that the pens were up, next job was kitting them out with equipment, logs, branches, and toys. Anything to make the animals feel more comfortable.

Tonight was the big winter lights switch-on in the village. Bronte never enjoyed Christmas, but she had to admit she was looking forward to tonight. For the first time in her life, Bronte felt like she didn't have the shadow of her mother looming over her. In Rosebrook she could be the Bronte that she wanted to be.

That might be enjoying a Christmas celebration with her new friends. Everyone was friendly and that had helped let down some of her barriers, like accepting help.

Griffin.

Bronte found herself staring in the mirror. Mostly thinking about her building fences, attempting planks, and the sexiest of all, chopping wood with an axe.

Stop it, she told herself. *Friends are all you can afford to have— besides, she's leaving.*

Bronte applied her lipstick in the mirror.

But she did feel closer to Griffin than anyone else. Griffin had popped in each day this week to see if she could help, and Bronte looked forward to it.

The doorbell sounded, and she quickly gave herself a once-over in the mirror. In this cold and frosty weather, it was hard to dress up the way she'd like to, but she wore a pink and purple headscarf, a light purple quilted jacket, tight jeans, and purple and white trainers.

Bronte hurried downstairs, and it wasn't just exertion that was making her heart thump—it was who was waiting for her at the door.

"Okay, okay. Take a breath." Why did this feel like a date?

She opened the door to a smiling Griffin. She had dressed differently too. She wore an extremely cosy looking quilted black jacket, really nice jeans instead of her usual combats, and what looked like brand new leather Timberland boots.

Bronte wished she could pull her in, take off that jacket, and pull her into a kiss.

"Hi, I'm not too early, am I?" Griffin said.

"No, I'll just grab my purse and my phone."

They were soon walking down the road, heading to the centre of the village.

"Hold on, the paths are icy." Griffin offered her arm.

Bronte gladly took it. "Thanks. You can hear the band playing from here."

"Yeah, I think Fox has pushed the boat out on this. Partly because it's Fox and partly because we don't have Guy Fawkes night on the fifth like other villages."

"You don't? Oh, that's a relief," Bronte said.

"Right from the start we all agreed fireworks were bad for the animals, especially in a rural community."

"I thought I would have to try to persuade everyone to give fireworks a miss for next year. I'm so happy it's already part of your culture here."

"I think our village was made for someone like you, Bronte," Griffin said.

"You too. It's a shame you're leaving." Silence then loomed over them. There was no answer to that as long as Bronte didn't know her reasons for leaving.

By the time they got down into the throngs of people, the awkwardness had dissipated. "I don't think I've ever seen as many people in Rosebrook before," Griffin said.

"People from the town and surrounding villages have turned up. It's wonderful."

There were food and drinks stalls, a brass band playing Christmas music, jugglers, fire dancers, and other performers. The atmosphere was smoky and cold and was certainly good for getting you in the mood for any winter celebration.

"I'll go and get us a drink—Jonah's got a stall over there," Griffin said. "Lager and lime? Or mulled wine?"

"He won't have lime, will he?" Bronte said.

Griffin smiled. "I asked him to bring some."

"Then I'll have that, please." Bronte sighed. *Why did you have to come into my life now, just when you are going to leave it?*

"Bronte," Clementine shouted. Both she and Kay came over.

"Hi," Bronte said, "this is wonderful, Clementine."

"You'd have to thank Fox for this. It's turned out well," Clementine said.

"And so many new people," Kay said, "Fox is really putting our little village on the map. I saw you arrive with Griffin. You've put a smile on her face."

Bronte was about to reply when Griffin returned with two cups of lager and a big paper bag carried in her teeth. Bronte took the bag from her.

"Hi, Clem, hi, Kay, can I get you a drink?" Griffin said.

"No thanks, Griff," Clementine said, "we've both got mulled wine."

"Where's Ash?" Griffin asked.

Kay laughed. "Trying to persuade Archie she doesn't look stupid in the Santa Claus costume."

"I think the number of people who turned up has given her cold feet."

"I don't blame her," Griffin said. "Here, I got us these. There's a food truck selling roasted chestnuts, like from the movies."

"Really?" Bronte took her lager, then took a chestnut out of the bag.

Griffin offered the chestnuts to Clementine and Kay, who each took one.

Bronte bit into it and loved it. "Hmm, that's tasty and salty."

"Nice," Kay said. "That's a new experience for me."

"Where are Casper and the boys?" Griffin asked.

"He's taken them to see the fire-eaters. Gives me some peace. Anyway, Clementine, we better go and help with the final prep. The lights go on in about ten minutes, you two."

"Thanks, Kay."

When they were gone, Bronte said, "Let me give you some money for the drinks and chestnuts."

Bronte brought out her purse and Griffin pushed it away. "Don't be silly."

"Well, I'll get the next ones."

"We'll see," Griffin replied.

Bronte started to wonder. Was this a date?

Just then Lucy stopped by them.

"Hi, Lucy, enjoying yourself?" Bronte asked.

"Yeah, it's great. This is Ola, Dr. Blake's daughter."

"Hi, Ola. Nice to meet you," Bronte said.

Ola whispered in Lucy's ear. "Bronte, Ola wants to know if she can come and see the rescue one day."

"Anytime, Ola. Come with Lucy one day."

Lucy handed Bronte a leaflet. "We're giving out leaflets for The Big Dip. See you later."

"What's the Big Dip?" Bronte asked Griffin.

"Fox wants us to go for a swim at the beach on Christmas Day."

"What?" Bronte couldn't believe her ears. "In this weather?"

"I'll explain later. Look, they're getting ready for the switch-on. Let's get closer." Griffin led her by the hand to the side of the crowd near the road. Quite naturally Griffin stepped behind her, protecting her from being jostled. "Here comes Fox," Griffin whispered in her ear, making Bronte shiver.

"Good evening, everyone. Thank you for coming to our winter light-up."

The crowd cheered, and just as it was dying down, Fox put her hand to her ear. "Wait a minute…I hear hoof beats. Could that be Santa Claus arriving?"

Bronte turned her head back to Griffin. "Here comes Archie."

"She'll be hating every minute of this," Griffin said.

Griffin put the chestnuts in her pocket so she could put her hand on Bronte's waist, and she didn't shift or resist.

Griffin loved this closeness with Bronte. She'd loved getting to know her from their frosty start till now. Bronte made her forget all of her worries while she was with her, and Griffin didn't want it to stop.

"Here comes Santa," Fox shouted.

Griffin's attention was caught by two car headlights at full blaze, on the road down to where they were. A woman stood at the side of the car, trying to shout.

"Bronte? Look—I wonder what she wants."

Bronte gasped. "It's my mother. What in God's name is she doing here?" Bronte handed her cup to Griffin and walked off at a fast pace.

Griffin followed her. She had to know why Bronte was so spooked.

The countdown for the lights had started, so she had to get closer to hear what was going on.

"What are you doing here," Bronte said. "I didn't invite you, and you're not welcome."

Bronte's mother said, "Who was that scruffy looking oik that was plastered around you?"

"Who?" Bronte asked. "That was nobody. Just Griffin, a neighbour."

That sentence cut Griffin deeply. *Nobody. Just Griffin, a neighbour.*

Bronte turned around and saw Griffin had followed her. She grabbed her mum and got into the car with her, which then turned and drove back up the hill.

The countdown had apparently ended because the village lit up brightly, there were huge cheers, and snow machines sprayed fake snow into the air.

All this happiness and excitement all around Griffin, and she couldn't have felt lower.

Nobody, just Griffin.

❖

"Why did you come here?"

Bronte didn't want her new friends and neighbours to meet her overbearing mother, so she took her back to her cottage.

"Is it so unusual for a mother to want to see a child?"

"For you, yes. This is my new life, Mother, and you will not approve of it, nor do I care, so why don't we cut to the chase. No skirting around the issue, just tell me."

Her mother sat on her couch and put down her handbag. "Just business? Fine with me. I had a meeting with the bank. We have six months to pay off our debt on the second mortgage or the bank takes it."

Bronte sat on the armchair opposite. As much as she pretended not to to her mother, Bronte did care about Lawton House and the history of the family there. It wasn't the house's fault that her mother was money-grubbing and a tyrant with her family. She did care, but there wasn't much of a choice.

"The only choice is to sell to the National Trust, mother. You must face it."

"I will not have my house turned into a tea room for the lower classes, while they stomp their way around my beautiful carpets."

"I just despair of you, Mother. We aren't living in the Regency era. There is no class system any more."

"You, my dear, are a fool if you think that. Why on earth then are Antonia's family so eager for you two to meet and hopefully date? Because they may have money, but they are new money. Their daughter Antonia could bring a great deal of respectability to their family if she married a future baroness."

"It's not going to happen. I'm sure she's very nice."

"You were at school with her, you should know," her mother said.

"She was the year below me, and we didn't have much to do with each other."

Her mother looked her straight in the eye and said, "I won't sell to the National Trust, and if you don't meet and win the favour of Antonia, the house will be gone and all our artwork, your father's books, six hundred years of unbroken history will be gone. Our family's home will be gone."

Bronte closed her eyes and pinched the bridge of her nose. She didn't want that as much as anyone in her family, but the price was too high.

"This is the last time I'll ask you, Bronte. Come and meet Antonia. Her parents are willing to pay off our debt if they can marry into the family of a baroness."

"You know what my answer will be. I won't be pimped out to pay off the family debts."

Her mother got up and lifted her bag. "Six months, Bronte. That's all you have. All I can say to you is to think about when you became a baroness with all the prestige it brings—but there's no Lawton House for you to live in with your family. Nothing to bind your title to the land of England. I can only hope that the guilt will eat away at you."

How dare her mother lay this at her door. She honestly couldn't dislike her mother more at the moment.

"Get out, Mother."

"You once told me that I had ruined your chance for ever loving, so why not consider an arrangement that would suit us all?"

Fury built up from her stomach, and rage poured out. "Get out now," she shouted.

"That was always your problem, Bronte. Too overemotional." She left without looking back.

Tears burst forth from Bronte's eyes and wet her hot cheeks. Her mind played and replayed the movie that tortured her. Waking up in the morning to find her girlfriend gone, drawers and wardrobe empty of her clothes.

Bronte could still feel the pain and panic of that moment. The experience of all the air in her lungs being sucked out. She still hadn't recovered. Her mother had played her part in the pain, yet she thought Bronte would help?

Never. The bank was welcome to Lawton House.

Chapter Ten

Bronte hated the way she ran from Griffin. It was the shock of her two worlds colliding—the woman her mother ruled, and the one she had shaped for herself in Rosebrook. When her mother asked who Griffin was, she didn't want her mum to know, not because she didn't care, but because she did.

Bronte didn't want her mother ruining any sort of friendship she was developing with Griffin. To prevent that, she had denied Griffin was anyone of consequence to her.

At first Bronte didn't think Griffin had overheard her, but when Griffin never came to see her that night, the next day, or the next, Bronte knew she had heard, and that she had hurt Griffin.

She didn't have the courage to go to her. Every night when Bronte did her walk in the woodlands to check for hunters, she thought Griffin might be at her campfire, building her den, as she often was, but there was no sign of her.

Bronte couldn't leave it any longer. So she decided to walk down to the brewery one afternoon, to try to see her on neutral territory. When Bronte got there, she saw a van being loaded at the main entrance, so she looked for a door at the side, which helpfully had an intercom on the door.

She pressed it and a voice said, "Hello?"

"Hi, this is Bronte from the animal rescue. I was hoping I could see Griffin."

"Come up."

The door buzzed open, and she followed some metal stairs up

to an office. Patrick, who Griffin had pointed out to her before, was waiting for her.

"Hi, Bronte. Nice to meet you properly at last."

Bronte shook his hand. "You too. Is Griffin in today?"

"I'm sorry, she's gone to London to take care of some business," Patrick said.

"Do you know when she'll be back?"

"She didn't put a firm date on it. She mentioned maybe a couple of weeks."

Great, you've messed it right up now. "Okay, thanks."

"Do you want me to get a message to her?" Patrick offered.

"It's okay. I've got her number. Thanks, Patrick, and it was nice to meet you."

"You too, Bronte."

That was that, then.

❖

Griffin's feelings of melancholy hung heavily over her as she sat in a leather armchair in the waiting room of her lawyer's office. Trent, Trent, and Masters had been her father's lawyers, the ones Griffin had dealt with when her inheritance had to be sorted out.

Griffin had gotten on well with the younger Trent. They both were gay and had similar outlooks on life, and Griffin decided to keep Trent as her own lawyer, dealing with all legal matters to do with her estate and banking affairs.

When Trent called asking her to sign a few papers, it was the perfect opportunity to get away for the week. It wasn't until Bronte's mother arrived and she overheard their conversation, that Griffin realized how much her burgeoning friendship with Bronte was getting her through the emotions of learning the truth about her father.

But apparently, she was the only one enjoying her so-called friendship.

No one. Just Griffin.

She felt like a fool having put herself out for Bronte, when Bronte clearly thought she was forcing a friendship. Since then, Griffin's feelings had been all over the place.

Griffin didn't want to deal with it all and couldn't wait till she could be on the road again. Sitting in the one place, with long winter nights in Rosebrook, gave her too long to think. Although she couldn't leave yet, having made her promise to Fox, there was one step she could make to gain some distance from her emotional luggage.

The buzzer on the secretary's desk went off, and she said, "Trent will see you now, Griffin."

"Thanks."

As she approached the door, it opened to reveal the well-dressed and ever dapper Trent. They were quite the contrast, Griffin in her slouchy combat trousers, heavy boots, and floppy hair, and Trent with her immaculately cut short blond hair, and equally immaculate grey suit and tie.

"Come in, Griffin. Great to see you."

"You too."

"Take a seat. You didn't have to come all the way from Rosebrook to sign these papers. We could have done this next time you were in London."

Griffin sat down at Trent's desk. Trent's office was like one you would imagine in a Dickens classic, all dark wood furniture, leather seats, and leather-bound books on the shelves.

"No, it's okay. I wanted to talk to you about something anyway." Griffin looked to the picture on Trent's desk and said, "How are your wife and children?"

Trent's face was now wreathed in smiles. "Wonderful. There's a more up-to-date picture on the wall behind you. Alice and Noah have grown up so quickly. And Wendy has had her first children's book published."

Griffin turned in her seat and saw a beautiful, smiling family, something that she would never have.

"They are beautiful. You're very lucky."

Trent sighed with contentment. "I know I am, believe me. I put the picture right across the room from my desk, so that whatever bitter divorce or client I'm dealing with, I know that a truly loving family is possible, but that you have to work at it, and that I'm extremely fortunate to have learned that."

"I'm glad for you, Trent."

"I wasn't always this privileged, so I never take it for granted. Anyway, enough about me. What did you want to talk about?"

"I want to sell the house and estate."

Trent looked extremely surprised. "You want to sell everything?"

"Yeah, it's what I should have done from the beginning. It's a weight around my neck. I just want to be rid of it."

"Okay, but what about your great-uncle?"

Her father's uncle had been living in a cottage on the grounds since she inherited the family lands and fortune. He had sent messages via Trent asking to meet her since the beginning, but Griffin had such a coloured view of her dad's family that she wasn't interested, but did allow him to remain in his cottage.

Griffin realized it probably sounded as if she was turfing him out. "Oh no, I don't mean his cottage. The land his house and garden are on, keep that. He can continue to live there rent-free for as long he lives, and make sure his house is up to date as well please, Trent. If it needs new kitchen, new bathroom, anything."

"Of course I will do that, but I think he would dearly love to meet you if—"

"No," Griffin said firmly. "I can't do that, but make things comfortable for him."

Trent was silent for a moment. "Griffin, I understand you had a difficult relationship—or no relationship—with your father. You're a lot like me. I had a terrible relationship with my father, hated everything about him, but at least I knew him. Your uncle could help you know him."

Little did Trent know that she was running away from the fact that everything she had thought about her dad was wrong, and she just didn't want to face it.

Trent continued, "I've been up there, as you know, when business required, and it's strange. It has a spirit of place, if you believe in that kind of thing. You can feel a unique atmosphere. I would advise you to visit it, and your great-uncle, at least once, before deciding to sell."

"No, I don't want to, Trent. I just want it sold, and then I'm leaving the country as soon as Fox gets someone to replace me at the brewery," Griffin said.

"Has something happened?" Trent asked.

Trent didn't want to reveal that she'd found out her dad wasn't as her mum had told her all her life. It cut too deep to deal with those emotions here and now, in Trent's office.

"No, just sell it, Trent."

"If that's why you want, I'll set the wheels in motion."

"It's what I want."

But was it?

Chapter Eleven

A week had passed since Griffin had left for London. A week was a long time for Bronte to harbour guilt at the way she had spoken about Griffin.

Bronte was going on her daily walk to check on wildlife and to see if there was any sign of the hunters being back again.

It was bitterly cold today, and the first snowflakes had started to fall. The weather forecast had been predicting snow for several days, and now it was finally here. Bronte walked further in, checking on the trees, on any tracks on the ground.

There hadn't been any significant signs that the hunters had been back since the night Griffin had seen them. That didn't mean they hadn't been—there were just no telltale signs.

The snow was already coating the ground in a light white blanket. Bronte would need to be quick, or any tracks left would be covered and snow would cover any evidence she might find. And find it, she did.

Beside a tree lay the mutilated body of an adult badger. She gasped in horror at the state of the poor creature. From Bronte's experience, this animal had been ripped apart by dogs. This was awful. She had to make sure the rest of the badger sett was okay. Bronte set off at a run towards the tree where the badger sett was burrowed.

As she was running, she felt a painful tug at her ankle. In an instant she fell at speed towards the ground. Then everything went dark.

❖

A week away from Rosebrook didn't help Griffin. Why she thought being alone in a hotel room and going for drinks in her once favourite bars would help, she didn't know. Bars, loud music, and extremely happy people were the worst things for her mood. She was past that kind of diversion.

At one time Griffin would have been in the middle of the dance floor, drinking to quell the pain of her father's abandonment, but not now. Everything had changed.

When she arrived home, she went to Patrick's house to check in with him. Griffin felt guilty. She'd left a lot of responsibility on Patrick's shoulders because she was having a hard time. Patrick, on the other hand, didn't seem fazed, which was good. It meant Griffin had trained him well.

Just as they were finishing off their catch-up, Patrick said, "Bronte stopped by looking for you."

Griffin gulped her tea, and her heart thudded a few times. "Did she?"

"Yeah, said you promised her a tour of the factory, and she said to tell you that she wanted to apologize."

That made her heart sore more that she'd imagined. Griffin had tried not to think about Bronte while she was away, but she couldn't help it. Even though Bronte had hurt her with her words, Griffin wanted to believe it wasn't her, deep down.

When Bronte's mother arrived, Bronte changed. There was some stress or strain that Griffin didn't know about, but now that Patrick had told her this news, Griffin was determined to find out.

Griffin put her cup on the coffee table. "I better get going, Paddy."

They both stood up, and Patrick pointed out the window. "Look, the snow's really flying now. The locals say Rosebrook's never had as cold a winter as this."

"Yeah, and we've agreed to do Fox's big dip in the sea come Christmas morning. Think about that," Griffin said.

Patrick rubbed his arms. "That makes me shiver at the thought. I think she might kill all the younger people of the village with this idea."

"Hope not."

Griffin opened the front door and walked down the steps to the path, her feet making that characteristic crunch on snow as she went. She took a big cold breath in. In all the snowy places Griffin had been on her travels, she always swore that fresh, newly fallen snow had a fresh scent all its own.

She looked up to the dark grey sky. "Looks like the snow's here for the night, Paddy."

"Yeah, a night for being inside in the warm."

"Have a nice meal with Alanna." Griffin grinned.

Patrick had let slip he and Alanna were getting closer, and Patrick had a romantic meal all planned out for her tonight.

Patrick gave her a shy smile. "Thanks."

Griffin closed Patrick's gate and walked, more slowly than usual, up to Bronte's animal sanctuary. She didn't bother with the front door, knowing, more often than not, that Bronte would be either outside or in the heated conservatory, or in the kitchen.

Griffin was nervous. They hadn't parted well, and she just hoped that Patrick had conveyed Bronte's message correctly.

There was no one in the garden, nor in the conservatory. She walked up to the indoor pens and saw Hedge and Hoggy looking much better.

"I don't suppose you two know where she is?"

When no reply was forthcoming, she turned around and listened for any noise. There was nothing, and Griffin was starting to get a bad feeling. She hurriedly checked the workshop. Nothing. Then out to the back fields, which were empty.

Griffin looked at her watch. Where would Bronte be at this time?

A sweep of the woods.

Griffin jogged through the garden and out to the front, after a quick look into the living room window, to check Bronte wasn't there, then over the road into the woods. She remembered all the places that Bronte checked, the burrows and the dens.

It was when Griffin approached her own clearing in the woods, where she was building her shelter, that she noticed signs the hunters were back. There were cans of beer strewn around the fire, and burnt wood was all over the place—clearly the fire hadn't been put out correctly.

The snow was getting heavier. Griffin could be worrying about nothing. Bronte could be having a cup of tea inside one of their neighbours' houses, but something in her gut told Griffin otherwise.

Griffin followed the path that Bronte had led her from this spot, and before long she was shocked to find a badger that had been torn apart.

"Bastards." Griffin knew badgers were a protected species, and even if these men had permission to hunt on Clementine's land, which they didn't, they were breaking the law by letting their dogs do this.

Griffin heard a moaning up ahead, then weak shouts. "Help!" She ran towards the sound and got the shock of her life when she saw Bronte lying in the snow.

"Bronte!" Griffin ran and knelt by her side. "What happened?"

She lifted Bronte up to lean against her, and Bronte grabbed at her to steady herself.

"I'm dizzy."

"And cold." Griffin saw she was shivering and took her jacket off, leaving her in her T-shirt. Griffin wrapped the jacket around her, and Bronte held it closed tightly. She noticed a bloody injury on Bronte's forehead. "What happened?"

"I saw a badger that had been mutilated and ran to see if the rest of its sett mates were okay. My leg caught in one of the hunters' traps, and my leg was jerked back. I hurt my ankle, tripped, and hit my head on a rock."

"Did you lose consciousness?"

"I—I think so. Everything went dark, and then when I came to, my ankle was so painful."

"Okay, let me look at your ankle. Can you hold yourself up?"

"Yes." Bronte braced her arms against the ground, and Griffin moved down to her ankle. Straight away she saw the blood seeping into the white snow. The twine—God, not twine. It was metal wire. An animal would have had its leg sliced clean off.

"How's it looking?"

"Were you running when this happened?" Griffin asked.

"Just a light jog, thank God. I think I've sprained my ankle because I couldn't push myself up on it."

"Probably. Hopefully the wire hasn't gone too deep. I'll cut away the loose wire and let the doctor look at the rest."

Griffin took her survival knife out of her back pocket and tried to gently move Bronte's ankle.

"Argh!"

"Sorry, sorry, I'll be more careful."

Griffin cut the wire and then pulled the trap from the ground so that it couldn't hurt anyone else or any animal.

"If I catch these hunters," Griffin said, "they won't know what hit them."

"Did you see the badger?"

"Yeah, poor creature."

"I took a picture. This is a police matter now. Whoa."

Bronte appeared to be hit by a wave of dizziness.

"Let's get you to Dr. Blake. I'll pull you up, but don't put your weight on your foot," Griffin said.

As Griffin pulled her up, Bronte clung to her T-shirt for support. "My head's going round and round."

"You've probably got a concussion. I promise you I'm going to find these men," Griffin said angrily.

"We'll find them, if you forgive me for—"

"Shh. Don't say any more. We'll talk about that later."

Before Bronte could protest, Griffin scooped her up in her arms.

"Griff, no…"

"Do you propose hopping on your foot through the woods? The snow is getting heavier."

"You're right."

As they walked on, Bronte wrapped her arms around Griffin's neck and rested her head on Griffin's neck. Griffin loved it. Bronte felt so right in her arms.

When she'd seen Bronte lying motionless on the snow, her stomach dropped, and panic spread throughout her body. Griffin had to admit she cared for Bronte a lot, and she was so glad that she knew Bronte had wanted to apologize. It meant she could be close to her new friend again.

Griffin looked down at Bronte in her arms and said, "I'll have you at Dr. Blake's in no time."

"What about Hoggy and Hedge? They need to be fed and their water bowl checked."

"Don't worry. I'll call the duchess and ask her to bring Lucy down. She'll know what to do, right?"

"Yes, yes, she will, but I don't want everyone to know, Griff. I don't like a big fuss," Bronte said.

"Don't worry. Everything will be fine."

❖

Whatever Dr. Blake had given her when she arrived at the surgery made Bronte extremely drowsy. She had flitted in and out of sleep as Blake worked, but this time when she woke, Bronte felt much more clarity.

"How is it looking, Doctor?"

Blake smiled. "Oh, you're back with us."

"Yes, I was knocked out cold there."

Blake was taking bandages from her nurse and wife, Eliska.

"I got the wire out. The damage could have been a lot worse. I've cleaned it all and bandaged it. You have sprained your ankle. We were worried you had dislocated it."

"So I'll be okay in a few days?"

"A few days is maybe a bit optimistic. You also have a concussion. Griff said you lost consciousness when you fell."

Bronte rubbed her head and found she had a sticky bandage across her forehead.

"Would you like a drink of water?" Eliska asked.

"Yes, please."

In a few seconds Eliska was back from the water dispenser with a cup of cool water.

"Thank you." Bronte took a sip and remembered about her animals. "Did Lucy come for my keys to the sanctuary?"

"Yes," Blake said, "Clementine brought her, and you gave Eliska your keys to take out to her. Ola went to help her."

"That's your daughter, isn't it?" Bronte asked.

"It is indeed," Blake said with a huge smile on her face.

Bronte caught a sweet, loving look that passed between Blake and Eliska. They must be newly married.

It must be nice to find someone who would look at you the way

Blake looked at her wife. She'd long ago dismissed the idea of falling in love. Most of the time Bronte was stoic about it, but every so often, she longed for the feeling and cried for the two people who had broken her heart.

"I'll finish up bandaging your leg, and you'll be good to go. I'll give you some painkillers to take away with you."

"Thank you, Doctor." Bronte hated being ill or injured. She was so independent and hated asking anyone for help. But she would cope. She always did.

❖

Clementine got the keys for the sanctuary and set Lucy and Ola off to look after the animals. Soon after, both Ash and Kay arrived. Word got around the village very quickly.

Clementine had her eyes glued to Griffin since she first arrived at the doctor's surgery. Griffin was pacing backwards and forwards, tension and stress pouring off her. She knew Griffin and Bronte had become friends quite quickly, but Clementine felt there was something different going on here.

Did Griffin like Bronte more than as a friend? It would be lovely for Griffin to find someone, but then again, she was leaving soon. That thought put a downer on her romantic ideas.

"She'll be all right, Griffin," Clementine said.

"Just wait till I catch those bastards." Griffin said with anger.

Clementine was furious herself. "We'll find out who they are. Cameras will be going up."

"Their dogs ripped a badger apart. Bronte has a picture for evidence," Griffin said.

"It's disgusting," Ash said.

Kay shook her head. "I'd never have imagined we'd have traps and badger-baiting in our forest."

"Don't worry," Clementine said. "As soon as Bronte is up to it, we'll go to the police station, and I'm going to go full duchess-mode on them. This better be taken seriously and stopped."

Kay gazed at her approvingly. "They have no idea what's coming their way. Full duchess-mode is dangerous."

"Well, I only use it under very special circumstances."

The doctor's office door opened, and Bronte came out on a pair of crutches. Griffin was immediately by her side.

"How is she, Doctor?"

"You can ask me, you know."

"Sorry, how are you?"

"I'm fine. Dr. Blake has bandaged me up."

Dr. Blake cut in, "She has a concussion, though. Is there someone who could stay with her, or could Bronte stay with someone?"

"Yeah, me," Griffin said instantly.

"No, there's no need for that. I'll be okay."

Clementine, Kay, and Ash all walked up closer to them.

"If you don't let Griffin take care of you, then I'll drag you up to Rosebrook, and one night of Fox on her high horse because of what's happened will have you jumping from the windows," Clementine joked.

Bronte sighed. "Okay. Griffin can watch me like a hawk then." She turned to Griffin. "I did say not to tell anyone. I don't like a big fuss."

"There's no secrets in a village," Ash said.

Kay joined in. "It might seem like we're nosy, but really we just want to help."

"Exactly," Clementine said, "now I'll drive you two back to the sanctuary and pick up Lucy and Ola." Clementine then said to Blake and Eliska, "I'll drop Ola back to you on the way back."

"Thanks, Clem," Eliska said.

Dr. Blake said, "Griffin, watch out for vomiting, confusion, slurred speech, memory problems—and call me straight away."

"I will, Doctor, thanks."

Clementine saw Bronte's knuckles turn white on the handles of her crutches. She was clearly so independent that it was hard letting others look after her.

Before she exploded, Clementine said, "Okay, let's get you home, shall we?"

❖

Bronte was sitting in her living room, quietly cursing whoever put down that trap, not only for trying to injure the animal, but for leaving her in the position that she had to accept help. Her sprain wasn't that bad, and her concussion was a headache that wasn't nice, but Bronte was sure she'd sleep it off.

She would have sent Griffin packing if the doctor and her new friends hadn't made such a fuss, and if not for the fact that she owed Griffin an apology. How did you send someone packing if you needed to say sorry to them?

Maybe she should have gone up to Rosebrook and braved the larger-than-life Fox. Griffin made her feel uncomfortable in a way that was difficult to understand.

When she looked at Griffin or Griffin was near her, her skin prickled and her chest and throat tightened. It was such a strange sensation. The uncomfortable sensations posed uncomfortable questions, but she wasn't going to go there.

Bronte normally kept people at arm's length, but in such a short space of time Griffin had become entangled in her life, in a natural way, and whether she liked it or not.

No, here she was, in pain, staring at the flames in the fireplace while Griffin made her dinner.

Griffin came through the double doors that led to the kitchen and said with a flourish of her tea towel, "Dinner is served."

"I never knew you knew how to cook."

Griffin offered her hand to help Bronte up on to her feet, with the aid of her crutch.

"I've travelled the world, learning about all the world's cuisines, and I bring that knowledge with me."

"You know, something small like a sandwich would have been perfect." Bronte hopped through the doors to the kitchen while saying, "You didn't need to go to all this trouble—" Then Bronte saw two plates filled with beans on toast, and she started to laugh. "All the world's cuisines, eh?"

Griffin pulled out Bronte's chair. "Yeah, a British classic." Bronte took a seat and handed her crutches over to Griffin. "I saw you had them in your cupboard and thought, you can't go wrong with beans on toast, although there is a special difference."

Bronte felt a tiny bit worried now. "Something from your travels?"

"Nah, I melted cheese through them. That's the way my mum always did it. One of my favourite childhood meals. It's called cheesy beanos."

Bronte furrowed her brow. "Cheesy beanos?"

"I take it you never had these as a kid at private school?"

"No, it wasn't on the menu, but I'll give it a fair taste test."

Bronte took a forkful of the beans, and they were surprisingly tasty. "They're quite nice actually."

Griffin sat at the other end of the table and pointed a fork at her. "You're not just saying that, are you?"

"Absolutely, I'd never tell you a lie," Bronte said.

Griffin just gazed at her then with an unreadable look upon her face. "Thank you."

It was true. Despite seemingly worldly experience, travelling the world, being a survivalist, and a beer maker, Bronte felt there was a wounded animal behind those eyes.

As they both tucked into their food, Griffin said, "Being someone who camps a lot, I'm a connoisseur of canned food."

"Tell me the most beautiful place you've been camping."

"Eastern Canada. On the edge of a frozen lake"—Griffin pointed at the snowfall outside the window—"in weather much like this."

"You camp in the snow?" Bronte said with surprise.

"Yep, thirty degrees below zero it was."

Bronte dropped her fork. "Thirty below? Are you serious?"

"Hot tent camping. You have a woodburning stove inside the tent with a metal chimney taking the smoke outside. It gets too hot inside."

Bronte couldn't believe it. "I've never heard of that. I bet I'd be too cold."

"Picture it."

Griffin had this passionate intensity come over her as she explained. "You're sitting on the side of a frozen lake, you've just finished eating, and the campfire is crackling. Darkness falls and the sky is inky black, and the stars are shining brightly. You feel like you're at peace, connected to the earth and the galaxy above your head. It's almost spiritual."

Bronte was lost for words, and that chest tightening that she felt when she looked at Griffin turned another few notches. Beneath that floppy blond hair and the unkempt look lay a heart that felt deeply.

"Wow, you make it sound beautiful."

"It is. You should try it sometime."

They gazed into each other's eyes until Bronte realized what she was doing.

She cleared her throat. "Maybe I will. If I get to eat your delicious canned food delicacies."

Griffin laughed. "You would love them."

They ate their meal in silence for a few minutes. It all seemed to be going well, Griffin thought. She hadn't scared Bronte off with her cooking, anyway. It was good they were having this time together. Obviously, Griffin wished she wasn't hurt, but after not seeing Bronte for a week, but thinking about her for a week, she was happy to be near her.

Bronte was so beautiful and could make her heart pound with just a look. It wasn't the same feeling Griffin usually got when chasing a girl—this was deeper and more intense.

"Griff? Griff, did you hear me?"

Shit. Griffin had been caught daydreaming about the woman across from her. Bronte would probably be thinking, *Why do I have to have this scruffy character here?*

"Sorry?"

"I wanted to talk to you about what happened before you left for London."

"You don't have to explain," Griffin said.

"No, I do. I was rude and said things that I didn't mean. I'm really sorry about what I said. I didn't mean it."

"Your mum seemed to upset you," Griffin said.

Bronte took a sip of her juice. "She did. My mother is a difficult woman, and she's been overbearing and into all of my business since I was a little girl, telling me who I can and can't be friends with, and as I got older, who I could date."

"Do you have brothers or sisters? Is she like that with them?" Griffin asked.

"I have a little sister—she's called Jocasta. No, Mother wasn't bothered so much with her. She married a suitable man young and all was well. But I'm the oldest, you see, the heir to the title and family seat."

"Does she bug you to get married all the time?"

"Married to a man with money. It's a long story. I shouldn't bore you," Bronte said.

"No, I want to know about you. Why don't we go back through, I'll bring us some tea, and you can tell me more."

"If you want."

❖

Five minutes later, Griffin brought through the mugs. She handed Bronte a mug and sat on the other end of the two-seater couch.

"I just want to say before we talk any more, that you don't have to apologize to me," Griffin said.

"I do," Bronte said firmly. "I did come to say sorry sooner, at the factory, but Patrick said you were in London on business."

"He told me."

"That night, I was having so much fun with you, feeling a close connection with you and the village, that I didn't want to spoil it. She wants to spoil things when I try to make my own life away from her. So when she asked about who you were, I said nobody, so that you wouldn't be of any consequence to her, but I know how it sounded."

"Then I accept. Let's hear no more about it."

Bronte squirmed as she couldn't get comfortable with her sprained ankle.

"Here." Griffin patted her knees. "Put your feet here, and then you can lie back comfortably."

"Eh no, I couldn't."

Griffin rolled her eyes. "Stop being politely upper class and get your feet up."

"No, no. I'm okay."

"You're not okay. You can't get comfy. I won't accept your apology if you don't."

"You've already accepted it," Bronte shot back.

Griffin leant forward and said menacingly, "I can take it away."

Bronte sighed. "Oh, for God's sake, fine."

Griffin carefully lifted up her feet and placed them on her knees. "There. That's more comfortable. Admit it."

"Yes, yes, okay."

Bronte took a drink of tea and placed the mug back on the side table Griffin had placed there for her.

"How's your head?" Griffin asked.

"It's sore but nothing to worry about."

"You're due more painkillers soon. That should help."

Bronte nodded. "So where were we?"

"I accepted you apology, and you were going to tell me about your sister."

"Yes, Jo Jo married a lovely man, a wealthy man, and they have two children. Perfect for my mother, and less pressure on me."

"Didn't you want to meet someone?"

Bronte said nothing for a few seconds and got a faraway look in her eye. "At one time, but I'm certainly not marrying some wealthy guy or woman just to bring money into the family."

"I'd have thought a family like yours, you know, with a title and stuff, would have plenty of money to go round."

"Just because we have a title? No, my grandfather had no money, my father made some bad investments, and history repeated itself with Jo Jo's husband. So here I am, the only marriageable asset, the only one who can save Lawton House. That's the way my mother sees me, anyway."

"Lawton House? Is that your family home?"

Bronte checked herself. Why was she suddenly opening herself up and telling Griffin this? She normally kept her emotional cards close to her chest. Years of being brought up in the de Lacey family had trained her to not show any emotion, but here she was, letting all her walls down.

"Yes. It's the oldest building in London. It used to be a nunnery before Henry VIII got hold of it after he closed down all the monasteries and nunneries. Historians come to study it sometimes."

"Sound like an amazing place to grow up," Griffin said.

"It was cold, damp, and musty. Terrible house to upkeep. It just drains money, hence why my mother is obsessed with money. It's mortgaged up to the hilt, and the bank have given her six months to pay."

"That'll be tragic if your family lose the house."

"I've told my mother repeatedly to sell to the National Trust. It's the right thing to do. Then the public can enjoy its history," Bronte said.

"But your mum won't hear of it, I guess?"

"You guess right. It's an ego thing. She won't be the baroness who lost the family seat."

"So she wants you to marry a nice rich guy or woman?" Griffin asked.

Bronte nodded. "She's finally accepted that I'm gay and never going to marry a man, so she's been finding all the most suitable women to introduce me to. Can you believe it? She doesn't care about my happiness."

"I'm sorry."

"She's a total snob. Thinks herself so above the man or woman in the street, and she is broke herself. Mother could be walking by someone in the street who is rich but wouldn't give them the time of day because of how they looked, dressed, or what class she believed they were from."

Griffin cleared her throat and shifted uncomfortably in her seat.

"Sorry, are my legs too heavy? I can move them—"

Griffin grasped them softly as Bronte started to move. "No, no, keep them here. I'm fine."

Maybe I'm boring her? "I'm sorry, Griff. I never normally talk this way with people, and it's a long way around explaining why I needed to apologize to you."

"Hey, just blame your head injury and unburden yourself. I'm right here, trapped by your stinky feet."

"They're stinky, are they?" Bronte said with horror.

Griffin laughed. "No, I'm only winding you up. Go on with your story."

"Mother hatched a plan with a friend of hers, a wealthy friend of hers, that I should marry her daughter. A girl I went to school with. She was all subtle about it at first, but then the day I packed up to come here, she laid it all on me. Coming here was meant to be my dream." Bronte slapped her breastbone. "My chance to get away from London, from her, and pursue my dream of saving animals. She's already interfered with my life too much as it is."

"I'm sorry, Bronte. You shouldn't have that much pressure put on you," Griffin said.

"Then I'm having fun with my new friends—you, and she turns up, sees me close to you, and makes assumptions."

"That you and I…?"

Bronte nodded. "I still feel bad for what you heard."

"Well, don't, because I accepted your apology, remember? I understand the pressure you were under," Griffin said.

Griffin was kind and forgiving. A gentle wandering soul.

"Thank you. I really mean that."

"Did she leave soon after?"

"She came back here and decided to put a guilt trip on me. Mother's been told by the bank to have the debt repaid in six months or they take the house. If they do, it's all my fault."

Griffin's face turned angry. "It's like she's pimping you out. What did you say?"

"I said she better sell to the National Trust because I was never marrying or getting involved in any long-term relationship with anyone with money, just for her to get her hooks into it."

Griffin became quiet.

"You okay?"

"Yeah, yeah. You must be tired. Why don't we get set up in here for bed?"

Bronte was a little surprised Griffin cut the conversation dead. *She must really be fed up with my tale of woe.* "You don't really have to stay, Griff."

"The doctor said you needed someone overnight, and I'm it. Get used to it."

"Okay, okay, if you say so."

Griff rubbed her face. "Sorry if that sounded harsh. I'm just tired, I think."

They both agreed that Bronte would sleep on the couch with Griffin sleeping on her camping mat in front of the fire. She had hurried home to get it after Clementine dropped them off.

Bronte eased her feet off Griffin's lap. Just before Griffin stood up, Bronte caught her hand. "Thank you for rescuing me today. You saved my life."

"Shush. Someone would have found you."

"Maybe, but not as quickly. You knew my routine and all the places I visit in my rounds of the woods. Not everyone would pay attention. You're a really good friend. Thank you."

"You're welcome."

❖

Griffin was glad of the fireplace. The wintery wind was still howling outside the window. The snow flurries had been on and off all evening so far. Lucky Hedge and Hoggy were in an indoor pen, all toasty and warm.

She watched the flames dance together and heard the comforting crackle of wood. Despite the comforting sounds, Griffin felt low.

On one hand Griffin knew so much more about Bronte, the woman she had to admit was getting under her skin, but what she learned hadn't helped her cause. Bronte was not impressed by anyone with money and pledged not to enter a relationship with anyone wealthy.

Unbeknownst to Bronte, here Griffin was with more money than she knew what to do with. Like Bronte's mother, Bronte had made the assumption that she was just your average working-class person.

Griffin didn't blame her—it's how she liked to be perceived. She was who she was and didn't let money change her. She pulled her blanket up to her nose and inhaled Bronte's scent. Bronte had given her a blanket from her bed.

When she closed her eyes, Griffin could imagine Bronte spooned in front of her. Nothing would make her happier. She supposed that both she and Bronte weren't what they seemed. With her tattoos, animal T-shirts, and general festivalgoer's look, people wouldn't ever think Bronte was the heir to a baroness.

Why was she even thinking about this? Bronte had said she wouldn't be with someone with money, and anyway, Griffin was leaving Rosebrook to wander the world again, while Bronte was just starting her new life here.

No, there couldn't be anything in these feelings. She had to ignore them. Griffin fluffed her pillow, then thought, *I better tell Clementine not to tell Bronte about my money, just in case.*

❖

Bronte opened her eyes as she heard Griffin ruffling her blanket. She never thought she'd be lying on the couch, with Griffin lying in front of her fire.

She touched the side of her head and grimaced at the pain. Between that and her ankle pain, she was grateful it was time for painkillers just before bed. What a day it had been.

The snow, the hunting of the badgers, her accident—Bronte couldn't wait to get to work and find out who these illegal poachers were. She was sure she'd have the full backing of Clementine and Fox.

Her eyes focused on Griffin. She cringed when she thought of how open she'd been. Maybe it was the painkiller Blake had given her, or the head injury, but it had felt so important to explain the background of why her mother's appearance had affected her that way.

Bronte smiled when she thought of Griffin's gourmet meal. Cheesy beanos was the most romantic meal she'd had in years.

Wait. She didn't just think *romantic*, did she?

Was she going to deny those long looks over the kitchen table? Or the chest tightening?

Bronte couldn't deny it. She was like one of those old-fashioned wind-up dolls. She had a big key at the side of her heart, and every smile, each funny thing Griffin said, that key was turned a notch.

Griffin had pulled the whole blanket up under her chin, for some reason, leaving her back and long legs exposed. She had a loose vest on that was pulled over to one side, exposing her spine and shoulders.

Bronte had noticed those strong shoulders the first time she'd seen Griffin, and they were only more sexy close up. Griffin was tall but not lanky, more athletic, like a basketball player. Her left arm had a full sleeve gothic art design, and a map and compass—to represent her wandering all over the world, Bronte supposed.

Griffin's back was just as strong and looked so incredibly sexy with the flicker of the flames caressing her skin.

She reached out her hand and imagined her fingers tracing Griffin's shoulders, then the top of her spine, ever so slowly and softly. In her mind she heard Griffin moan as she touched her, and that made Bronte moan out loud.

Griffin, the real Griffin, jumped out of her sleep and sat up. "What is it? What happened? Are you okay?"

"Sorry, sorry, I'm okay. I just forgot about my ankle and moved it the wrong way."

Griffin crawled over, and her face was right over Bronte's. "How's your head? Any dizziness? Do you feel sick?"

Now Bronte was wet, a heavy drumbeat pounded low in her sex, and Griffin's face and lips were an arm's length away.

"None of that. I'm sorry I woke you."

Surprisingly Griffin smiled and stroked her hair. "That's what I'm here for. You wake me up any time you need anything."

Bronte was frozen. Griffin hadn't stopped stroking her hair, and she was gazing into her eyes. *Kiss her, kiss her!* Bronte's subconscious was saying. Trapped between her subconscious wants and needs, and her logical brain, she did the next best thing. She froze.

Griffin pulled away after what seemed like forever. "You need anything, don't hesitate, okay?"

"Okay," Bronte squeaked.

As Griffin went back to her bed in front on the fire, Bronte felt like that big old brass key had tightened at least four more full times, and a prickle broke out over her skin that made her shiver.

She had to take deep breaths and calm. Her heart was beating so fast. This hadn't happened with someone in a long, long time, and never to this intensity.

How could she feel like this already? She hardly even knew her. All she knew was her mum made her cheesy beanos as a kid, she travelled the world, and she had a love of microbrewing.

Griffin Harris, I wish I knew your story. She had to find out.

Chapter Twelve

Clementine sat up in bed, making notes on her iPad for her police visit. She was looking up laws, rules, and regulations regarding hunting in the countryside. As much as she tried to concentrate, her mind kept turning over today's events. She felt so badly for Bronte. Bronte was here in Rosebrook to be a positive addition to their little village, and she had been injured just trying to do her job.

Clementine was so angry and embarrassed that this happened on her estate. Thank goodness Griffin found her, or things might be very different. There had been a strict no-hunting policy on Rosebrook land since her grandmother Isadora's day. Her wife Louisa was a great animal lover and got Isadora to stop allowing fox hunts to cross onto their estate from nearby landowners.

This was not going to happen on her watch.

The shower that was running in the bathroom came to a halt and she knew Fox would come bounding out. Fox had been out for a night-time run in the deepening snow. She was trying to get acclimatized to the cold for the Big Dip on Christmas Day.

Why had she married such a maddening woman? Clementine had volunteered to take the video for the event. There was no way she was going in—Clementine didn't do well in the cold. Lucy wanted to do it with Fox, but she'd said no way. Not in the worst winter in generations. Lucy always was enthusiastic to try anything Fox did. She hero-worshipped her, and that generally made Clementine very happy.

Fox burst out of the bathroom in her usual fashion—loudly, with her music playing on the bathroom speaker.

"Could you turn that down a bit?"

"Sorry, Mildred, stop music."

The music stopped, and Clementine rolled her eyes. "Why did you have to call her Mildred?"

Fox had installed the most up to date home automation system, and as part of the set-up, you could call your computer whatever you chose.

"It's funny."

Clementine watched Fox slip into her boxers and T-shirt and walk over to the window and noticed she was still shivering.

"Foxy? Why are you still shivering after having a hot shower?"

Fox leaned into the window to look outside and didn't turn around. That was a sure sign there was something she wouldn't approve of.

"Fox?" she repeated.

"It wasn't a warm shower. It was a cold one."

Clementine put her iPad down hard on her knee. "So now you not only run in the mornings of an unusually cold winter, but you also decide to go out running on an evening when it's even colder and the sky has dumped a huge amount of snow on the ground, then come in and have an ice cold shower?"

Fox turned around and held up her hand. "I never said ice cold shower."

"Was it set as low as it can go?"

Fox screwed up her face. "Ah, I can't lie to you."

"I'm glad you can't lie to me. Why do this to yourself?"

Fox hugged herself. "Because it's cold exposure training. It helps keep the mind sharp, helps the body heal, and gets my body ready for the Big Dip."

"Get in here," Clementine said firmly.

Fox ran and jumped under the covers. "Can you heat me up?"

"Snuggle into me. I've got work to do."

Fox snuggled her face into the side of Clementine's breast and continued to shiver.

"How's the snow looking?" Clementine asked.

"Heavy. I think the roads will be impassable tomorrow, but the temperature is supposed to be going up a bit for the rest of the week. Hopefully it'll thaw on the roads and paths."

"That reminds me…" Clementine opened Messenger and typed out a message. "I'll call in the emergency group."

The duchess's emergency group, or Duchy Gang as Kay and the others called it, was formed after the severe flooding nearly destroyed all they had rebuilt in the village. If a call was put out, then anyone not committed to other work would meet at Rosebrook and decide what was required to help the village and its residents.

"I better make a list, actually. We'll need care packages handed out, like bread, milk, eggs, and I'll get the gardeners started with gritting the paths and roads. We'll muck in when we've made sure everyone's okay."

"What a woman," Fox said.

"What?"

"You've really come into your own, in this duchess business. You might have studied as an architect, but a duchess running an estate was what you were born to be."

"Ah, thank you, Foxy." Clementine leaned over and kissed her on the head. "That means a lot to me."

Fox, who had her eyes shut, mumbled into her breast, "Only telling the truth."

"I see you're not shivering now." She got no response. "Fox?"

But Fox was already asleep.

Clementine chuckled. "Goes off like a firework, goes out like a light."

Now she could get on with her planning.

❖

Bronte awoke to Griffin pulling on her boots, as if she was in a rush. Maybe a rush to get away from her?

"What's wrong?"

"Oh, you're awake. How are you feeling?"

Griffin helped her sit up and swing her legs down. "A dull ache in my head, and my ankle—" She tried to put it on the floor but yelped in pain. "Stiff and sore."

"I need to rush, but I'll make you tea and toast and get your painkillers," Griffin said.

Bronte hated letting people look after her, but she didn't have a lot of choice, at least until the painkillers started working. "Are you late for work?"

"No, the factory isn't opening today. The roads are impassable with the snow. The duchess has called everyone in Rosebrook to help with clearing the paths and taking food out to people. It's an emergency group the duchess started exactly for this kind of time."

"The bat signal goes up, and you all run to help."

Griffin smiled and snapped her fingers. "Exactly. It's an amazing place to live. Everyone is willing to help."

"Why are you leaving then?"

Griffin's smile fell from her face and she mumbled, "My own reasons."

"You can talk to me, you know. I have told you almost everything about my life, which I don't normally do."

"I'll go and put the kettle on."

She was hiding something, Bronte realized.

❖

Fox leaned against a side table, with her arms folded, watching as Clementine took command of the living room, now the operations room of the Duchy Gang. She, Archie, and Mrs. Murdoch had been handing out cups of tea and biscuits to everyone and letting Clementine get on with her planning.

She was so proud of Clementine. She had managed to turn the ancient feudal role of a duke or duchess into something relevant for the modern era. A leader, a figurehead for the people to rally around and accomplish tasks for the benefit of others. A bit like the Queen was to the country.

Everyone who could turn up had, so far, except Griff, but she'd texted and said she was on her way. There was Kay, her husband Casper, and their two boys, who were running around wild with Prisha's toddler Rohan. Lucy and Ola were sitting chatting and keeping an eye on the young kids.

Patrick was there, but Alanna stayed home and off the icy roads, and Jay and Erika were keeping the shop open for essentials. Blake and Eliska had managed to get through the snow, as well as Jonah and

Rupert, and Ash's dad James O'Rourke. Their two farmers, Mr. Mason and Mr. Murdoch, were there, as well as Christian and Whitney, who had taken charge of the community gardens with Casper. Finally, the gardeners were there too.

"Okay, gather round, everyone," Clementine said.

As Fox made her way to the table, she heard Mr. Mason say to Clementine, "If you find those hunters, tell them I've got a shotgun and lots of ground to bury them in."

"You tell 'em, Mr. Mason," Fox joked.

Clementine gave Fox a look. "Let's hope it doesn't come to that." She turned and beckoned Lucy over. "Luce? Come over see what we're doing."

Clementine took every opportunity to teach Lucy what her role would be as duchess when it would be her turn.

"Okay, everyone." A large map was placed out on the table. "You'll see I've shaded the areas into red, amber, and green teams. Our red team is Mr. Murdoch and Mr. Mason. They are going to use Mr. Murdoch's digger to clear as much of the snow on roads through the village, especially at the two entrances to the village. When the other teams are finished with their tasks, they'll join them to help."

"We'll do our best, Your Grace," Mr. Murdoch said.

Clementine smiled. "We know we can count on you."

Just as Clementine was about speak again, Griffin hurried in. She looked flustered. "I haven't missed too much, have I?"

"Not at all, Griff," Fox said. "In you come."

"How's Bronte?" Dr. Blake asked.

"She had a good night's sleep. The concussion seems to be fine. It's her ankle more than anything. Sore and stiff. I gave Bronte her meds and some toast and tea to take along with them—that's why I was late."

"Excellent. Come and join us," Fox said. "Over to you, Your Graceship."

"Griffin, you'll be part of amber team with Jonah, Christian, Casper, Archie, and Fox, along with my gardening team."

She pointed to the older member of the gardening team. "Bill, my head gardener, will take charge. They have the buckets of grit and shovels. If you can, concentrate on the pavements and garden paths, especially for the Tucker twins, Fergus, and Alanna, so she can get in and out with her wheelchair."

"Got it," the team replied.

"Now for Green team—oh, but first…" She looked to Lucy. "If you and Ola can look after the boys and Rohan, it lets Prisha and Kay help outside. That okay?"

"Yes, no problem."

Clementine kissed the side of her head. She was so proud of Lucy.

"That's sorted, so me, Kay, Prisha, Rupert, Whitney, Eliska, and Blake. We're going to hand out care packages. Jay and Erika are making up bags with essential items, bread, milk, eggs, things like that, for us to hand around."

"How are we going to take them around? That's a lot of bags," Whitney asked.

"There are a few old wooden sledges in the stable block out back. We're going to be like Santa's elves."

"Brilliant." Whitney laughed and clapped her hands.

"Blake, I want you on green team just in case anyone needs medical reassurance, especially the Tucker twins and Fergus."

"I'd like to check up on Bronte too."

"Excellent. Bill is going to get the sleds out for us. Any questions, anyone?"

A chorus of *no*s replied.

"Okay, let's all get ready. Keep in touch, everyone."

Fox walked over to Clementine and said, "You are remarkable."

"Shut up, silly. You know, I was thinking that we should buy a few Clydesdale carthorses, and buy some carts. They would be invaluable at a time like this. They had them in my grandmother's time."

"Very good point. We are trying to teach people to return to more traditional methods, and we should lead by example."

"And they are cute. Lucy would love them. I can teach her how to take care of them. My mama taught me."

"Sounds perfect. Let's do that." Fox beamed at her wife.

"Fox? Clem? Can I have a word." Griffin seemed nervous and jumpy.

"Sure thing, Griff," Fox said. Fox slipped her hand into Clementine's and they walked to the other side of the room.

"I wanted to ask you a favour," Griffin said.

"Absolutely," Clementine added.

"If you're talking to Bronte, can you not tell her about my position—I mean, my estate, the money, the whole nine yards."

Clementine frowned in concentration. "We wouldn't gossip about you, Griff."

"No way," Fox agreed.

"No, I don't mean you would do that, just if it came up naturally in the conversation."

Fox and Clementine looked at each other. This was a bit strange.

"Is there something wrong, Griff?" Fox asked.

"No, it's difficult to explain. Her mum's putting pressure on her to marry this rich woman, you know, to bring money in to save the family kind of thing. So she doesn't want to be with anyone…"

Fox was totally lost, but Clementine seemed to get it straight away.

"Bronte doesn't want to be involved romantically with someone who might please her mother?"

Griffin nodded.

"You have feelings for her?"

Fox finally got what was going on here. Griffin was into Bronte?

Griffin's cheeks flushed. "Yes, no, I don't know. I don't know how I'm feeling, but I just want a chance to know her as this Griffin, without all the other baggage."

Fox saw a big red warning ahead. She lowered her voice. "Griffin, you're leaving in the new year. You asked me to get people interviewed for your job. You can't get involved and then leave."

"I'm not—look, everything is the same. Just don't tell her, please? I'll handle it."

"Of course we won't," Clementine said. "Just be careful, okay?"

"I will, thanks."

Griffin left to join her team. "Uh-oh. I see trouble ahead," Fox said.

Clementine kissed her hand. "But maybe that trouble will change Griffin's life. Let them get to know each other. There may be romance ahead."

❖

Clementine's teams worked hard to make sure the snow was causing as few problems as possible. Paths were cleared, and everyone was safe. The snow on the roads was starting to melt and they were passible with care.

Clementine came to visit Bronte in the evening with the aid of one of the Land Rovers.

Bronte used her crutches to get to the door. "Hi, Clementine, come in."

"I brought you a casserole. How are you feeling?"

"A bit sore but okay. I wish I could have been out there helping with the snow," Bronte said.

"Don't you worry, there will be plenty more chances for you to help in the future. Today, we help you. I'll put this in the kitchen. You go and sit down."

Bronte went to sit on the couch and Clementine soon joined her. "How are the Duchy Gang faring?"

"Exhausted, but in good spirits at the pub. Fox has put quite a large amount behind the bar to thank everyone for their efforts."

"They'll be very merry then."

"I should think extremely," Clementine joked. "To business—do you think you'll be up to going to the police station in a couple of days?"

"Absolutely, this has to be dealt with as soon as possible. I'm okay, as long as I've got my crutches, and you can get through the snow."

"It seems to be turning to slush on the roads now. Hopefully it won't freeze, but we'll get there. Can you email me a copy of the photo you took of the badger, and we can maybe take some of your injury?" Clementine asked.

"Sure, let's just hope Griffin is up to coming with us, and not still nursing a hangover."

The two women laughed.

Later that night, Bronte was in bed reading her book. She heard a voice outside. She got to her feet and used her crutch to hop over to the window. When she pulled up the blinds she saw Griffin waving at her.

Bronte opened the window. "What are you doing, Griff?"

Griffin, her speech slurred, said, "I wanted to say hi. I've been at the pub."

Bronte giggled. Griffin was sweetly drunk. "So I see."

"I'm going home, but I wanted to say hi, and I missed you today."
Bronte's heart melted. "Go home to bed and I'll see you soon."
Griffin saluted her. "Yes, ma'am. Miss you."

Then she blew kisses as she walked away. How was she going to
stop herself from falling for this adorable, gorgeous, wounded soul?

❖

"Are you sure you are up to this, Bronte?" Clementine said.

"Yes, let's do it. Griff, are you up to it or is your head too sore
still?"

"Ha ha. What did I say to you anyway?"

"I'm saying nothing," Bronte said.

This pair were so sweet together Clementine thought. "Right,
game face on people."

Clementine raised herself a little taller and walked into the small
police station. Sergeant Wexford, who she had seen before. He had
silver hair and a silver moustache, like he'd been taken from a 1950s
detective novel.

He looked up and he narrowed his eyes. Someone was not too
happy to see Clem. "Hello, Your Grace. Don't often see you in our little
village."

"I have a crime to report, sergeant, and you being the closest,
you're it."

He sighed and lifted his pen to take down the details. "What crime
would you like to report?"

"Trespassing, poaching, and the killing of a badger with dogs, a
protected specious as I'm sure you know."

He put down his pen again, obviously uninterested in the details.
"With the greatest respect, Your Grace, why are you concerned with
hunting? It's been the way of the country since time began."

"Because an innocent animal was killed," Bronte said fiercely.

"You obviously live in the country, *Miss*. Controlling animals is
necessary."

Clementine put her hand up. "Let me handle this, Bronte."

She heard Griffin say in a calming tone, "It's okay. Let Clem do
her stuff."

"There is no need to control the animals on Rosebrook land,

Sergeant. We are quite happy with them walking around minding their own business."

Clementine lifted up his pen and offered it to him. "Now I hope I won't have to phone the police commissioner and say that you wouldn't take a criminal report, because as Duchess of Rosebrook, the commissioner would always be available to take my calls."

He held her gaze for a few moments and then took the pen.

"Right, tell me what happened."

"As I wasn't there, I'll let my friend Bronte tell you the details. Bronte runs the new animal sanctuary in Rosebrook."

"Of course she does," Sargent Wexford said under his breath.

Bronte stepped forward while leaning on Griffin's arm. "Hi, my name is Bronte, and just so you know a little of my background, I'm an animal rehabilitator, and have worked within an anti-fox-hunting group, travelling up and down the country sabotaging illegal fox hunting. So I speak from great experience in dealing with hunters."

Griffin looked at a smiling Clementine and winked her approval. Griffin loved this side of Bronte. She was strong, confident, and passionate about her cause.

"My friend Griffin informed me that she had seen hunting and poaching going on when I first arrived in Rosebrook. So I made daily rounds of the woods to check for any evidence and any injured animals. Last Sunday I took my usual route and found the body of a dead badger."

She turned to Griffin and asked for the folder. Bronte placed it on the desk and opened it to pull out the picture of the badger. She handed it to the sergeant, and he glanced at it dismissively.

"Right, I see."

"What you should *see* is the badger was obviously torn apart by dogs. Illegal, as I'm sure a country man like yourself knows all too well."

Go Bronte, Griffin said silently.

Bronte continued. "Eager to find out if the badger sett had been disturbed, I ran towards it. A trap set by the hunters grabbed my ankle, and I was pulled to the ground and knocked myself out on a rock."

"Maybe you should have taken more care, Miss Bronte."

Griffin couldn't stop herself from reacting protectively. "Hey, Bronte shouldn't have to expect traps put down by poachers to be underfoot. That was the day the snow started. Bronte was knocked out. If I hadn't gone looking for her, I don't know what would have happened."

"Thank you, Griff," Bronte said. "If you'll look here in this folder, you'll find pictures of the trap that you can keep for you records."

Clementine came forward and Griffin watched Wexford reading over his notes. They were so brief that there was no way he'd written down the full statement.

"The way I see it, Your Grace, you have a few problems. First of all, you're right, badgers are protected, and I will take a report about that. But the hunting and poaching? Most woodland is common land, which would therefore make it impossible to be accused of poaching."

"What are you talking about? The woodland is part of the Rosebrook estate."

Wexford dropped his pen and stuffed his hands in his pockets and rocked back on his heels. He smirked as he said, "Oh yes, your *wife*, is it? Bought the estate back for you. But If I know my history well, your grandmother sold off a lot of land, and the area in question may have been part of what she sold."

"Are you kidding me, Sergeant?" Clementine said.

"No not at all, Your Grace. As you know, your grandmother sold land to the local council and the government when they used the facilities during the war."

"You're very well schooled in the history of Rosebrook." Clementine thought it would be hard getting the police to take it seriously, but not this hard.

"Oh yes. I used to ask my father what happened to the dying village next door to ours, and he told me the history of it."

"What are you saying then?"

"I'll need to see proof from your papers that you own that woodland. Otherwise it's common ground," Wexford said.

Clementine forced a smile onto her face. "Then we will return with that. In the meantime if you could let it be known to anyone who might be thinking about poaching that we are putting up cameras to protect our woodland and every animal in it."

He nodded and they walked out.

"Both of you were amazing," Griffin said.

Bronte shook her head. "He was brushing us off like he knew something."

"I know," Clementine agreed, "but we have to follow along with what he asks for. He has to take the report about the badger killing, and he knows it'll gather dust in the files with no evidence, but we can actually get hold of the culprits. Bronte, you know what you're doing with the cameras. If you and Griff source them and get them installed, I'll go through my papers to find the proof of ownership."

Bronte nodded her head. "We will do that straight away."

"Remember, get the best cameras you need, and pay with the Trust bank account."

"Will do. Griff? Can you come with me after work?"

"It's fine. We can go straight away. Paddy and I told the staff to take the next days off. We don't want any accidents while the roads are treacherous. Production is slowing anyway. We have enough stock for the Christmas markets."

"Okay, we'll drop you home, Clementine, check on Hoggy and Hedge, then head into town."

"Let's do this," Clementine said. "I'm not going to let people like Wexford win on my land."

CHAPTER THIRTEEN

A re you happy with these?" Griffin asked as they came out of the
electronics shop.

"Yes, they're perfect. Once they are up, we both can use our
phones to monitor what's happening there, anytime day or night. Night
vision, infrared, they'll be so useful."

"Did you say they alert you too?" Griffin asked.

"Yes, the app will send a notification."

Griffin nodded and they continued walking back towards the car
park. Griffin had enjoyed following Bronte around in the shop and just
spending time with her. She didn't want it to end. *Ask her for dinner*,
Griffin told herself. But she was nervous. Griffin had a lot of experience
with women, but not like this.

Usually she met them in clubs or on the beach while travelling,
and both parties generally wanted to move to the endgame quickly.
They didn't want to walk around the shops or go to dinner.

"Bronte?"

Bronte turned to her. "Yes?"

Griffin gulped. "How's your ankle?"

"Much better. A bit achy after walking around the shop, but the
crutch helped. I only need the one now."

Griffin nodded. "Good, good."

Ask her, you fool.

Instead of listening to her inner voice, she said, "They've handled
the snow a lot better in town, haven't they?"

The snow was all cleared from the pedestrian walkways, piled up by the sides of the pavements and roads, and the leftover snow had turned to slush after being treated with salt.

"They have the right equipment, I suppose, but you all did a good job," Bronte said.

Now, now, now!

Griffin gave herself a huge mental kick up the backside.

"Um, Bronte, since we're just going back to our empty cottages, do you want to get some dinner before we go home?"

"I'd love to." Bronte smiled.

"Great." Griffin kind of squeaked with excitement. *Keep it cool.* "Where would you like to go?"

They stopped and Bronte looked around. There were a lot of chain restaurants in the retail park where they were. Indian, Chinese, pizza, fish and chips.

"What about pizza? Pizza is my guilty pleasure."

"Pizza it is then. Let's go."

Griffin offered her arm to Bronte, and she took it. She felt such a buzz. This was going to be fun.

But in the very back of her mind she said, *You're leaving in the new year.*

But Griffin dismissed it quickly.

Clementine was in Isadora's study upstairs looking through the old papers. Some of them were very delicate, and she had them inside protective wallets.

She saw the oldest and smiled.

"Lucy, come and see this, you'll like this."

Lucy was at the bookshelf going through the old steward's books. She came over and took a seat beside Clementine. "What is it, Aunty Clem?"

"This is the original paper granting the Rosebrook lands to our family."

Lucy's eyes went wide. "From King Charles II?"

"Yes," Clementine said with a grin, "do you want to see?"

"Uh-huh."

"Put these white gloves on first, okay, and I'll tell you all about it."

Clementine took the precious document out of the folder. It was in another protective plastic sleeve, and she carefully took it out. "Can you remember what you learned about our family's beginnings?"

"Yeah, our ancestor was the mistress of King Charles II," Lucy said.

"Exactly right. She had many children with him, and they were given the name Fitzroy, meaning son of a king, *fitz roy*. Can you remember what our ancestor was called?"

"Was it Maria?"

"That's right, Maria Warwick."

Clementine loved teaching Lucy this stuff, just like the way her father taught her.

"She was from poor farming stock. She came to London to be a dancer and entertainer, met the king, and the rest is history. To give Maria and her children an income, he made their first son a duke and gave him these lands, which were much vaster at the time than they are now. When the son died young, there were only daughters, and without inheriting the title they wouldn't have the lands and money. So she persuaded the king to change the dukedom to one where females could inherit. The oldest daughter Charlotte then became the new duchess."

"Is this the original?" Lucy asked with a smile on her face.

"This is it. Let me show you the part that allows you and me to inherit the title."

Clementine pulled the document out extremely carefully and placed it down on the desk.

"Wow, this is so cool," Lucy said. "Would the king have touched this?"

"Yes." Clementine nodded. "Although a scribe would draw it up, the king had to put his seal on it."

"A king is my ancestor, and this is his seal. It's really weird in a cool way when you think about it."

"Next to his seal is the seal accepting the title deed. *Duchess Charlotte*. But the most important part is here in the text. It can be hard to read this old way of writing, but if you look closely, where it did ordinally say the title would be handed down though *male heirs of the body*, the word *male* has been crossed out and signed by the king."

"That's what makes us be able to be duchesses?" Lucy asked.

"Yes, just that one word change. Amazing, isn't it? There are very few titles that go down the female line. They do exist, but there aren't many."

"That's what made my dad so mad he couldn't inherit," Lucy said.

"I imagine he wasn't too pleased."

Clementine was always careful not to talk badly about Lucy's dad Peter in front of her. Lucy and Peter might not have had the best father-daughter relationship, but he was still her dad.

"I better put it away now before it gets any damage."

Clementine slipped it back into the sleeve and then the folder. "We need to find a similar document that mentions the forest woodland. I know I've seen it in here before."

Before they could continue looking, there was a knock at the study door. "Come in."

Clementine got very excited because she knew what was coming. Fox's voice came through the door.

"Lucy could you open the door for me?"

Lucy got up quickly and opened the door. When she saw Fox holding two cat carriers, she covered her mouth with her hands and jumped up and down with excitement.

"You got the cats? How did you?"

"Archie and I went in one of the estate Jeeps with snow chains on the tires, and we made it." Fox put the carriers down on the floor. "These are the two cats you chose at the cat protection league."

Lucy looked back at Clementine, and she had tears in her eyes. "Thank you, Aunty Clem, thanks, Fox. I've always wanted a pet."

"Now you have two. Open the carriers," Clementine said.

Fox opened one and Lucy the other. "Just let them find their own way out, Luce. Be nice and calm."

Two heads popped out. "Aww, they're so cute," Lucy said. "Hey, girls."

Both cats were only one year old, and sisters. They were an ideal pick for Lucy, Clementine thought. The sisters would keep each other company.

One cat was jet black, and the other was an almost blue grey with four white socks. The black cat seemed to be more confident of the two and went straight for Lucy's lap, the grey following soon after.

Lucy stroked and scratched their chests and ears. "You're both two beautiful girls."

"Have you thought of any names?" Fox asked.

"I had, actually, but I wanted to run them by you, Aunty Clem."

"What did you come up with?" Clementine asked.

"Dora and Lady, for Lady Louisa her wife."

Clementine and Fox burst out laughing.

"Do you think it's too disrespectful?" Lucy asked.

"No, I think my grandmothers would take it in good fun. It's a nice idea to have a Dora and Lady Louisa about the house again."

"Which will be which?" Fox asked.

"The black one takes the lead more, so I think she's Dora, and the grey, Lady."

"Perfect," Fox said. "Now, first things first. We'll leave Clem to keep looking here and you can put out the litter trays and food and water, okay?"

"Yeah, and then I'll show them my room. Thank you so much for them. They are the best Christmas present."

Lucy didn't know what was going to hit her on Christmas Day. Fox was determined to give Lucy the Christmas she never had with her miser of a father. Clementine didn't want to spoil her, but she knew Lucy was the kind of girl who was very appreciative of what she had.

"Off you go, you two. I'll keep my head in the papers."

I just have to find this document.

❖

Bronte was glad Griffin had asked her to dinner. It was just nice to be in her company, and maybe she could get Griffin to open up about her family background.

"Are you a vegan like Fox?" Griffin said out of the blue. "Just in case I ever have to cook for you again."

Griffin gave her the sweetest smile. She must have girls with just a smile and a wink.

Bronte lifted her menu. "How could I describe what I am? A vegetarian with pretentions of being a vegan, or just a really bad vegan. It's the cheese. Cheese has always been a big thing for me, hence why I love pizzas and your cheesy beanos."

Griffin slapped her forehead softly. "What a loser. I never ever asked you. Ugh."

"I would have told you. Don't worry about it. Anyway I want to go vegan, and I'm determined to make it. I can only keep trying."

"Yeah. Do you not like any of the vegan cheeses? They do vegan pizzas here."

"No, I've tried them. There's something...*chemical* about them. Maybe I could make giving up cheese my New Year's resolution."

Griffin laughed. "Good luck with that one."

Bronte saw a Christmas menu on the table and picked it up. This could be a great conversation opener. "Look, a Christmas menu. Yuck! Christmas dinner pizza. That sounds awful."

"I could probably force it down. I love to eat," Griffin said.

"You've got a big frame to fill."

She saw Griffin blush.

Now maybe if she opened up a bit about her family life, it might encourage Griffin to do the same.

Here goes. "This will be my first Christmas away from the family. I've been trying to get away for years, but Mother always guilt-trips me."

Griffin leaned forward on her hand and said, "I thought you aristocracy would have an amazing Christmas Day. Lots of expensive food, nice drinks, great presents..."

"I suppose we did have good quality food and drink, but that doesn't make a nice Christmas. Everything is regimented. You're frightened of saying the wrong thing, using the wrong cutlery or the glass for the right course. My mother sucked all the joy out of the day. My sister and her family feel the same. This year after everything she's said and done, I'm finally standing up for myself and not going."

The server interrupted to take their order just then.

"I'll have a stuffed crust veggie sizzler, Griff?"

"A stuffed crust meaty sizzler." Griffin grinned.

"Would you like garlic bread?" the server asked.

"Griff?" Griffin nodded. "Yes, a large garlic bread, please."

Once the drinks were ordered, Griffin said, "We both like spicy."

Bronte leaned forward. "It seems that way."

They lost themselves in each other's eyes, just like their first meal together. Griffin cleared her throat. "So, you're staying in Rosebrook?"

Bronte nodded. "Christmas without Mother will be present enough in itself. What about you?"

As soon as Bronte said that, she saw the wounded look she had seen a few times from Griffin. She kept it well hidden, but it was there.

"My mum's on a Christmas cruise, with her sister. She had a heart attack not too long ago, so it's a kind of recuperation type thing."

Bronte didn't hesitate to reach across the table and clasp Griffin's hand. "I'm sorry to hear about your mum. Is she doing better? I suppose she must be if she's going on a cruise."

"Yeah, yeah, she is."

Griffin was clamming up.

"Did you not want to go with her, or—"

Unfortunately, the order arrived just as Bronte was asking the question. Griffin dived into her pizza, probably so she didn't have to answer the awkward questions. Maybe she could try a new path of questioning?

"What was Christmas like when you were a child, Griff?"

Griffin swallowed her bite of pizza and said, "We had nothing, virtually. My mum was a single mum, no dad or help…"

Bronte was sure she could see Griffin's eyes well up at that point, but then she appeared to shake it off.

"She had two jobs, three in the run-up to Christmas. Mum saved all year just so we could have a nice meal together, and maybe one present. I respected her so much for working that hard, and that she had to work that hard. We maybe didn't get food from the same sort of shops you did, but we enjoyed it."

"I think I would have enjoyed yours much better. All the fine food and drink in the world doesn't make up for the cold, loveless atmosphere we had. You and your mum sound as if it was full of warmth."

Griffin stared down at her plate. "Yeah, it was."

The woman's fortunes must have turned if she was now going on a cruise. If Bronte read between the lines, she would guess that there was some sort of estrangement with her mum. You didn't go from a loving, warm childhood like that to leaving your child alone on Christmas, even though she might be an adult herself.

"What are you going to do for Christmas dinner?" Griffin asked her.

"Fox and Clementine asked me to join them. I think they are having those lovely elderly ladies, the Tucker twins, too."

Griffin smiled. "Yeah, Clem said the same to me."

Bronte's heart started to beat faster. Was it the hot-chilli pizza, or the chance to spend Christmas lunch with Griff?

"Would you like to go together?"

The tension disappeared from Griffin's face. "That would be nice, yeah."

"You're going to need a big warm meal after the Big Dip in the morning. How are you feeling about it?"

"Dreading it, to be quite honest," Griff said. "I mean, I'm used to the cold. I've told you about the temperatures I've camped in. But then I've always warmed up, worked up a sweat, by putting up the tent, chopping wood, catching dinner. This is just get undressed and walk into the waves. Cold water is a whole other level. What did Dr. Blake say about you doing it?"

"He said my ankle wound isn't healed enough. Now you might say that's a convenient excuse to get out of doing it, but I was actually looking forward to trying. I love new experiences."

"Fox is enthusiastic about it all. Cold water therapy. She cornered me a few times to tell me about it. Sounds interesting."

"I'll be there cheering you on. I'll hold your towel if you want," Bronte said cheekily.

"Oh, you're too kind."

"When can we put these cameras up?"

"Can you wait till the weekend? We're going to try to open the factory this morning."

"Of course. I've taken enough time from you as it is."

"I want to help keep the woodland safe and secure. The forest has been an escape for me. That's why I wanted to build the shelter."

"That's another thing I've kept you from doing. Instead you've been helping set up the animal rescue," Bronte said.

Griffin shook her head. "Helping the animal rescue is much more important, believe me. Have you got much more to do before you can start taking the bigger animals in?"

"Everything is basically ready. I want to make the field at the back more habitable. It will probably be used by foxes mainly, so I need to add quite a few things. Dig out some ditches, some tunnels, that kind of thing. I thought I could source some old fallen tree trunks, things like that."

"I'll keep an eye out for you," Griffin said.

They both fell silent and ate their food. Griffin reached out for another slice of garlic bread just as Bronte did, and their fingers brushed.

"Sorry. After you," Griffin said.

Bronte didn't remove her fingers straight away, causing tingles to spread up Griffin's arm. But she eventually moved them, and Griffin felt their loss.

Griffin felt so much inside that she had to say something.

"Bronte, it's been nice spending time together today. In fact it's been special since you first came."

"Since I first came?" Bronte raised an eyebrow.

Griffin remembered with embarrassment how she'd greeted Bronte when she first arrived. "Oh, forget that. I was just in a bad mood."

"I forgive you, but only if you'll share a dessert with me."

"Done. What I was trying to say was that a lot of my friends here are now in couples. Even Paddy has found someone," Griffin said.

"Alanna?" Bronte said.

"Yeah, they've been spending a lot of time with one another, and I'm really happy for Paddy. Nobody deserves happiness more than him, but it's just awkward if everyone is together."

"Yes, I suppose it would be. So I'm a convenient friend?" Bronte said with an annoyed tone to her voice.

Panic shot through Griffin's body. "No, no, I didn't mean that. I mean it's been nice to get to know you, spend time with you, and not spend time down the pub being a gooseberry."

Bronte chuckled. "I know what you meant. It has been nice."

Griffin let out a sigh of relief. "I always think I say the wrong thing at the best of times."

"Please don't ever think you say the wrong thing with me. Since I've come to Rosebrook, you have been nothing but a good friend to me, even when I was being stubborn and wanted to do everything myself. I'd never have gotten this far with the shelter without you. I really appreciate your friendship."

"Thank you."

"You're welcome. Now are you are going to share dessert with me?"

"Which one?"

"Triple chocolate death," Bronte replied.

Griffin was dazzled by the playful twinkle in Bronte's eyes as she said it. She was so beautiful, not just on the outside but on the inside too. Everything was different since she got to know her. The pain and confusion Griffin felt coming back to Rosebrook hadn't gone away, but she felt happy and distracted in Bronte's company.

Bronte made her heart feel lighter.

"Triple chocolate death it is."

Clementine put the document she was reading back into the folder in front of her and held her head in her hands. She couldn't find anything that mentioned the woodland specifically. Clementine did find the deeds to the land and original house on the site—Humbledon Hall, as it was then called. Humbledon Hall and estate had been owned by a colonel in Oliver Cromwell's New Model Army. After Oliver Cromwell's death, when Charles II was invited back to the throne, he had many involved in his father's death executed and all their lands taken back to the Crown.

That gave him the land around Rosebrook village to give to his mistress and her children, but the original deeds mentioned only the size of the parkland.

She was sure that Sergeant Wexford wouldn't accept that, especially as it was well known her grandmother sold a lot of their land when her housing project was in trouble. There was nothing more she could do tonight. She'd been reading the documents for too long, which required a lot of concentration, especially when they were written in a mixture of English and Latin, and some in French.

Clementine was determined to find something, though. She could go to the council for their opinion, but the wheels of local government turned so slowly that many animals would be harmed in that time.

No, she needed something clear to stop this behaviour in its tracks. Clementine left Isadora's study and walked along to Lucy's room to check up on her. She heard the TV on low in the background as she knocked.

"Luce?"

"Come in."

She opened the door and walked into a lovely sight. Both cats were lying on Lucy's bed. The one Lucy had called Dora was lying across her feet, and Lady cuddled into Lucy's side as she looked at her iPad.

"These two girls have settled in quickly."

Lucy had the biggest smile on her face. "They are the best. Thanks again, Aunty Clem."

Clementine sat on the edge of Lucy's bed. She stroked each cat in turn.

"Hello, Lady Louisa, and you, Dora." Clementine turned back to Lucy and said, "I hope they'll keep you company in this big house."

"I'm used to it now. My school friends keep trying to freak me out, saying that there were two ghosts who walked the house and grounds."

"Don't tell me," Clementine said, "the white lady and green lady?"

"Yeah, how did you know?"

"Every stately home in Britain has a white lady and a green lady. It's a bit silly," Clementine said.

"Don't worry, I'm not scared any more. Not since you told me about ghosts when I moved in," Lucy said.

"And what did I tell you?"

"That your mother, Isadora, and Lady Louisa all died in this house, and they wouldn't allow any ghost to scare me."

"That's right. You are their heir, remember. The one who is going to look after and protect Rosebrook House for them one day. They've got your back."

Dora the cat chose that moment to roll onto her back, wanting a belly rub. Clementine obliged. "She's so soft."

"I know," Lucy said, beaming, "so cute. Did you find anything about the woods?"

Clementine sighed. "Nothing as yet that's going to help us, but I'm not giving up. There's got to be something. I know Louisa absolutely loved those woods, but Dora sold off a lot of land by the end."

"Would Dora mention it in a diary? I remember you said that you had some," Lucy said.

"Yes," Clementine said excitedly, "that could be it. You're a genius."

Chapter Fourteen

Saturday was a big day for Bronte. She and her new friends were putting up the cameras to try to help protect the woodland, and she was going to release the hedgehogs back to the wild.

Hedge and Hoggy would come later. First of all the woodland had to be safeguarded for them.

Archie, Ash, Clementine, Fox, and Lucy came to help Bronte and Griffin. As they walked through the woods, Bronte looked to Griff and thought how natural it had become to be with her. She'd never been a person who made deep, long-term friendships, mostly because she had nothing in common with her schoolmates. The girls she went to school with were not going to go into a path of life like animal conservation. They were going into business or banking, living on their parents' fortune, or becoming the wife of a rich name. Bronte shared nothing in common with these people.

Griffin was different from her in so many ways but in the fundamentals, loving and caring for the world and people in it. She wasn't affected by wealth or greed, had an ordinary job, and even better, Mother would not approve of their friendship.

"Are we near where you want the first camera, Bronte?" Archie asked.

Bronte took out her sketch of the forest areas where she wanted to install cameras. "Griff and I thought we'd put the first at her little shelter in the middle of the woods, because the hunters use her fire ring to drink when they are out."

The group walked on, their shoes crunching the layer of snow underfoot. It hadn't snowed since the big storm they'd had, but temperatures hadn't risen as much as the weather forecasters had predicted, so a snow layer had frozen rather than melted.

When they arrived at the spot in the middle of the woods, Fox joked, "You haven't got very far with your log cabin, Griff. I was hoping we'd be having a few beers with you here by now."

"It's only a shelter, Fox—don't be getting the idea you can come here and hide from Clem. It's not going to be a sports bar."

"She wouldn't dare hide from me." Clementine narrowed her eyes at her partner.

Everybody laughed and even Fox smiled. "Let's get on with it then, smart-arse."

Griffin carried one of the two ladders they brought over to a large tree across from her camp area. "I thought here would be a good place."

Archie came over with a bag of grit to melt the ice and make it safe for the ladder.

Griffin said, "I'll get the fire going first."

Fox said confidently, "You carry on."

"Have you made a fire before?" Griffin asked.

Archie tried to hide her laugh.

"Shut up, Archie. I can make a simple fire."

"Of course you can," Archie replied.

Griffin wasn't convinced, but she wasn't going to embarrass Fox in front of her wife and Lucy. "Okay, well, the dry wood and everything you'll need is under the roof of the shelter. It wasn't finished by any means, but there is enough of a roof to keep the wood and kindling dry."

Bronte said, "Be careful up there, Griff."

"I'll be fine with Archie stabilizing the ladder. Could you go over and make sure Fox doesn't set the woodland alight?"

"Okay. Archie, make sure she's safe. I don't want the two of us to have injured ankles."

"Will do."

Bronte walked over to the fire area where Clementine and Ash were getting out some of Griffin's camping gear. It had been Clementine's idea to have a picnic of sorts while the cameras were going up. She and Ash made sandwiches and brought tea bags and cakes. From Griffin they got the kettle and other equipment they would need. Bronte took a seat next to Lucy, who seemed really excited.

"I've never done something like this before. It'll be such good fun."

"You were never in the Girl Guides, Lucy?" Bronte asked.

"No, nothing like that."

Bronte didn't know all the details but could tell that life with her father wasn't great, and coming to live with Clementine and Fox changed her life for the better.

"Well, we'll have lots of fun today. I hear you got your two cats."

"Oh yeah, they are gorgeous. Dora and Lady—her full name is Lady Louisa. After Aunty Clem's grandparents."

Clementine brought out the kettle and the boxes of food. "You should see them, Bronte. It's like they have known Luce their whole lives. They are very attached to her."

Lucy had a big smile on her face. "They sleep cuddled up to me all night. Let me show you some pictures."

"I'd love to see them."

While Lucy was opening up her phone, Fox arrived at the fire pit with logs that even she could tell were too big.

"Fox, maybe—" Bronte said.

"I'm okay. Don't worry."

But Bronte kind of was. She'd realized Fox wasn't exactly the outdoors type when she turned up for a day in the woods in a pair of crisply ironed designer jeans, a button-down shirt, and a pair of blue boat shoes.

Forty minutes had gone by, and there was still no fire. Clementine gave an apologetic look to Ash who, like her, was shivering.

"Fox?"

Fox was so frustrated by this point she barked, "Look, I can do it. Just give me five minutes."

But Fox had been asking for five minutes for the best part of forty. All sense of protecting her dapper look was now lost. Fox was on her hands and knees trying to blow on the kindling underneath these three hulking great wood logs.

Fox now had two big dirty wet knee patches on her very expensive jeans and muddy marks on her shirt and jacket. Clementine didn't even want to look at the state the boat shoes would be in.

Lucy shuffled up to Clementine and leaned into her looking for warmth, so she put her arm around her and hugged her in tight. It was a cold winter's day, but they had been expecting to be drinking warm tea and eating sandwiches by this point.

Clementine heard Griffin climb down the ladder and announce, "That's the first one done."

She looked at Bronte and mouthed, "Help."

Bronte nodded, then went over and whispered to Griffin. She nodded and Griffin came striding over.

"Hey, Fox, let me get that fire for you, and then you can look after it while I do the next camera." Griffin handled it very diplomatically.

Fox stood up and brushed down her clothes, as much as she could. "I thought I had it a few times there," Fox said.

"Fires are tricky beasts. Don't worry about that."

Griffin went to work immediately, taking away all of Fox's wood pile. She went back to the shelter and started cutting little bits of wood into small sticks and using the axe she'd brought to cut the logs down to a more manageable size.

Fifteen minutes later there was a fire going, and Griffin got a round of applause. Ash, Lucy, and Clementine stood up close to the fire to allow the warmth to enter their bones.

Bronte was showing Griffin where she wanted the next camera on her map of the area.

Clementine said to Fox, "Why don't you go with Archie and Griffin, I'm sure they'll need your help. We'll get the tea on."

"Excellent idea, Clem. They'll probably need a hand with the wiring or lifting something heavy."

Once they were out of sight, Ash said, "Oh, thank God. I was freezing to death."

Clementine nodded. "I know, I just needed to ease her bruised ego. Fox has an amazing business and technology brain, but she's not so good with this kind of stuff."

"She'll be needed when we need to set the app up for the cameras," Bronte said.

"You okay, Luce?" Clementine asked.

"Can we have tea quickly? I'm so cold, Aunt Clem."

"I'm on it. Water, Ash, please?"

Clementine opened the kettle and Ash poured in the water from a metal canteen. She hung the kettle on the hook above the fire.

"The fire's nice and strong now. It shouldn't take long."

Fifteen minutes later, the three women and Lucy were holding piping hot cups of tea and feeling nice and toasty by the fire.

"Sandwich, anyone?" Ash handed around a box and they each took one.

"Hmm," Lucy hummed. Then she asked, "When can we release the hogs?"

Bronte looked at her watch. "Maybe half past four? I'll go back and pick them up from the cottage about four."

"Why as late as that?"

"It's because they're nocturnal, so they'll be awake then. If you put them out during the day, they'd be sitting ducks for predators. Tonight they'll find some food and probably try to find a safe place to sleep."

"Are you sure they are well enough?" Lucy asked.

"They probably could have had a few more days at the rescue, but they are due to go into hibernation anytime now, so I didn't want to disrupt that."

"Oh, that's interesting," Ash said. "I hope they have a nice long sleep."

"Without any disturbance from these poachers. Oh, did you find the deed for the woodland yet?" Bronte asked.

"Not yet. I've looked through the papers I have a few times, and I can't find mention of it."

"Do you think it could be common land then?" Bronte asked.

Clementine shook her head. "No, it can't be. The family owned land for miles. Isadora did sell off some land, but Louisa loved this woodland. She used to come and do sketches here for her paintings. Dora wouldn't have sold it."

"I hope you're right, or the animals here will be in danger," Bronte said gravely.

"Lucy here had the great idea of reading through Dora's diary for clues. She wrote about a lot of the estate business in there. I just need some time."

Bronte nodded. "Okay, I'll keep everything crossed then."

"This is nice," Ash said. "Sharing a cup of tea around a fire in the forest. It always amazes me to think that just a few miles that way, there's the cove and a beautiful beach."

"You're right," Clementine said, "this village has everything. A seaside day out, or a day for rambling through the trees. I feel really lucky to live here. Especially now that my grandmother's dream of revitalizing the village has come true."

"I should probably go and check on them. They'll need the plan to put up the next camera," Bronte said.

"Wait a second," Clementine hesitated. "Lucy, this is a top-secret conversation."

"Got it."

Clementine nudged Ash. "Oh yeah. How are you getting on with Griff?"

Bronte looked confused. "Good, I mean, we're friends."

Ash shrugged. "Friends? We're all friends."

"I like her, but she's leaving, so there's no more to say. I better go and help."

❖

Griffin and Bronte walked home painfully slowly, Bronte leaning heavily on Griffin.

"You should have said your ankle was this painful."

"I didn't want to spoil anyone's fun," Bronte said.

"The cold will have made it feel worse."

Bronte stopped to rest for a moment. "I've wanted it to be better so badly that I pushed it too far, I think, but we had two important jobs to do—get the cameras up, and release our two hogs."

"You need to take care of yourself too, or you won't be able to look after any animals that need your help," Griffin said.

"Thank you, Mother."

Griffin shivered dramatically. "Just...no. But I've got an idea," Griffin continued. "We're closer to my cottage. Why don't we go there, get you warmed up and some painkillers into you, and then I'll take you home?"

"Good idea. Let's do that."

"Oh? Right." Griffin was expecting to have to gently persuade

Bronte, but no. Now she began to worry about how tidy her cottage was. "Eh, you'll need take me as you find me at the cottage. I don't think I did much tidying yesterday."

"Do I look like someone who cares about tidiness, Griff? Come on, my ankle is throbbing."

"Got ya. Let's go."

They made it to Griffin's quite quickly. Griffin took them in the front door and into the living room. She quickly lifted some discarded clothing from the couch and mail from the coffee table. "I'll just get you some water for your painkillers. Take a seat."

Bronte let out a sigh of relief when she sat down. She had overtaxed herself today. "Argh."

Griffin came back through with a glass of water. "Are you okay?"

"Yes, I think it's just taking the pressure off it caused some sharp pains."

After taking the glass from Griffin, Bronte took out her tablets and swallowed them quickly.

"What would you like? Tea, coffee, juice?"

"Coffee would be nice. Perk me up a bit."

"On its way," Griffin said.

"Strong and—"

"Strong and one sugar, I know," Griffin said.

"Well remembered."

Griffin walked backwards into the kitchen, while pointing at her head. "I remember everything about you."

Wow. That comment took her aback. Was Clementine right? Did Griffin have more than friendly feelings towards her?

She couldn't deny her own confusing feelings. Confusing because it had been so long since she'd had feelings towards another.

Bronte decided to leave those thoughts filed away under *deal with later* because for just now it was too much on top of everything else.

She turned to her side, where there was a small side table, and put her glass of water down. Something caught her eye on the table. It was a card. Bronte picked it up, and she realized it was a hand-drawn card with some goofy kids' characters on it.

She should not be doing this. It was clearly private correspondence, but she just couldn't help herself. She so desperately wanted to know Griffin better. Even though Griffin had opened up and discussed her mum when they had dinner together, it was clearly only scratching the surface.

Griffin had deep wounds and a reason why she wasn't going to see her mother at Christmas.

Bronte flipped open the card and read what was inside.

To Griffin,

> *You are, as always, in my thoughts. Especially on your birthday. Each year that goes by makes me feel sadder that I don't get to see you. But never doubt that I love you.*
> *Love always,*
> *Daddy xx*

God, Bronte was welling up with tears. Was this the emotional wound that Bronte could sometimes see on Griffin's face? Intriguingly there was a five thousand pound cheque stapled to the inside of the card that was uncashed.

There was something really wrong with this picture. Griffin had described how poor she and her mum were when she was little, and that her mum had to work two or three jobs just for them to survive.

Yet here she was, leaving a five thousand pound cheque uncashed. Was this a one-off? She put the card down before she was caught.

Griffin was even more mysterious than she thought. She looked around the living room. Decor was sparse, but the furnishings there were, like the TV, were high-quality, expensive makes.

Bronte jumped when Griffin came back into the room, she was so deeply in her thoughts.

"Coffee, strong, and one sugar."

"Thanks, I was just admiring your TV on the wall."

Griffin handed her a coffee and plonked down on the couch beside her with a can of Coke.

"You know that's not good for you," Bronte said.

Griffin rolled her eyes. "It's my only vice, and I only have one at night."

"I'll let you off then."

"How the ankle doing now?" Griffin asked.

Bronte tried to rotate it a few times. "Throbbing, but only to be expected, I suppose."

"You need to look after it, so I can have a dance with you at the New Year's party."

"New Year's party? Where is it?" Bronte asked.

"Rosebrook," Griffin said. "There was one last year, and Fox said she wanted to make it a tradition. It's a lot of fun, and I want a dance out of you."

"Oh? Why are you so determined?"

"One, because you're going to be a baroness one day, and it would be nice to say I've danced with a future baroness."

"Baroness Lawton," Bronte said. "The thought is just awful to me."

"Why?" Griffin asked.

"Because Baroness Lawton makes me sound like my mother, and that's horrifying. Besides, the title will be useless by then."

"Why?"

"Well, because Lawton House will be gone, because the bank will have taken it, and it just won't mean anything," Bronte said.

"I don't get what you mean. Explain to this working-class subject."

Bronte laughed. "A title is only worth having if it is useful. Like, my family's usefulness was safeguarding the oldest building in London, and the historic items within its walls. Antique furniture, paintings, books in the library, even historically significant scientific instruments, wall hangings, all sorts."

"Did your mum not try to sell some of those to pay the bills?"

Bronte smiled. "She couldn't, and believe me she would have if she could. It's a bit of a family story."

Griffin pulled her long legs up on the couch and said, "Oh, tell me, tell me."

"You really want to hear this kind of stuff?"

"Uh-huh. It's fascinating. The aristocracy is a whole other world to me, I suppose."

"It was down to my great-grandfather. Back then we did have some money, but my great-grandfather knew he had to do something or my grandfather would fritter it all away. He was a gambler, you see."

"It's a terrible addiction. I've seen good people lose their whole lives through gambling," Griffin said.

"Exactly. He set up his will to protect what the family had at that point. He left the money in a trust that would only pay out yearly, and any items in the house at the time of his death could not be sold. So my grandfather and my mother were stuck. The money in the trust ran out because it wasn't invested wisely, and she can't sell anything worth money."

"That a shame. Because the house will be lost and selling some of the paintings would help."

"I don't think so—the paintings wouldn't still be hanging on the walls if my great-grandfather hadn't set up his will that way," Bronte said.

"True."

"So, besides safeguarding national treasures, the other reason a title can make sense in this modern world is community responsibility."

Griffin narrowed her eyes. "No, you'll have to explain that one to me."

"Clementine is a perfect example. The Duchess of Rosebrook. She has the house, the focal point in the wider area, and most crucially, she plays a leadership role in the community. She has the power, with Fox of course, to make the village aim to be a greener place, a safer place for the LGBTQ community. She's a leader in times of disaster, like the snowfall, or the big storm they had before we got here. It's remarkable what she and Fox have done here, but I don't think they would have just listened to Fox, but they would listen to their duchess."

"You make a lot of sense," Griffin said.

"When I'm baroness, I won't be able to do that. There's no village community in the middle of London, and the house won't belong to the family by then anyway."

Griffin blew air from her lips. "That's depressing and sad."

Bronte shrugged. "I don't know how many times I've told Mother to sell to the National Trust. At least then the public could enjoy it. But she's so stubborn. It's simple vanity. She won't be the de Lacey who hands over the keys to the house."

"That's a shame."

"The National Trust would even let her stay there for her lifetime. Instead she'd rather pimp me out to a daughter of a rich friend."

"What is this woman like?" Griffin asked.

"I didn't know her at school, I just knew of her. She won everything you could win. Maths, science prizes, chess, debating competitions, passed all exams, went to Oxford. Perfect person, I'm sure, to carry on a family multinational company, but certainly not my type," Bronte said.

Griffin cleared her throat. "What is your type?"

Before Bronte could censor what she was saying, she blurted out, "Someone who can make a fire?"

It was meant to be a joke, but Griffin didn't laugh. She gave her a smoky look. "Oh yeah? What else?"

Bring it back to my rich suitor, it's safer, Bronte told herself, but her mouth wasn't connecting with her brain. "An outdoors person. Strong, maybe can chop wood with an axe. Antonia is far too femme for me."

An awkward silence fell upon the room as Griffin obviously realized who fit that bill. Bronte picked up her coffee and took a few long gulps.

"Nice coffee."

"Thanks. About what you—"

Bronte wasn't ready for this conversation so she interrupted with, "You've got a lot of Christmas cards on your mantelpiece."

"Eh, not too many, really. Only the older members of the village send cards. The younger ones listen to Fox about environment stuff. No, the rest are from charity organizations. I support a lot of charities, mostly child and animal welfare charities."

That was it. The large brass key tightened her chest and her heart another notch. Could Griff get any more desirable? In the silence her stomach gave her a hint of what to talk about by rumbling loudly.

"Excuse me, I'm starving. Do you have anything else on your culinary repertoire?"

Griffin thought for a second, then snapped her fingers and pointed at her with a big smile. "Cheese on toast. Because you love cheese."

"How sweet, you remember all the special things I like, coffee and cheese."

"I'm a good listener," Griffin said. "I'll be back shortly."

❖

Clementine was lying on the sofa in the TV area in the kitchen while Lucy and Fox played with the cats. Dora and Lady had taken to

Lucy so well. They followed her around the house, and Lucy just loved it.

Clementine was methodically going through Isadora's diary looking for any clues about the woodland. She was sure there had to be something, anything. A crumb of information that would lead her to what she needed.

"Aunty Clementine? Have you found anything yet?"

"Not yet, Luce, but I'm not giving up."

"It was nice but sad letting Hedge and Hoggy go today. I mean, they could get hurt again."

"I know it's difficult," Clementine said, "but they would have gotten stressed if they weren't able to hibernate in the wild. The wild is their home."

Fox was waving around a tiny fishing rod with a feather on the end for her cat friends and was giving them good exercise. Lady had long since given up and was curled between Lucy's legs, but Dora was leaping all over the place.

"There'll be more animals for you to look after soon," Fox said, "that's the sad thing. There will be a need for space at the animal rescue."

"Bronte says I have to get used to being happy for the animals to be released. There's only a few that don't to go back," Lucy said.

Clementine let the diary fall on her chest. "Have you got much more to do at the rescue, until it's fully open?"

"Yes, we're working on the field at the back. We've split it into two, and one area we're setting up as a fox yard. Bronte says rescues get a lot of foxes in the country."

"Foxes are the best," Fox joked.

"Foxes are full of themselves," Clementine said quickly.

"Ow, you wound me, dear wife."

Clementine ignored her. "What makes it a fox yard? What do you have to do to the area?"

"Dig ditches, make the beginnings of burrows for them to finish off. Lots of toys, because they are clever, dog toys, and children's nursery playthings. Like chutes and climbing equipment."

"Really?" Clementine said. "I didn't know that. Lots more for you to do then."

"Lots more billable hours too." Fox raised her hand and Lucy high-fived it.

Clementine smiled and shook her head. When Lucy came to live with them, she came with only herself and her clothes. Peter was in so much debt that selling their house only covered a portion, and Clementine and Fox had to pay off the rest of the estate.

They wanted Lucy to have a regular allocation of pocket money each month so she could feel a bit more independent, but the kind of girl Lucy was, she wouldn't like just being handed money for nothing.

Fox told her about how her mum and dad handled her pocket money, and they adapted it for Lucy.

Every environmental task she helped with in the community, she got paid for. Litter picking, cleaning up the beach, helping at the rescue, even reading important books on the environment.

Fox took charge of that and encouraged Lucy in everything she did. It had been working perfectly and gave Lucy great self-esteem that she could buy things that she had earned.

"Do you want to go litter picking on the beach tomorrow, Luce?" Fox asked.

"Yeah, that would be fun."

"Great, I want to try another training swim—well, I say swim, paddle mostly."

Clementine still couldn't believe Fox was holding this event. She pointed at Fox and warned her. "You wanted this huge big Christmas, and I've planned the food to perfection. If I have to sit in Accident and Emergency all Christmas afternoon, I'm leaving you there."

Fox held up her hands. "Calm down, calm down. It's all going to be safe and done properly. I've got volunteers from St. John's Ambulance coming, and security, there'll be waivers for participants to sign, I even got the events manager at Fox Toys to plan it."

The Big Dip had grown arms and legs since Fox announced it. It was shared on social media and people were coming from surrounding villages, towns like Bournemouth and Poole. It was going to be much bigger than she thought.

"Just make sure you are safe."

"I will," Fox said.

"I wish I could do it." Lucy sighed.

"The medics have advised no under-sixteens, so unfortunately it's out," Fox said.

"Okay. I think I'll go and watch some Netflix before bed."

"Okay, sweetheart."

Fox got up too. "I think I'll have a cold shower. Keep up the cold water training."

Dora the cat climbed up Fox's back, sat on her shoulder, and hit her with her paw three times.

Clementine and Lucy laughed. "I think Dora's spirit is in that cat and trying to tell you you're a fool."

"Very funny. Come on, Luce. Let's get these two ragamuffins upstairs. Are you coming up, Your Duchess-ship?"

"I'll be up in twenty minutes or so. I just want to finish a few more pages," Clementine said.

"Don't be up too late." Fox leaned over and gave her a kiss that left her wanting more, but Fox was already on her way with Lucy and the two cats.

"Back to the diary, with some nice peace and quiet."

Clementine turned over the next page and saw a blank page, then another, then another. This was strange. Dora's diary was meticulous. Why had she left those pages out?

The next page after them had an entry.

May 1st

> *I am so ashamed. I've let my family down, my community, but most of all my wife. I've never had anything but love from my Lou Lou. She goes along with every plan I come up with, but I went too far.*
>
> *In desperate need to keep the beer factory and refurb of cottages going, I had to sell some land. I sold the forest land to keep my dreams from going under.*

Clementine sat up quickly and covered her mouth with her hand. "You sold it? You couldn't do that, surely?"

> *It was a step too far. The woodland has always been a special place for Lou Lou. She could spend whole days down*

there drawing, walking, with a flask of tea and a sandwich. She took our son and taught him about the birds and the woodland animals. I took that from her, and I've never felt so guilty in my life. She hasn't spoken to me in days. That has never happened in our marriage before.

I am so selfish, and I couldn't let this stand. I went back to the purchaser and managed to persuade him to sell it back to me, at twice the price. It puts me in an even deeper hole, but that is better than hurting my poor, dear wife so much.

"Oh thank God. You bought it back, Dora. Now where's the deed? Please help me?"

Now I have to work on earning the trust of Lou Lou back again. To help, I made things different this time. I had the seller put Louisa's name on the deed. Now in the future, no matter how much I want to sell it, I can't. I told her to put it away somewhere safe, away from my office. Lou Lou decided to keep it in her jewellery box, the one I gave her on our first Christmas together. I will never repeat such a mistake.

Clementine got up so quickly that she tripped on one of the cat toys. "Bloody toys."

She tried again and raced up the kitchen stairs, then up the main stairs. She knew exactly where the jewellery box was.

It was passed on to her mother, and Clementine had played with the jewels inside all the time. It played "Greensleeves," and that made it almost magical to her as a child. When she married Fox and moved back to Rosebrook, she placed it back in her mother's dressing room, which both she and Lady Louisa would have wanted. But as she tore along the corridor, she thought in all the times she played with the box, she'd never seen a piece of paper in there.

"Please don't say it got lost in the move to the gatehouse."

She heard Lucy's voice behind her, "What's wrong, Aunty Clem?"

"I think I've found something."

Lucy soon caught up with her and they entered the dressing room.

"The diary…" Clementine tried to catch her breath. "It said that

Dora had sold the woodland but felt so bad about taking it from Louisa that she bought it back and titled it in Louisa's name, and she kept the deed in her jewellery box."

"Yes." Lucy punched the air. "You did it."

Clementine sat at the dressing table. "Don't celebrate yet. I played with this box as a child, and I never saw any paper in it."

"Open it up and see."

It was a big box, intricately carved, and a treasured family possession. Clementine prayed she was mistaken, and the deed was inside.

She opened it and it started to play. There was nothing inside, and her heart sank.

"It's lost."

Lucy looked at it, then ran her fingers around the bottom. "There's a tiny gap all around the bottom."

"Is it not just the design?"

Lucy felt around the back. "There's a little, tiny button—"

All of a sudden a hidden compartment popped out, and there was an aged looking envelope.

"Lucy, you clever girl. Please be inside."

On the envelope was written, *Forgive me, Lou Lou.*

"Is that Dora's handwriting?" Lucy asked.

"Yes, it is. Keep your fingers crossed."

Clementine carefully opened up the envelope and eased out the paper within. She opened it, and her heart started racing. She read, "Land deed for private woodland in Rosebrook village. Yes!"

Clementine jumped up and Lucy threw her arms around her. "We've done it, Yes! Yes!"

Clementine could smell Fox's gorgeous cologne before she'd even had time to talk.

"What's going on?"

Clementine turned around and saw Fox shivering in her T-shirt and boxers. It felt like most times she saw Fox now she was shivering.

"Aunty Clem found the deed for the forest."

Fox rushed to them and put her arms around them both. "Yes, we can protect the animals now." Fox kissed them both on the cheek.

"It was clever Luce that found it," Clementine said.

"You did all the research with the diary," Lucy said.

"We are all a team," Fox told them.

A sly smile came to Clementine's face. "I'm going to enjoy showing this to Sergeant Wexford."

Fox laughed. "He didn't know who he was dealing with."

❖

Griffin and Bronte walked slowly back to Bronte's house. Griffin had a great evening eating cheese on toast and just being near Bronte. She hadn't known the happiness of just being in the company of someone she was falling for, and she was falling for Bronte, in every way.

It made her heart ache when Bronte described her type, but she was probably just joking. Could a woman like Bronte like her? Bronte didn't even know the truth about her and her wealth.

"The temperature's really dropped again, hasn't it," Bronte said.

"Yeah, make sure you hold on to me tightly. All the snow and slush is freezing right up. We don't want your ankle hurt any more. If it snows on this, it will be bad."

"We think it's bad enough here on the coast, but I saw on the news it's going down to eighteen below zero in Scotland and the North of England."

"Crazy world we're living in," Griffin said. "How's your ankle holding up?"

"Not too bad. The rest and cheese on toast helped."

Griffin smiled. "Glad I could help."

Bronte's mobile rang. She took it out and then immediately stuffed it back in. "Bloody woman."

"Your mum?"

"How did you guess," Bronte asked with sarcasm. "You'd think she'd give up haranguing me. I just have to keep ignoring her—that's generally what I try to do. She's probably got some unfortunate seventy-five-year-old who would just love to marry me for the price of a house."

"If only you had money in another way, keep your family off your back." Griffin just wanted to test the water, just to see Bronte's reaction to someone with a lot of money who might be falling for her.

Bronte stopped. "What do you mean?"

"Um…just, if you were rich in your own right by some strange set of circumstances…" Griffin fumbled.

"Like, win the lottery kind of thing?"

Griffin snapped her fingers. "Yeah, lottery. That's it."

They began walking up Bronte's drive. "I suppose then yes, I would pay off the house debts, shut my mother up, and I suppose it would be nice to keep the title with the house in some ways. But I'd hate to be rich, wouldn't you?"

"Um—" Griffin was on uncomfortable territory now.

"Wouldn't you rather be like us? Living free and doing what you want?"

"You could help a lot of animals, or look at Fox and Clem. They do amazing things with their money."

They were at Bronte's front door now. "I suppose. I've just seen money do terrible things to people."

Bronte's phone rang again. "Argh, I'm going to switch this thing off. Oh, it's Clem…Hello? Uh-huh?…You are kidding?"

"What is it?" Griffin whispered.

"It's Griffin. She's with me. I can't wait to see the look on his face. Yeah, I'll tell her. Goodnight."

"Well?" Griffin asked.

"Clementine found the deed to the woodland. We can protect those animals any which way we want. Wexford is going to be sick."

"Yes!"

Bronte threw her arms around Griffin's neck and they both jumped up and down in celebration. Until Bronte hurt her ankle and fell back against the front door.

Griffin caught her. "It's okay. I've got you."

Bronte grasped the floppy hair at the back of Griffin's neck. Their heads were so close that their breath in the cold air was intermingling. And Bronte was getting lost in Griffin's beautiful eyes.

Her fingers stroked the side of Griffin's neck, and without even thinking their lips came together with such passion Bronte had to hold on tightly to Griffin's neck.

Griffin's lips were so much softer than she'd expected, and the intensity of the kiss was so much that her knees were weakening.

The brass key on her chest had been turned so tight that the cogs and wheels felt like they burst out of her chest. She felt Griffin's tongue slip softly into her mouth and the cold of her fingertips reached under her short jacket onto bare skin.

That was enough to give her a jolt. It took everything in her, but she pushed Griffin back.

Griffin looked a little dazed. "What? I'm sorry if I upset you."

"No, no, I wanted you to kiss me more than anything, but we can't."

"Why? I felt this thing between us since I met you."

"I felt it since I saw you chopping wood in the forest, but it makes no difference," Bronte said.

"Why?"

"Because you're leaving in the new year, and I'm not going to have a few months' fling with someone like you."

"What like me?"

"Someone I could fall for."

Griffin lost all of her fight and stared at the ground. "No, it's not a good idea then."

Bronte was angry at that response. She was secretly hoping Griffin would say, *I don't have to leave.*

"Why are you leaving anyway?"

"I'm going travelling."

"I know that. Where?" Bronte pressed her.

"Wherever the road takes me."

"Why?"

Griffin shot her a look of extreme annoyance. "Why? What do you mean why?"

"I'll tell you *why.* I tell you everything about me. My impossible mother, my family debt, my sister, everything. You tell me nothing."

"Yeah, I do," Griffin said angrily. "I told you I was from Manchester and my mum was a single mum."

"Yes, and leaving you all of a sudden after a heart attack and not being with you at Christmas. There's a whole lot you're not telling me."

"There's nothing," Griffin said.

"There's a whole lot. I can see it in your eyes. The hurt, the anger, you're wounded."

Griffin let her head fall back in frustration. "Jesus Christ. It was just a kiss—I wasn't proposing marriage. I don't normally get this much trouble from women I kiss."

"No, you probably just jump into the sleeping bag with them when you're travelling."

"This is childish. I'm going." Griffin turned and started to walk away.

"Is it about your dad?" Griffin stopped dead but didn't turn around. "I saw his card on your table. It was beautiful. Tell me about yourself, Griff. That's all I want. To know you."

Without saying another word, Griffin started walking away.

Bronte sighed. How did they go from kissing to this?

She unlocked the door and went into the house, making sure to lock up well. She walked as carefully as she could upstairs and got changed for bed.

Bronte looked at her phone and was desperate for Griffin to call or text. But it stayed silent. She went under the covers and pulled them under her chin. She had made a big mistake. She could see it clearly now.

If Griffin was the wounded animal she thought she was, then Bronte had done the completely wrong thing—she'd backed her into a corner. That was the very worst thing to do because the animal would snap and bite to get away.

Why did she do it? Maybe to get Griffin to realize she didn't have to run away, maybe to get her to stay. This was not the way to do it.

Do you truly want her to stay? Bronte asked herself.

Yes, yes, yes, her heart said.

When she worked with animals who couldn't go back to the wild, she made them a safe haven. Somewhere to live with freedom and safety, without the pain and torment of what waited for them out in the wild.

She needed to make Griffin a safe haven. She had to make Griffin feel safe here, no matter what happened between them.

Bronte picked up her phone and texted Griffin: *Griff, I'm sorry we argued, and I brought up some of your personal business. Can we start again as the good friends we were? Bronte xx*

She closed her eyes and drifted off with the memory of Griffin's lips upon hers.

❖

Clementine walked out of her en suite to find Fox lying in bed waiting. She was under the covers, up on her elbow, with a cheeky twinkle in her eye.

"What's that look for, Foxy?"

"You promised me full duchess-mode," Fox said.

"Oh, did I?" Clementine took off her dressing gown and draped it over the dressing table chair.

"Yeah, you did."

Clementine pulled back the cover and saw that Fox wanted to use her strap-on tonight. The thought of it made her wet, but she didn't show Fox that.

"I see you've come well prepared for your duchess." Clementine lay on her side and trailed her fingernails teasingly slowly down the centre of Fox's chest.

"I'm always well prepared for my duchess."

Clementine leaned over and kissed Fox. Fox moaned when she slipped her tongue into her mouth. But Clementine pulled her lips away and stroked her palm down Fox's stomach until she grasped hold of the strap-on.

Fox moaned.

"You like that?"

"You know I do. You know exactly how to touch me, Duchess."

Clementine loved the feel of the strap-on in her hand. It was a realistic one, firm but soft to the touch.

"I want you, Foxy."

"I am yours, always yours," Fox said.

Clementine went up onto her knees and took off her nightdress. She straddled Fox's stomach, not mounting the strap-on just yet.

"Give me your hands."

Fox offered them up, and Clementine placed them on her breasts. She loved Fox's touch on her breasts.

"You're beautiful, Duchess," Fox said.

Clementine's nipples hardened, and she could wait no longer. "I want you to put your arms above your head and keep them crossed."

Fox loved this when the duchess came out to play. It was such a turn-on. The sound of her posh voice, the demeanour that Clementine had when she took on this role. She would do anything she said.

Her wife leaned over and whispered, "I'm going to ride your cock till I come, Foxy, and you can't touch me."

Fox could have come right there and then. "Yes, Duchess."

Clementine positioned herself and slowly eased herself onto the strap-on. Fox groaned, and she felt her wife slip onto her cock.

Clementine groaned as she did, and Fox had to force herself not to move her hands onto her wife's hips. She started to move her hips slowly, in time with Clementine. She could see the pleasure was starting to take over when Clementine closed her eyes and let her head fall back.

"God, Clem. Let me touch you?"

"No," Clementine said breathily, "don't you dare."

The frustration was making Fox's orgasm approach more rapidly than it should.

"It's too fast, Duchess." Fox thrust her hips faster and faster.

"Don't come yet, Foxy. I want to ride you a bit longer."

"Fuck," Fox breathed. How was she going to hold on?

Clementine upped her pace and said, "Yes, Foxy, yes. Go, come inside me now."

In her rush of pleasure, Fox forgot about the rules and grasped her wife's hips. She thrust faster and faster until she went extremely still and tensed up her whole body.

Fox rode the wave of pleasure until she let go and shouted, "Fuck."

Clementine came in one long groan, grinding on Fox's strap-on. She fell forward and found her partner's lips. "Oh, Foxy."

They shared long, languid kisses until Fox turned Clementine onto her back for more. But when she did, she came face to face with a big black cat.

She jumped up out of bed in a millisecond. "Jesus Christ!"

"What is it?"

"Dora." Fox pointed at the black cat, and Clementine burst out laughing. "How did she get in here? It's not funny, Clem."

But Clementine didn't stop laughing.

❖

Griffin came back into the house and slumped onto the sofa. She picked up the card that Bronte had mentioned and started to well up. She was so confused, as she had been since she'd found all these in her mum's papers.

Her brain struggled to function every time she wanted to process the information. It wasn't so much the 360 she had to do to accept her father did care. It was the tragedy of never having the chance to know the man who obviously cared about her, and of course the knowledge that the mum who she had idolized had lied to her.

Tears started to fall as she gazed at the card. His words and the care he'd taken to draw such a beautiful card made her emotional, but every time she read the words *Love, Daddy* she went to pieces.

She threw the card to the side and held her head in despair. The only way she could deal with it was not to deal with it, and to push it down so deep that she could carry on with life on the surface.

Why did Bronte have to bring it up? She was doing so well, trying to forget.

Just then Griffin's phone beeped with a text. She wiped away her tears and looked at her messages. It was Bronte. Her stomach clenched.

Griffin was scared to open it. Everything had been going so well. The kiss they shared was seared on her mind.

Griff, I'm sorry we argued, and I brought up some of your personal business. Can we start again as the good friends we were? Bronte xx

Griffin wanted to know if that meant friends and more, or just friends.

It was selfish, Griffin supposed, to expect Bronte to get involved with someone who was leaving. All that was true, but when they kissed, none of that reality mattered.

Why did reality have to ruin everything?

Griffin texted back, *Yeah, I'm sorry we argued too. I'd like to be friends.*

Bronte replied, *Do you want to help me with the fox yard tomorrow? There's a lot of digging to done, but not with my ankle.*

Oh God. She would have loved to spend her day with Bronte, but she'd promised Patrick she would be in at the factory. She was going to see this as a rebuff. *I'm sorry, I need to go into the factory.*

The Christmas market in Kirkswell is on Friday and we've got a stall. Sorry.

That's no problem. Goodnight.

So Bronte thought she was trying to keep away from her, and Griffin felt like a fool.

CHAPTER FIFTEEN

Griffin, Patrick, and two of the brewery staff, Max and Andrew, were in a meeting room at the factory, making up gift packs to sell at the farmer's market.

Griffin looked at her watch. "It's midday already? Max, Andy, go and have your lunch hour. Tell Jonah I'll be up for lunch later and I'm starving."

"Will do," Max said.

"I think these are looking pretty good," Griffin said.

They had old-fashioned mini beer crates with one of each beer and lager they produced, plus their new Christmas label, the recipe Patrick had come up with.

"Yeah, the crates are cool. Thanks for putting my recipe in as the Christmas beer. It means so much to me."

"Mate, I wouldn't have put it in there if it wasn't such a good lager. It's all your hard work in learning and listening."

Griffin carried the pile of crates over to the others sitting on the floor. "Okay, just the smaller multipacks to do now. Oh, how are you and Alanna getting on now?"

Patrick flushed a little bit. "Uh, good. We're kind of dating now."

Griffin's heart soared. She knew the terrible time Patrick had after coming out as a trans man. "That's amazing. Give me a hug, mate." Griffin pulled him into a hug and slapped his back.

"Thanks. Alanna knows about my transition and likes me just the same."

"You deserve a woman like Alanna, Paddy. She's a great person," Griffin said.

"It's hard sometimes to believe I'm good enough for her."

"Of course you are, and knowing Alanna, she's told you the very same thing, hasn't she?"

Patrick scratched his head bashfully. "Yeah, she has."

"I knew that. Are you bringing her along to the Christmas market?" Griffin asked.

"I was going to ask you if that was okay," Patrick said.

"Yeah, that'll be great."

"Are you bringing Bronte?" he asked.

That question surprised Griffin. Was he implying they were dating? "Not with me, but maybe she's going with the duchess and the others. I don't know if Clem is going after her face-off with the police sergeant in Kirkswell."

"Sorry, I thought maybe you and Bronte were—"

"No, I'm leaving soon, remember?"

"Why are you leaving?" She heard Bronte's words in her head so many times since she'd last seen her. Griffin knew the answer. Because she was scared. It was three days since she'd seen Bronte. Although they were quite busy at the factory, she could have found some time to visit. But Griffin had thought about her constantly.

"Oh, okay," Patrick said.

Griffin wanted to change the subject. "Have you been training for the Big Dip like Fox, or are you just going to wing it like me?"

Patrick smiled. "I heard Fox was having a lot of cold showers. I think that would put me off. I'd rather just not know what it's going to feel like and go for it."

"That's my thinking."

"Alanna is doing the challenge too," Patrick said.

"Is she? Good for her."

"She doesn't want to have any limitations on her. That's one of the things I love about her." Patrick stopped all of a sudden and realized he'd said more than he wanted to.

"You're in love, Paddy?" Griffin smiled.

"Yeah, I haven't told her yet. I don't want to seem pushy or putting pressure on her. I've never been in love before. It makes you feel weird."

"I've never been in love either." Griffin felt like she was trying to convince herself of that fact. "I'm happy for you, Patrick. I hope you'll be happy."

❖

"What do you think, Dr. Blake?"

Bronte was having her ankle check-up at the doctor's surgery.

"The wound is healing nicely. I know you're not using your crutch any more, but you do a lot of walking on uneven surfaces, so just be careful."

"I will."

Blake turned to Eliska. "Can you give Bronte a strong bandage and tape it up? I'd like a good support on it."

"Of course," Eliska replied.

Dr. Blake went to her desk to write up some notes while Eliska brought over the things to bandage her foot.

"Doctor, are you sure I can't do the Big Dip challenge? I'd really love to be involved."

"No," Blake said firmly. "You'd be risking all sorts of infections. Just be a cheerleader for everyone else."

Bronte sighed. "Okay. What are you two and Ola doing for Christmas?"

Eliska started to wrap the bandage around her ankle. "Kay and Casper have invited us for dinner," Eliska said. "The children love to play together, and Kay has been a very good friend to me, helping me settle into British life."

Bronte knew that Eliska had come from the middle of a war zone in her country. It seemed surreal to get used to a new life in Britain.

"We'll be at the Big Dip in the morning, though. Fox has me working as one of the medics on scene. I'd have loved to have done it myself."

"I'll just have to support everyone there too," Bronte said.

Eliska finished with the bandage, and she said goodbye.

When she walked out onto the street, the cold almost cut her in two. She didn't have anything planned until Lucy came after school. There was lots she could be doing, but with this ankle she needed help with lifting and carrying.

Bronte saw the sign for the pub and thought, *Why not have some lunch with the locals?* She pushed through the door and at once heard, "Hello, m'dear."

It was Fergus.

"Come and share a table with me."

"I'd love to. I'll just get a drink."

"No young lady buys her own drink when Fergus is around."

When he went to get a drink, Bronte heard a notification and quickly opened her phone. It was the woodland camera system letting her know there had been movement.

She pressed to see the live camera and immediately saw Griffin. She was hammering some wood to her shelter. Bronte should have closed the camera straight away, but she just had to keep her eyes on her. Griffin was absolutely mesmerizing.

Unfortunately, she hadn't stripped down to her sleeveless T-shirt—today was too cold for even Griffin to do that. She had dispensed with her jacket, though, and was wearing a loose plaid shirt and a pair of leather work gloves.

Her old axe sat ready for use in a holster around her waist, ready to cut each piece of wood to size.

Why did she keep building that thing when she was leaving in a few months?

By the time Bronte finished her lunch, she'd had a blow-by-blow account of the history of the village from Fergus. He was a lovely man and such a brave person to have moved to this village decades ago with his partner. Much like Fox today, Isadora had wanted to create a safe place for people who felt they had to live on the fringes of society, through fear.

Fergus went to chat with one of his friends. Bronte felt a blast of cold air when the pub doors opened. It was Griffin. Oh no, this could be awkward. Would she have guessed that it was Bronte watching?

Only Bronte, Griffin, and Clementine had access to the cameras. Hopefully Griffin would assume it was the duchess.

After going to the bar, Griffin came over to her table with two glasses, a pint and a half-pint, of beer or lager. "Hi, don't normally see you in here," Griffin said.

"I was at the doctor getting my ankle checked out, and then I thought why not treat myself to one of Jonah's famous meals."

"Good idea. How was your ankle?"

"Dr. Blake says it's healing really well, and Eliska bandaged it up for me, but I'm still banned from the Big Dip."

"That's a shame," Griffin said. "You can cheer me on and have the warmest towel waiting for me. That's if you want to be helping me—you don't have to."

"Of course I want to."

"Great. I nearly forgot. I know you don't normally drink beer, but this is the new Christmas one that Patrick came up with himself."

"Yes, I want to taste it if Patrick made it."

"I got you a half-pint."

"Thanks."

Bronte took a sip and found it was lovely. "Really nice, refreshing."

"I'm so proud of him. We've made Christmas gift packs of our beers to sell at the Christmas markets, and the supermarket is carrying it."

"Wow, that's amazing. You must be so proud of him."

"I am, I am."

Griffin was clearly just wiping her mind of the kiss and their heated discussion.

"Bronte, I was wondering if you wanted to come to the Christmas market with us? Alanna is going to come with Patrick."

Was this a double date or just a friend thing?

"I'd like that."

Griffin looked really happy with that answer.

"Yeah, it'll get us in the Christmas spirit, although we're not very popular with the police in Kirkswell. Oh, were you on the cameras when I was building my shelter?"

Oops. Caught out. "Yes, I got a notification on my phone so quickly checked."

"That's good. It's working well then," Griffin said.

If only she knew that Bronte was lusting after her as she watched. That axe…

❖

"Griff, it's starting to snow again."

Bronte and Griff were setting up the market stall with Patrick and Alanna.

"It couldn't be nicer for a Christmas market," Griffin said as she smiled at her.

That smile could melt the hardest of hearts. It was going to be horrendously painful to say goodbye to her.

Bronte stayed with Alanna at the front with samples while Patrick and Griffin sold the gift packs.

"I need more samples, Bronte," Alanna said.

"No problem."

Bronte opened another few bottles and filled up the sample cups. She put them on Alanna's tray.

"It's going really well," Bronte said to Alanna.

"It sure is. People are loving it."

The market was so busy. It was only halfway through the night, and their stall only had one box of gift packs left.

Bronte filled up her own tray and started to offer it to passers-by. She saw a young man with curly red hair approach Alanna. Something gave her a bad feeling, so she wandered over beside her.

"Can I offer you a taste of Rosebrook beer?" Alanna said.

The man took a cup, tipped it upside down on the ground and dropped the cup. "I wouldn't drink anything that comes from that queer village."

"Hey, there's no need to be like that."

He stamped his cup into the ground and walked off. Griffin and Patrick were with them in seconds.

"What happened?" Griffin asked.

"Just a homophobe. We can handle his type, can't we, Alanna?"

"Yep, he was just a loser."

"Are you sure you're okay?" Patrick asked Alanna.

"One kiss and I'll be fine," Alanna said.

Bronte wished she could say that to Griffin.

They packed up early, as they had sold out of beer, and drove home. Griffin walked Bronte up to her door.

"That was a good night," Griffin said. "Thanks for coming."

"Thanks for inviting me."

There was an awkwardness in the air. It felt like they should kiss goodnight, but after the last time it didn't seem like a good idea.

Instead, Bronte leaned in and gave Griffin a kiss on the cheek. "Goodnight."

"'Night. Remember and lock up tight," Griffin said.

❖

Bronte was awakened by the incessant beeping on her phone. She grasped for it on the bedside table and dropped it. Now more awake, she got it off the floor. Notifications from the cameras at the woodland.

She opened the app and turned on the motion detector. What she saw shocked her.

"Oh my God."

A group of people, all dressed in black with black balaclavas, had arrived in the clearing. They also had baseball bats.

"Oh no."

The people climbed the ladder and started knocking the hell out of the cameras. Bastards.

She got up and ran to her clothes, but what was she going to do? Arrive in the pitch darkness, to face a gang of men? Yeah, like that was safe.

She had to phone Griffin, but before she could one of the men climbed up to the camera she was watching on. Bronte could see the rage in his eyes, the only part of the man Bronte could really see through the mask.

"Leave the countryside to those that understand it, bitch."

Then, seconds later, the feed from the cameras was gone.

She had to get there. Bronte pulled on her clothes quickly. She could phone Griff on the way.

Bronte got down to her front door. When she opened it, snow that had just fallen already piled up a good few inches. It was still snowing, big heavy flakes. She would just need to get this cleared up later.

She took a step out of her cottage and saw the most horrifying sight, a dead fox with horrific injuries dumped in the snow.

Bronte clasped her hands to her mouth. God, who would have done this? Tears started rolling down her face. Next to the fox was a laminated piece of paper, with a message: *This is our countryside, dyke. Fuck off, queers!*

Bronte's hands shook. She needed Griffin. She managed to dial her, but all she said was, "I need you, Griff."

Griffin needed no explanation. "I'm on my way."

❖

Bronte sat in front of the fire staring into the flames when Griffin appeared at her side. "I've taken care of the fox's body, but I've kept the message for the police."

"They'll be no help."

"Breaking the cameras is criminal damage. It's gone beyond hurting animals."

"We should have checked the woodland, there might be clues," Bronte said.

"It's piling it down out there. It would have been too dangerous at night. We'll go and see Clem in the morning and take it from there."

Bronte gasped Griffin's hand. "Thank you for coming to me."

Griffin pulled Bronte's hand up to her lips and kissed it. "I would do anything for you."

Bronte looked into Griffin's eyes and saw nothing but sincerity. "I know. I believe you."

She got up and got some big cushions from the couch, and some blankets.

"I'd like to lie by the fire. Would you lie with me?"

"You know I will."

Griffin helped Bronte make up a makeshift bed. Bronte settled down first, and she patted the space behind. She really did want to be close, Griffin thought.

She stripped down to her T-shirt and got behind Bronte. Was she meant to be so close to her? Would she mind if Griffin placed her hand on her hip or back?

Griffin decided to follow her instincts and spooned up close to Bronte and put her hand on her hip. Bronte immediately took her hand to her breastbone and held it there.

This was what she dreamed of doing, being close with Bronte. She had the urge to pull Bronte so much closer to her, pulling Bronte's bottom into her sex.

"I'm sorry I wasn't helpful and got emotional with the fox."

"Don't be silly, you got a shock. That was a terrible thing to find on your doorstep."

"I'm meant to be an animal rehabilitator. I've seen worse sights than that poor fox when I was recording illegal fox hunting, but the frustration at not being able to protect these animals, the vandalism, what the guy said to me, and finding the fox took me back to the pain of losing Sox. It was just another I've failed."

"You haven't failed the animal." Griffin squeezed her tighter. "You and the duchess have been fighting to get the woodland secure. Those men are the ones to blame. How anyone could treat an animal like that is beyond comprehension to me, but don't worry—we will win this fight with all of us pulling together as a team."

"It feels good to have someone backing me up for a change, someone who'll give me a hug," Bronte said.

"You haven't had that before?"

"No, I've never given anyone the chance, well, apart from my one and only girlfriend."

"You've only ever had one girlfriend? A beautiful woman like you?"

"Shut up," Bronte said playfully. "You are talking nonsense. Besides, one was enough."

"Want to tell me what happened?"

"I was eighteen and stupid. I was in love, or so I thought, with a woman who ran the anti-fox-hunting group I was part of. She was older than me and everything my mother hated. I was trying to be rebellious as well as in love."

"What happened?" Griffin asked.

"My mother happened. She found out about it, offered my girlfriend money to get out of my life, and the woman I loved dropped me like a stone. I was so hurt as a young woman, and I promised myself it would be the last time I was made a fool of."

"Why don't you mind getting a hug from me?" Griffin asked.

There was a silence for a minute. "You're not my girlfriend, are you?"

"Eh, no, but I wouldn't break your heart either."

"You could easily break my heart, but you're leaving, aren't you?"

How did this conversation get so deep so quickly? It felt like they were on the precipice of something, that they were both negotiating with each other about the next step, without being straightforward about it.

The phrase from the night they kissed jumped into her mind, as it had nearly every waking hour since. *Why are you going travelling?*

Running away? Trying to make sense of her messed-up head?

Griffin couldn't answer a question when she was so confused about it. So she agreed with Bronte.

"Yeah, I'm leaving."

Griffin felt Bronte's body go limp from what she could only guess was sadness.

Bronte turned her head around and gave her a forced smile. "Then you can't break my heart, can you?"

"I suppose not."

There was a long silence after that, until Bronte said, "It's so nice to be in front of the fire with the snowstorm howling past the windows. So cosy."

"Yeah, especially hugging someone you care about," Griffin said bravely.

Bronte squeezed her hand on her breastbone. "Yes, especially then."

Griffin pressed her nose to the back of Bronte's neck and inhaled her scent. Griffin's body was alive and told her it needed Bronte. Everything in Griffin wanted to kiss her neck, kiss her shoulder, and make Bronte moan, but she couldn't.

The conversation had been clear—*Don't make me fall for you and leave.* Griffin never wanted to hurt Bronte for a second, so she would be the best friend she could be while she was in Rosebrook, but she longed for so much more.

CHAPTER SIXTEEN

Griffin awoke and felt a weight on her chest. When she opened her eyes, she saw Bronte's beautiful reddish-blond hair fanned across her chest. Bronte's head rested under her chin, and her leg wrapped around hers.

Bronte must have gotten into this position during the night, perhaps as the fire burned down and she got cold. No matter the reason, Griffin loved it. She imagined waking up like this every morning, and it would make her so happy.

But then her stomach sank when she remembered their conversation last night. The conversation that skirted around the fact that they both clearly had feelings for each other but established that they couldn't have even a short relationship because it would probably break both their hearts.

Quite clearly both physically and mentally she and Bronte wanted each other, but...

Why did there have to be a *but*?

Griffin lifted her fingers to the edge of Bronte's sleeve and, barely touching, stroked her fingers down her arm.

Bronte started to squirm, and eventually her eyes flickered open. She looked up at Griffin and realized her position.

"I'm sorry, I must have—"

"Don't apologize. You must have been cold during the night."

Bronte raised herself up on her arm and gazed down into Griffin's eyes. "That must have been it."

Griffin could see passion in Bronte's smoky eyes. She leant down as if she was going to kiss her, then pulled away sharply.

"We better get dressed and call Clementine."

Bronte was up and away in seconds. Griffin was left with her arms empty. She should be begging that woman to give her a chance, not running away from her.

Maybe it was better in the long term. Bronte might have had one experience of a relationship—Griffin had none. Women were characters that passed through her life, but she never held on to them. Who was to say she'd manage to be everything Bronte needed and not hurt her?

Griffin got up and said to Bronte, "I'll make coffee for us if you ring Clementine."

"Okay, I'll just be a minute."

Griffin pulled on her jeans and made her way to the kitchen. She gazed out of the kitchen window and saw the snowfall from last night lay heavy on the ground. A trip to the police station was going to difficult today.

The kettle boiled, and she made two cups of coffee. She thought of the kids in the village and how they would enjoy having a white Christmas. Such an unexpected white Christmas was pleasing to Griffin, if everyone in the village was safe. She'd always loved snow.

Her mum came into her mind as she was more and more as Christmas approached. She would be on some part of her cruise, enjoying the warm weather. Her mum had never liked the snow. She saw it as a hindrance to getting to work when they desperately needed the money.

Although now she knew that there had been no need for her mum to work three jobs—her dad would have supported them. This was how it generally went in her head every day. She'd miss her mum, then go over the fact she kept secret that her dad did want to be part of her life, and end up resentful and hurt.

She had to stop thinking like this. Griffin hoped her friends would distract her at Christmas because no matter what her mum had done, it would be her first Christmas without her.

Griffin stirred her coffee and heard Bronte on the phone to Clem.

She supposed she should get some presents for the kids of the village and to take to her hosts on Christmas Day. Maybe Bronte would help.

She took a sip of coffee. Griffin wanted to get Bronte something, but what to get her? She looked up at the picture of Bronte's pal Sox the fox. Maybe there was something she could come up with to remember Sox.

She quickly went over to the picture and took a snap of him on her phone.

Bronte came in and said, "Clementine is phoning the police and some other contacts above Wexford's head to make sure this is dealt with properly this time. She'll phone me back."

"Your coffee's there."

"Thanks."

"Did Clem already realize something had happened?"

"Yes, she woke up about twenty minutes ago and saw the footage on the app. She was just giving me a chance to wake up, and she was horrified about the fox left on my doorstep."

"Bastards, if I got hold of them—"

Bronte held her hand up. "We don't need any more violence, thank you."

"I can't help it if I'm protective of you."

Bronte smiled. "Thank you."

Then Bronte's phone rang. She was expecting Clementine, which must have been why she answered it without looking at the screen.

"Hello…Mother?"

Bronte mouthed the word *fuck* to Griffin. Griffin shook her head.

"Mother, I'm not going to talk about it again. I've made my position clear. I'm quite aware of our six hundred year history…Mother, I need to—there's a work call coming in. Talk to you later. Bye."

She ended the call and threw her phone on the kitchen counter. "She caught me out."

Griffin walked to her and opened up her arms. Bronte slipped into the hug.

"No matter what I do, she won't leave me alone."

The phone rang again, and Bronte groaned.

"Here, let me," Griffin said.

Bronte shook her head, checking the screen. "It's Clem."

Griffin waited impatiently for the news. Bronte even laughed when she was talking to Clem, so it was sounding good.

Once Bronte finished with the call Griffin said, "Well?"

"Wexford and his constable are fighting their way through the snow as we speak."

"We don't have to go in then?"

"No, Clementine phoned her MP, then he phoned the area's chief constable and told Wexford to come around ASAP."

"Well done, Clementine," Griffin said.

"Come on, we better get ready. It'll take some time to walk through the snow."

❖

The drawing room of Rosebrook house sat in uncomfortable silence.

"Thank you for coming, Sergeant Wexford. It must have been cold and difficult walking through the snow this morning."

Wexford had informed her that he and his police constable—Lambie—drove as far as half a mile from the village and had to walk the rest of the way.

They were freezing when they arrived, and Clementine got them blankets, plus Fox and Griffin were downstairs making tea. The central heating was on, but Clementine made a fire in the drawing room fireplace, just to make things a bit cosier.

Fox and Griffin entered the room with the tea tray. "Thank you, darling."

Clementine learned from her last encounter that Wexford wasn't exactly gay friendly, so she decided to emphasize her relationship with Fox to annoy him.

Once the tea was handed out, Clementine said, "As I say, it was good of you to come out in the snow. You know what, Wexford? Even in this day and age, when class barriers are breaking down, quite rightly, it's amazing to see how quickly you get a response from your MP and police commissioner if you have a dukedom."

"Yes," replied Wexford. "I was awakened this morning extremely early by the commissioner. And so here I am. Would you tell me what happened?"

"First of all, at the weekend we installed surveillance cameras in the forest to catch any illegal hunting. Then last night the cameras sent notifications. Bronte dealt with them, so I'll let her describe what happened then."

Bronte sat forward on the couch clutching her cup of tea. "I was just getting ready for bed when the notification pinged. I opened the app and watched a group of men, wearing balaclavas, with ladders and baseball bats. They proceeded to smash the cameras up completely, and when one of the men got round to the camera I was watching on, he talked directly down the camera and used some homophobic language—"

"Which is a criminal offence," Fox added.

"I am aware," Wexford said. "Make a note of offensive language."

"I got dressed, then ran downstairs to get my boots."

"Were you planning to go there yourself? A woman alone, in the forest that late at night?"

"I wasn't thinking straight, to be honest, but I was going to phone Griffin on my way. Anyway I opened my front door…"

Griffin sat on the arm of the chair and took Bronte's hand. Bronte was so glad of her strength. Bronte didn't usually let her guard down that much, but she trusted Griffin not to make her feel weak.

"There was a dead fox on my doorstep with a laminated card with a horrible message on it."

Clementine got up and handed them the message as well as a picture of the fox.

Wexford looked at both carefully before handing them to Lambie to bag.

"Seems you have riled up our hunting community."

"I have?" Bronte said in a high-pitched voice. She couldn't believe what she was hearing.

"Let me take this, Bronte," Clementine said. "I think you understand the pressure that you are bearing, from our MP and your commissioner, so if you know who these hunters are, you best make sure they are arrested."

Then it was Fox's turn. "You might also tell them this. Now that the cameras are broken, they will be removed, but in their place will go much better cameras. I am instructing my security team at Fox Toys to set up a complete surveillance system around the woods. It is, as the deed proves, a private woodland. And until we are confident that there will be no return visits, and the animals are safe, I'll have security guards patrol at night. Is that clear?"

Bronte could see the tension in Wexford's jaw. She had never seen Fox's hard business side before. There was steel under that funny, happy-go-lucky exterior.

"Crystal clear, Ms. Fox. With your permission, Lambie and I will visit the woodland area before we leave."

"Yes, that's quite all right," Clementine said. "Let me know if you find or hear anything, Sergeant."

Both officers stood up, and Griffin showed them out.

"Wow, Fox, that put them in their place," Bronte said, "Did you mean that?"

"Sure, I meant it. They are not coming onto our land and doing this kind of thing. That's twice you've been hurt or distressed by these people, Bronte. Clementine and I have a duty of care to you and everyone in Rosebrook."

Clementine agreed. "Can you imagine if it was one of the children got into one these traps? No, what happened to you and that poor fox has crossed the line."

"I'm so thankful for your support," Bronte said, "and Griff's. She came over as soon as I called last night and kept me company."

"I'm glad you had Griff with you," Clementine said. "They are quite obviously angry young men."

"I'll always be there. Call me day or night," Griffin added.

The four of them drank more tea and talked about the security of the village, the snow, and plans for Christmas. It was that discussion that reminded Griffin that she wanted to talk to Fox on her own. She tried as discreetly as possible to text her.

She simply typed, *Talk? Alone?*

When Fox read it, she looked over and winked.

"Who was texting you?" Clementine asked.

"Just Archie. That reminds me, Griff, I've got the new plans for the outdoor bar. Let's go to my office."

Clementine narrowed her eyes at Fox. She clearly had her suspicions, but they made it out of the room and through to Fox's office.

"Take a seat."

Fox's office was a mixture of old and new, the 1920s decor mixed with the latest technology, all to help Fox run her toy empire remotely.

"How can I help?"

Griffin leaned forward. "I want to give Bronte a Christmas present."

Fox grinned. "You like her, don't you. Is there to be a romance in Rosebrook?"

"No, I'm leaving, remember? I couldn't start something and then leave."

"Then don't leave. You can have a fantastic life here," Fox said.

"I have to leave, Fox. It's for personal reasons."

Fox let out a breath. "Okay, I suppose. We've had lots of applications for your job, by the way. We'll be having interviews in the new year."

Griffin hated the thought of anyone coming into her job, working with Patrick, making friends with Bronte—she couldn't even think about that.

But she had, and she felt jealousy form in the pit of her stomach.

"The gift I'm thinking of, it's probably impossible at this late stage," Griffin said.

"Nothing is impossible, Griff. Hit me with your idea."

Griffin really admired Fox's optimism. "It's a toy, so in your area of expertise."

"Excellent."

"I'll send you a picture. Hang on."

Griffin emailed Fox the picture, and she opened it up. "Ah, cute fox."

"It was a fox called Sox—no really, it was called Sox. Anyway, Bronte rescued it as a baby when its mother was killed. He had a deformed back leg so couldn't be put back in the wild. He became Bronte's pet, and she loved him like he was her pet dog or something. That picture is taken from one on her kitchen wall."

"What a great rescue story," Fox said.

"He died when he was three from natural causes, but Bronte's never forgotten him. Finding that fox last night brought it all back to her, I think. I'd love to have a Sox stuffed animal to give her to cuddle, but not just any fox stuffed animal, one that was Sox with the little leg and everything."

"Perfect idea, and it is entirely possible. I have a toy concept team. They work on new toy ideas, make individual examples before they go to mass production. Give me a sec."

Fox said, "Computer, call Andre."

The phone rang a few times and a poshly spoken man answered, "Fox, good to hear from you."

"You too, listen I'm in warp drive here, with a dream I need to make true, before Christmas, and I know you can help me."

Fox was hilarious to listen to. She had more energy than ten normal people.

"I'm sending the image now. It's a fox I need turned into a stuffed animal. Have you got it?"

"Yes, I have it."

"Okay the fox must look as much like the picture as possible, same marks, and the same small back leg."

"I've got you, and this is a one-off toy?"

"Yes, think of it as a private commission."

"It may be a bit tight to actually get it to you before Christmas," Andre said.

Griffin had known it would be too tight.

Fox got up and started pacing. "That's a shame, Andre, because I have two tickets for both women's and men's Wimbledon finals next summer, royal box too."

Fox winked at Griffin.

"I'll have some drawings for you tonight to look at. Can I have your authority to pay my team double time?"

"You can give them triple time if they make it more than a stuffed animal, a presentation case, and something to tie it in to the Fox Toys world."

"I've got you. We'll do it."

"That's what I like to hear. Talk to you later, Andre. Bye."

"You are amazing, Fox."

"I like to think so."

Griffin got up and shook Fox's hand. "I'll reimburse you for the materials and labour, of course."

"Don't be silly. This is my gift to you, for getting the beer factory up and running."

"No, no. It wouldn't be a gift from me to Bronte if you did that."

"Fair enough, how about cost of materials and drawings? I'll pay my staff." Fox held out her hand.

Griffin knew it was stupid to try to fight Fox on this. So she took her hand. "You have a deal."

It might not be the full cost, but the materials and drawings would probably make the most expensive stuffed animal ever, but well deserved. She just hoped Bronte would appreciate the sentiment.

Griffin and Fox walked back out of the office and found Bronte, Clementine, and Lucy in the hallway, admiring the Christmas tree. Lucy had one of her new cats up in her arms and Bronte had the other.

Griffin walked over to Bronte and stroked the cat. "Hello, what's your name?"

"This is Dora, and Lucy has Lady Louisa or Lady for short. Beautiful cats, Lucy," Bronte said.

"I love them," Lucy said.

Bronte nudged Griffin. "We were just admiring the Christmas tree."

"It gorgeous. Did you and Lucy decorate it, Fox?"

"With a little help from Archie."

"It looks great," Bronte said. "Do you need us to bring you anything on Christmas Day?"

Clementine said, "Nothing but yourselves, oh, but I think Fox was going to ask if you could help us transport the Tucker twins here on Christmas Eve."

Fox nodded. "It's going to be difficult with the snow, and the weather people say it's not going to ease up. Archie said she'd help too."

"We're going to have them stay to New Year, I think," Clementine said. "Once they are here, it would be safer for them to stay in this weather. I think they are looking forward to having a family Christmas."

"That's not a problem. We'll help," Griffin said. "Between us all we'll make it a nice Christmas."

Did I even say that? What is wrong with me?

Then she looked at Bronte. She was laughing and hugging Dora the cat, with Clementine and Lucy.

She knew why.

❖

"The tree was beautiful, wasn't it?" Bronte said as she and Griffin walked home.

"It was. Fox has got one in nearly every room," Griffin said.

"I believe it. She is quite the character, Fox. Ooh," Bronte said in pain.

"Are you okay?"

"Just my ankle hurting. The snow's hard to get through with an injury—" Before Bronte knew it, she was lifted into Griffin's arms. "Hey, what are you doing?"

"Giving your ankle a break. Calm down."

Bronte sighed. "Only if you carry me over to the railings at the beach. It's beautiful in the ice and snow."

"You've got a deal. I might collapse if I carried you any further," Griffin joked.

Bronte play-hit Griffin. "You could so carry me. I've seen those big, strong shoulders chopping wood…"

Bronte realized she'd said too much.

Griffin laughed. "You've been checking me out, have you?"

"Just get over to the beach, will you," Bronte snapped.

Griffin let her drop at the railings. "I love looking out at the beach and the sea," Bronte said. "It's such an amazing view."

"It was Fox that put this railing here, to be safer. It's a nice place to stop in the day, to think or whatever."

"I suppose you've seen a lot of beaches in your travels," Bronte said.

"Yeah, I've slept on some too."

Bronte raised her eyebrows. "I bet you have."

"I didn't mean with women. Well, okay, technically I did, but that's not what I meant."

"I bet you were very popular to spend a night under the stars with."

"That's not what I'm thinking about just now. I'm thinking about spending the day with you," Griffin said firmly.

"Okay, touchy."

"I don't particularly like being reminded."

"Why?"

"Because…" Griffin sighed. "Because I was drifting aimlessly for years, searching for my purpose, and I want to live in the now. I'm happy with you, my friends."

Bronte felt bad now for winding her up. Why she brought it up when the thought of Griffin with another woman hurt her, she had no idea.

"I'm sorry, back to the beaches. You saw nice beaches?"

"Yeah, but not like Rosebrook beach. In the summer, when the weather's warm, the cove is spectacular. We often have barbecues on the beach. The whole village turns out with food and drink, well the younger crowd."

"Sounds beautiful," Bronte said.

Griffin pointed to the right where the semicircle of cliff ended into open sea. "And see around that corner? There's a secret cove."

"A secret cove?" Bronte grinned.

"Yeah, only the locals know about it because you can only get there by boat. It's a beach for lovers, so I'm told."

"Oh, who told you?" Bronte asked.

"Ash. Archie took her there when she was wooing her."

"Wooing her?" Bronte laughed. "Archie?"

"Yep, Archie had to learn the art of wooing to get Ash's love. Ash is a great romantic. In the good weather, you'll see her reading her latest romance novel down there," Griffin said.

"Aww, that's sweet."

"Ash and Archie are the sweetest couple. I've never seen a beach in winter like this, though. I know Fox says it's bad and a sign of global warming, but it is stunning."

Bronte smiled at Griffin. She really was the sweetest person herself.

"How's the ankle?"

"Glad of the rest, but it's so frustrating. I'm supposed to be an animal rehabilitator, but I feel like a fraud."

Griffin turned to Bronte. "Why?"

"What have I done since I arrived? I should be digging the landscape for the fox yard, but I can't because of my ankle. If it wasn't for you and Lucy, I don't know where I'd be. I should be helping animals now."

Griffin shook her head. "What have you done? Are you kidding? You've put together an animal rescue with a little help—fair enough, you stubbornly resisted, but I wore you down. You did a complete survey of the wildlife in the forest, you saved and rehabilitated two hedgehogs, which have made social media all over the world, and you educated people about the animals. You've used your experience to advise Clementine on how to go about safeguarding her woodland, and you've fought tooth and nail, and been injured in the fight, to protect every animal in that forest. Is that enough for you?"

Wow. Bronte never had anyone speak so passionately about her before. There was nothing more to say. "Yes, that's enough."

"Good, now let's get you home, and you can rest your leg."

Griffin held out her hand, and Bronte took it without hesitation. There was one last cog that burst out of her chest. She was gone. No one made her heart feel like this. But she was leaving…

As they were walking through the snow, Griffin said, "I was thinking about Christmas Eve. We're both on our own, so why not spend it together?"

"That sounds nice. Do you want to come to mine or—"

"I've got a more interesting idea. Do you remember I told you about hot tent camping?"

CHAPTER SEVENTEEN

Griffin was so excited. It was Christmas Eve, something she never expected to be excited about after her huge fallout with her mum. Then Bronte came into her life, and things began to change.

She had planned today to perfection, she thought. Bronte had taken some persuasion that hot tent camping on Christmas Eve would be a fun thing to do. Griffin had reached the point that she had to tell Bronte her truth.

If she could take that step, then maybe she could have the courage to stay instead of running away from the woman she was losing her heart to.

Griffin was walking up the long drive to Rosebrook House to see Fox, her co-conspirator in tonight's adventure. Her mobile rang, and she was surprised to see it was her lawyer Trent calling. Griffin's heart sank. Maybe it was about her mother. Had she taken a turn for the worse?

"Hello?"

"Hi, Griffin. I'm just about to leave the office for the Christmas holidays, but we got a letter in from your great-uncle's solicitor, and I didn't want to leave it for two weeks."

"Is there a problem?"

"His solicitor says he hasn't had the best of health recently, and he wanted to ask again if you two could meet."

Griffin looked up at the sky and sighed. She felt guilty and didn't want to face it. She had always thought of her father's family as the bad guys, but now that she knew the truth, everything had changed.

"I'll need to have a think about it, Trent. Could you email me his contact details?"

"I will indeed."

"Thanks. Have a good Christmas with your wife and kids," Griffin said.

"Thank you. The place will be a madhouse by the time I get home, but I wouldn't have it any other way. Merry Christmas, Griffin."

"Bye, you too."

Just when Griffin thought she was getting a handle on her mixed-up mind, some more emotions came cascading down on her. She couldn't deal with it today.

Griffin carried on her walk up to Rosebrook. She saw Fox at the front door. She was positioning and repositioning some light-up reindeer.

"Fox, having some problems?"

"Not really. I thought they might look nicer set out with the baby ones to the front. To be honest, I was sent out by Clem."

Griffin chuckled. "What did you do?"

"I'm not sure, but I was told my presence was making everything worse. She and Lucy are in the kitchen preparing what food they can for dinner tomorrow. Since we have the Big Dip in the morning, it doesn't leave a lot of time for cooking on the day. That's my fault too apparently."

"You are in trouble, aren't you? When are your mum and dad coming?" Griffin asked.

"About five. We need to get the Tucker twins along before that."

A lot of their friends, Archie, Jonah, Fox, and Christian, had been out early this morning, trying to clear the loose snow from the road, so that Casper's Land Rover would be able to drive the old ladies to Rosebrook later. But under the loose snow was impacted snow, formed from the snow melting and freezing over the last few weeks.

"Do you think the Land Rover will get through?" Griffin asked.

"We can only hope. But if you, Jonah, and I follow with shovels, we can dig out the tires if they get stuck."

"I hope all the swimmers can get into the village tomorrow. There's more snow due tonight."

"I got the gardeners to cover the west end of the road in grit. If they can get that far and park up, at least they can walk down. My events manager is handling everything. Apparently with the cold weather, she says the medics advise only a one-minute dip and out."

"Thank God. The cold is going to be unbearable," Griffin said.

"Think about it this way—because it's so extreme, it'll make more headlines and more shares on social media for everyone's charities," Fox said.

"You never stop thinking, do you?"

Fox grinned. "Not even when I sleep. Let's get you the gifts from Santa."

She followed Fox into the reception hall. The cleaners were there. One was cleaning the marble floor with a sit-on buffing machine, while the other was dusting and cleaning the tables and ornaments.

"Hello, folks, don't mind us."

They went into Fox's office, and on the desk was a beautifully wrapped square and some smaller boxes.

"Thanks for wrapping them," Griffin said.

"My PA Violet organized that."

Griffin put her hand on top of the box. "I can't thank you enough."

"Is this a grand romantic gesture? You wouldn't normally go to these lengths for everyone."

"It's a let's see how things go tonight. I just want to make her happy," Griffin said.

Fox broke into a huge smile. "You are falling for her, aren't you?"

Griffin was squirming in her boots. "Maybe, anyway are you sure the security guards will be patrolling?"

Fox hadn't been kidding Sergeant Wexford. She brought in people from her Fox Toys security team, and they patrolled each night to keep the woodland secure. If it hadn't been for their presence, Griffin wouldn't have taken Bronte to camp.

"They will, and they know to keep an extra lookout for you. Don't worry."

"Okay, thanks."

"One more thing." Fox bent behind her desk and pulled out a hessian sack with a traditional looking picture of Santa Claus. "I thought you could put them all in here. Clem bought a bunch of these for gifts."

"Perfect. Thank you."

Fox held open the bag, and Griffin put the presents in.

"Lucy looking forward to Christmas?"

"Both me and Lucy are excited. Clem says I've bought too much, but I've never had a child to spoil before, and I think of her as my daughter. I couldn't love her more. Besides, she deserves it after the difficult time she's had."

"Quite right. Okay I better get back. I've lots to prepare. Just give me a ring when you're ready to pick up the twins."

"Will do."

❖

Bronte had all her Christmas wrapping odds and ends on the kitchen table. She and Griffin had jointly bought chocolates from a very exclusive chocolatiers in London for their hosts for Christmas dinner, as well as for the twins Agatha and Ada and, with Clementine's advice, some jeans and a hooded jumper from an expensive brand Lucy liked.

Bronte wanted to get her something big to thank her for all her help at the sanctuary.

She pulled over a wooden box. But this was her pride and joy. Bronte opened it up and gazed in happiness at what she'd managed to get for Griffin.

It was a hand axe, engraved with the name *Griffin* and in a beautiful tan leather holster.

"I hope she loves this."

She wrote the gift card inside and closed it up. Bronte had never been so excited for Christmas before, and it was all because of Griffin. Bronte wasn't so sure about the hot tent camping, especially seeing how cold it was. But it was an adventure.

Bronte began to wrap up the box. With the message she had put in the box, maybe it would persuade Griffin to come back sometime.

She was dreading the new year. Griffin would be helping choose her replacement at the beer factory and she be would gone.

Bronte had fallen hard and fast for Griffin. That wasn't what happened to her. She never got involved with anything that wasn't purely physical. Her first love had left her with a broken heart, and she'd vowed she wasn't going to let her heart get that badly hurt again, but then Griffin crept in when she wasn't looking. Yet she knew nothing about Griffin. That pain she had seen so early on was still a mystery to her.

But if Griffin was so determined to leave, why was she setting up a special night like this? Maybe it was a goodbye.

❖

Griffin bounded up the steps to Bronte's house, excited to start the evening. It was only four o'clock, but it was already dark, but that was perfect, given how she had set up the camp.

Griffin knocked and moments later Bronte arrived at the door. She had on a black rock band tour T-shirt and a purple headscarf.

"You look beautiful."

Bronte snorted. "I won't once I put my ten layers on. I've already got five pairs of socks."

Griffin followed Bronte into the kitchen. "You're going to be too warm."

"I'm yet to be convinced. Have you been out there? And it's going to snow again tonight."

"You have to trust me."

"I trust you in many things, Griff, but not in temperature levels. You're used to travelling, used to feeling the cold."

Griffin leaned on the table and said, "I'll just need to prove how hot I can make it."

"Oh, stop it you. Did you get the twins off to Rosebrook?"

"Yes, it wasn't too bad. They're going to stay there till New Year's. That way Clem can look after them."

"Clementine is a great duchess, isn't she? Born to it."

"She is. We're all lucky to have her."

"Okay, the big rucksack and these other boxes have to go."

Griffin looked at the size of the bag. "We're only going to the woods, not travelling around Southeast Asia."

"I'll need all those things," Bronte said as she started to put on her layers. "Okay—vest, T-shirt, long-sleeved T-shirt, fleece, and quilted puffer jacket. Now I can take on the cold."

"All I can say is you're going to be surprised, and you'll be taking off each one of those layers tonight," Griffin said.

"You wish, Griffy. Let's go then."

"Wait, who's Griffy?"

Bronte just laughed.

❖

Bronte walked through the woodland holding on to Griffin's hand. This sort of physical closeness had just happened naturally, and neither made comment on it. As they got closer to the clearing where Griffin had her campfire and shelter, Bronte's heart started to beat faster.

She could feel Griffin had more set up than just camping.

"Are you sure it's safe to stay out here?"

"Yes, for the millionth time. The hunters haven't been back since Clem and Fox warned Wexford, and there'll be Fox's guards making patrols all night."

"Okay, okay, I'm just a bit jumpy," Bronte said.

Griffin slowed down. "Are you ready for your lovely evening camping?"

Bronte nodded.

"Come through to my winter wonderland."

Bronte followed Griffin out into the clearing and gasped. "Oh, Griff."

The trees around the clearing all had Christmas lights hanging from them, the tent had lights around the entrance, and the shelter too.

"Oh my God. It's wonderful, Griff." She threw herself into Griffin's arms. "Thank you."

"Didn't I tell you it wouldn't just be a cold tent in the wilderness? I wanted you to have a Christmas like you never had before."

Bronte leaned in and gave Griffin a simple soft kiss. "You are a special person, Griff. I wish I could know you better."

"It's hard, but I'm going to try."

"Show me around then, and especially this hot tent."

"Personally, I think it'll be hot just because you are in it," Griffin said.

Bronte laughed and pushed her forward. "Show me around, cheeky. Oh, you've finished the roof on the shelter." Bronte went in and sat on the wooden bench. "It's perfect. You lit the campfire and everything."

"Yes, I'm quite perfect, aren't I? Come and I'll show you the tent."

At the entrance to the tent there was a thermometer hanging from one of the tent poles. "What's that for?"

"To prove a point later. If you take your boots off at the door here…"

"My feet will freeze," Bronte moaned.

"Not with five pairs of socks, you won't. In you come."

After taking off her boots, Bronte crawled inside. It was much bigger inside than she had imagined. There were two sleeping bags laid out, some cushions, and a kind of fire stove you'd find in a Victorian house, except much smaller.

"Is that where the heat comes from?"

Griffin nodded. "And the cooking."

Bronte looked up and saw more Christmas lights around the top of the tent. "You've gone to so much trouble, Griff."

"You're worth it. Sit down and I'll get the stove going."

"How does the smoke get out?" Bronte asked.

"You see the metal tube over in the corner? That's the chimney."

"Ingenious."

Griffin got out her kindling and fire starter. "I've got all the logs and wood sticks all prepared over by the chimney. I could have had it going, but then you wouldn't feel the difference. There should be a thermometer hanging near you."

Bronte looked around and saw it.

"Here, take this torch." Griffin threw over the small torch.

"Let's see. Umm…five below. Good God, and it's not even dinnertime yet. I can't sleep in cold like that, Griff."

Griffin grinned. "Just wait."

Bronte watched carefully as Griffin laid some small sticks into the stove. Then on top of the stove she got some kindling and lit it with the striker. She blew on the little ball of fire, as if it had now become a living thing, breathed into existence.

The kindling was pushed into the middle of the wood, and it started to catch fire. She shut the glass door.

"Once the fire builds, I'll put in a few larger logs. Then it'll keep going as long as I keep feeding it with logs."

Bronte sighed. In fact her heart was sighing. "You are amazing, you know that?"

"Why?"

"You did all this for me. Wait, are you leaving earlier than you thought? Are you leaving after Christmas?"

"No, I'm not. Fox hasn't even held any interviews. Let's enjoy the night together. I'm cooking for you again."

Bronte had to let it go and enjoy what time she had left with Griff. "What are you making me? More beans?"

"No, actually. Vegetarian fajitas. Peppers, onions, and veggie chicken."

"On a campfire stove?"

"Yep, hang on. I'll put a few logs in, and we can have a drink."

"Patrick's Rosebrook Christmas beer?" Bronte said.

"What else?"

Griffin got two of the bigger logs and fed the fire. It was going well so far, apart from Bronte's assumption that she was leaving early. It gave Griffin hope that she cared as much as she did. But could she stay? The answer would be if and when she could tell Bronte her truth.

The logs were burning, and the fire was burning nicely. She grabbed two bottles of beer from the cooler she had brought.

"Do you want to drink in here or out by the campfire?"

"The campfire. Then we can come in and enjoy this tropical heat you promised."

"Perfect."

When they got outside, they found the snow was starting to come down slowly. Griffin led her to the shelter and put a few more logs on the campfire.

"This is so Christmassy," Bronte said. "Look at the tent—it looks like it's been sprinkled with icing sugar."

Griffin used her camping utility tool to pop the beer lids off. "If it was in a film, you wouldn't believe it."

Bronte took a swig of beer and shivered. "Cold beer with this temperature? I'm looking forward to a hot tent."

"You just have to trust me."

"Is this the tent you go travelling with?" Bronte asked.

"Not always. I have different tents for different climates. Lighter ones for hot countries, ones for more rainy climates. I have all the right gear, GPS, flares. I've got a wildlife trail camera that you can attach to a tree, and it lets you watch the wildlife on night cam."

Bronte looked at her quizzically. "That's right. You do have all the right gear."

Griffin wasn't sure what Bronte was getting at. "Yeah?"

"I mean, it must have cost a fortune."

Shit, the money. That's what she was getting at. "Well, you pick up bits and pieces along the way."

They were interrupted by Bronte's phone. Bronte looked at it and shouted, "Jesus Christ. It's Mother. She thinks she can't control me any more, so she'll harass me to death."

"Just ignore her. Don't let her calls rile you up, and then she can't win."

Bronte let out a long breath. "You're right."

"I'm often right." Griffin smiled.

Bronte laughed and took Griffin's hand. "That is true. I've never met anyone like you, Griff. You're the tough, woodcutting outdoorswoman, but gentle and kind. I wish you would trust me with your truth."

"I will. I want to share everything with you, but first we're going to have dinner, and then I want to give you your Christmas present."

"You got me a present? How sweet. I got you one. But we can't open them on Christmas Eve, can we?"

"I can't wait, and anyway we'll be rushing to get ready for the Big Dip."

"Hmm. I don't know. Shouldn't we wait for Santa?"

"The Queen opens presents on Christmas Eve. It's from their German heritage."

"Oh well, if the Queen does it, let's go for it."

Griffin clinked her beer bottle against Bronte's. "Perfect."

"How are you feeling about tomorrow? That icy water?"

"It'll be bloody horrendous, but a challenge. I like a challenge, and the medics have reduced the time spent in the water because of the extreme cold weather. But with Fox donating a thousand pounds to everyone who manages ten seconds, it's a no-brainer."

"Who did you choose in the end?" Bronte asked.

"A food bank charity in Manchester. Mum and I had to use food banks often, so I wanted to give back. I've supported them in the past."

Only Bronte didn't know that Griffin actually paid the rent for the food bank facility.

"That's nice. You're thoughtful. Just don't die of the cold. I'm looking forward to spending Christmas Day with you."

❖

"Are you trying to kill yourself?"

Fox's mother's voice boomed across the drawing room. Fox had just explained to her parents, Cassia and Donny, about the Big Dip.

Fox was standing by the fireplace holding her glass of champagne. Donny was on the floor with Lucy, playing with the cats, Agatha and Ada were in the two armchairs nearest the fire, and Clementine was on the couch with her mother-in-law.

"It's for charity, Mum. There's a big tradition of cold water swimming events at Christmas."

"Not when it's like the Arctic outside. This part of England has never been as cold and snowy in my lifetime. We nearly didn't get into the village."

Fox and Lucy had walked up to the west entrance to the village with Jonah and Archie, to carry their bags down to Rosebrook.

"I know, Mum, but it's a challenge. I've been learning a lot about cold weather training and how it helps the body."

Cassia looked at Clementine in despair. "Don't look at me, Cassy. I've tried, believe me."

"She gets this from you, Donny," Cassia said.

"What?"

"It's a challenge, the Big Dip."

Donny stood up and sheepishly shrugged. "It's what makes her a good businesswoman."

"Aggie?" Agatha turned at the sound of Ada's questioning voice. "What are they talking about? A big whip?"

"No, a big dip, I think."

That broke the tension in the room, and they all smiled at the sweet old ladies.

Donny got the decanter and took it over. "Can I top up your sweet sherry, ladies?"

"Oh yes, thank you," Agatha said.

"Such a gentleman," Ada added.

Clementine nudged Cassia and said, "I've already told her that if she freezes, don't come crying to me."

Cassia sighed. "Well, I've said my piece. Can we give Lucy her special Christmas present now?"

Lucy looked up quickly. "I get to open one on Christmas Eve?"

"Yes, just one," Clementine said.

Cassia got an envelope out of her handbag and handed it to Lucy.

Donny couldn't quite contain his excitement. "You are going to love this."

Lucy jumped up full of excitement too.

"This is just one of your presents."

Clementine looked at Cassia with a smile. Cassia was a huge environmental campaigner, much like Fox, and consumption was one of the things Cassia always said was an evil of today's society.

"Consumption, Cassy?"

Cassia softly smacked Clementine's thigh. "Shh. This is our first Christmas with our new granddaughter."

Clementine was so happy that Donny and Cassia had taken Lucy to their hearts as their granddaughter. It was essential to surround Lucy with many people to love her.

Lucy opened the envelope and pulled out tickets. She read them and let out a shriek. "Tickets to *Six: The Musical*?"

"Front row seats," Donny said, "and you get to meet the cast afterwards. I know the producer."

Lucy ran to Donny to give him a hug, then to Cassia. "Thank you so much, Grandma and Grandpa."

Six was Lucy's obsession. She had posters on the wall, played the soundtrack constantly, and followed all the cast on social media.

"We'll make a weekend of it. You come and stay for the weekend, we'll go to dinner. Take you to the Tower of London, so you can see where the queens got their heads chopped off. We'll have so much fun."

Agatha said to Fox, "What tickets did Lucy get?"

"It's a musical about Henry VIII and his six wives."

"Really? I didn't know Henry VIII and Anne Boleyn sang and danced."

Everyone laughed, and Lucy said, "I'll play you the soundtrack, Aunt Agatha."

Fox winked to Clementine, and she knew what she was saying. It couldn't be more perfect. Could it?

Chapter Eighteen

Griffin placed her frying pan on top of the woodstove. She had already dispensed with her jacket and jumper and was down to her plain white T-shirt. When they got back inside from their drink in the snow, the temperature had rocketed up dramatically. Bronte stubbornly kept all her layers on, but her face was bright pink.

"Ready for fajitas?" Griffin said.

"Absolutely, I'm starving."

Griffin got her food bags out of the cool box. Bronte crawled over to watch. "You pre-chopped all the veg? How clever of you. I think you're a better cook than you let on."

"I can do simple things. I enjoy this kind of meal, so I learned."

Griffin drizzled oil into the pan and added the vegetables.

As they sizzled, Griffin said to Bronte, "You're looking a little flushed."

Bronte gave a big sigh and took off her big quilted jacket and her fleece. "Fine, you win, it's really warm."

"Any more layers coming off?"

"Not at the moment."

"That sounds nice. Watch, you'll like this."

Griffin opened the front of her bag and brought out a zipped pouch. "This is where the flavour comes from." She unzipped the pouch, which was full of little tubes of seasoning. "We've got salt, pepper, fajita seasoning, all sorts."

Bronte laughed. "You like all your little gadgets, don't you?"

Dinner was ready in no time, and they both lapped it up.

Bronte put her last bite in her mouth and groaned. "That was amazing."

"Really?" Griffin was so pleased. She was just loving this night.

"Yes, really. God, I have to take another layer off."

"I told you so. Wait, I'll go and look at the outside temperature, and you can check out the inside."

Bronte crawled over to the temperature gauge. She was used to being wrong tonight. When Griffin went out of the tent, Bronte was hit by a blast of cold air.

Griffin came back in and zipped up the tent quickly. "Ten below outside now. What is it in here?"

Bronte looked at the gauge and laughed as she read it out. "Twenty-two degrees. Okay, you definitely win. Your hot tent camping thing really works."

"Thank you. Want another drink? Lager, beer, soft drink, I've even got mini bottles of champagne."

"You are fancy. Could I have a bottle of water? Just to cool down a bit."

"Sure, I'll shut the vents on the stove so it doesn't get any hotter."

"I just can't believe I would be worrying about it being too hot," Bronte said.

"I don't use this all the time when I'm travelling. It's mostly warmer countries I go to." Griffin handed Bronte her water. "Although I did camp with this hot tent in Canada when it was minus thirty. I needed this tent, or I'd be dead."

"Wow. I think even with this tent that would be too much for me."

"Can we do presents now?" Griffin said excitedly.

"If you'd like." Bronte couldn't think what Griffin would get her that excited her so much.

Griffin brought over an old-fashioned hessian Christmas sack. "Open up the sack—there's a few things in there."

"You haven't spent too much money on me, have you?"

"Just take them out."

Bronte pulled out a big box and three smaller packages.

"Open the big one first."

Bronte took off the paper and found a cardboard pet carrier. "You got me a stuffed animal? That's sweet."

"No, it's more than that. Take him out."

Bronte opened the door in front and took out a stuffed toy fox. She looked at the collar round its neck. It said Sox. She checked the white marking on his chest, just like Sox. Then at the back end, he had the same withered back leg.

"Oh my God, it's Sox." She held her hand to her mouth in shock.

"It's an exact replica of Sox that I took from the picture in your kitchen," Griffin said.

Bronte was overcome with tears. She held Sox to her chest to stop her heart from bursting.

"Hey, hey, don't cry."

Griffin came over to comfort her, and Bronte threw one arm around her neck while the other was keeping hold of Sox.

"Do you like him?"

Bronte was stunned. "I don't know what to say. You did this for me? You listened and understood how important Sox was to me?"

"Fox made it possible, but yeah, this was something important in your life, and nobody has recognized the bond you shared, but I do."

"Can I kiss you," Bronte said.

It was what her heart was asking for. Griffin nodded.

Bronte didn't think she was expecting that request. She got up on her knees, leant towards Griffin, and gave her the softest of soft kisses, then rested her forehead against Griffin's.

"Thank you."

Griffin cupped her cheek and then said, "Bronte—No, we can talk later. First open the rest of your presents."

"Okay." Bronte wiped her tears away. "Look at the state of me. Why did you have to make me cry on Christmas Eve?"

"Because I care. Now open them up."

❖

"That's so funny."

Bronte's extra presents were a T-shirt, a mug, and a blanket, all with an original drawing of Sox, which Andre made from Bronte's picture.

"He's a great artist," Griffin said. "He did that drawing from the quick snap I took while you were out of the room."

"It's amazing. Thank you so much," Bronte said.

"Anything to make you smile."

"Open yours now." Bronte crawled over to get the box and handed it to Griffin. "It's heavy."

Griffin felt the weight, "What is it? A paperweight?" she joked.

"Open up."

Griffin took off the paper to uncover a wooden presentation box. She opened it to reveal a hand axe with her name engraved on the head.

"Wow. This is a beautiful hand axe." Griffin lifted it out to feel it in her hand.

"Read the card."

"*When you're travelling all over the world, and you feel like you need a safe haven, come home to Rosebrook. I have lots of wood for you to chop.*"

Griffin realized then that Bronte knew she had feelings for her, and that Bronte had feelings as well, and yet, she was letting Griffin go. Even though Griffin had never shared her truth.

She had to get out.

Griffin put the box on the groundsheet and fled the tent, leaving Bronte nonplussed. "What happened?"

She grabbed her quilted jacket and boots and put them on before going outside. Griffin was standing at the campfire in only her T-shirt, shivering.

"Griff? What are you doing? You'll freeze to death."

She turned around and said, "You were right the first night we kissed. You know nothing about me, and you share everything about you. You offer me a safe haven even though you don't know what I'm running from."

"You are running, aren't you?"

Griffin nodded.

Bronte held out her hand, much as she would do with an animal in pain. "Then come inside and talk to me. I can't harm you no matter what you tell me."

Griffin walked towards her and took her hand. Bronte led them inside. "Why don't you put that stove thingy up full blast, and we can talk."

Before that Griffin picked up her present carefully and took it over to the side of the tent, next to the logs she had piled up.

"I love my axe, by the way. It's the perfect gift."

Once the fire was stoked up, Griffin sat cross-legged on the floor and then dragged her sleeping bag over.

Bronte could see Griffin was still shivering. "Wait."

She got the blanket with Sox's picture on it and draped it around Griffin's shoulders. "Sox will keep you warm."

"Thanks."

Bronte grabbed Sox and held him in her lap. "Tell me what you feel comfortable sharing."

"I don't feel comfortable with any of it, but I feel safe with you. Fox doesn't know this, doesn't know why I'm leaving. You'll be the only one to know."

"Take it slow." Bronte was using all her skills here, trying to keep Griffin from fleeing or feeling trapped.

"I told you my mum was a single parent, and how we struggled when I was growing up. I mean, really struggled."

Bronte nodded.

"This was what I knew about my dad. My mum met Gyles at a music festival—they were both part of that kind of festival crowd."

"Gyles?"

"Gyles Beaufort."

Bronte felt that name was kind of familiar. "I feel like I know that name."

"He was an artist, heavily into drugs and alcohol. My mum had a month-long relationship with him. She found out she was pregnant. Mum said he wanted nothing to do with her and demanded she never contact him again."

Bronte remembered the gorgeous card she saw, the loving words, and the cheque.

"But the card?"

"Listen to the story. We'll get there. I can't tell you how much I hated Gyles. We went without, my mum worrying about money, going to a food bank to tide us over. I despised the guy. I used to dream about what hateful things I would say to him if I ever met him, and my mum I thought a saint for dealing with all that and bringing me up alone."

"It's only natural to feel that animosity," Bronte said. "You were abandoned."

"When I was twenty-one, two lawyers came to our door. Gyles Beaufort had died, and he owned half of Hampshire. Mum knew he was rich, I didn't. It made me hate him more for all the struggles we had. If I was his daughter, then I was his only heir. He left the information in his will that I was to inherit his money and land, but a DNA test was required, because his sister was expecting the money. The DNA proved who I was. I got the lot."

"You inherited the Beaufort millions? Why didn't you tell me about the money? I kept going on about how I didn't want anything to do with anyone who had money."

"I know. I was afraid it would put you off me. I'm sorry. I hated his money, I didn't want it, but I had to take care of Mum, so our lives changed overnight. I hated it, but it made Mum's life comfortable. I decided the only way to deal with it was to use it for good. I travelled the world and helped needy charities in every country and learned from other cultures about brewing. I did my best, but always carrying this baggage of rejection from my dad."

"Then you came to Rosebrook?"

Griffin smiled. "I did, and it's been the happiest time of my life. Good friends, making the world a better place, and making beer. I told Fox it would be short term, just to get the factory up and running, but as time went on, I thought maybe I could finally settle down."

"Really?"

This was so much to take in. Bronte just wanted to hug Griffin for all she'd been through.

"Yeah, but then before you arrived, my mum had a heart attack and the bottom fell out of my world. I spent weeks by her bedside. Luckily, she pulled through. She just needed time to recover."

"It must have been a scary time for you."

Griffin nodded. "It was the worst time of my life. Then my world was turned upside down again."

"What happened?" Bronte asked.

"Mum was getting let out of hospital that day. She sent me home to get some clean clothes for her, that kind of thing. I did a little too much digging. I found a file hidden behind a whole load of boxes."

Griffin opened the zip on her bag and brought out a bunch of cards, similar to the one Bronte had seen.

"This is just a small selection." Griffin handed them to her, one by one. "Easter, birthday, Father's Day, one for the summer holidays,

Christmas. Each hand drawn, each with a large cheque. Hundreds of thousands of pounds. All of them had a loving message, asking to meet me, and if we needed any more money just to ask."

Griffin cried out, "Mum hid this from me my whole life. I had a dad who loved me, and now I'll never know him." Angry tears fell down Griffin's face.

"Hey, come here." Bronte took her in her arms.

Griffin clutched her like she was a life buoy. "He loved me, and she kept it from me for her own spite. He died thinking I hated him."

Bronte felt Griffin's pain and anger so vividly that tears came down her cheeks too. "It's okay, it's okay."

"That's why I wanted to run. I didn't want to run from you. I feel so much for you. I—"

Bronte felt Griffin's lips crash against hers. She was stunned for a second, then passion took over. She entwined her fingers in Griffin's messy hair and felt Griffin pull at her top and take off her bra.

"I want you, Bron."

"Yes," Bronte said.

Griffin took off her own T-shirt and sports bra and pushed Bronte back onto the sleeping bags. Her mouth was on her breast in no time. The feel of Griffin's wet mouth, sucking at her nipple, made Bronte desperate.

"Yes, yes, you've made me so wet, Griff."

Griff pulled off her jeans, and then kicked off her own. "You are so beautiful," Griffin said.

Neither could wait to be skin to skin. "I want to feel you, Griff."

"Yes, baby." Griffin slipped between her legs and began thrusting her sex against Bronte's. "I can feel you're so wet."

"Just like my mouth." Bronte pulled Griffin back to her mouth and kissed her deeply.

Griffin's hips got faster, and Bronte wanted her even closer. She wrapped her legs around Griffin's waist and brought them as close as they could be.

Griff pulled away from her lips and rested her forehead against hers. "Jesus, I'm going to come, baby."

Bronte gasped. "Yes, come on me. Please, please." Bronte's orgasm erupted. She thought she could wait for Griff but couldn't control it. "Oh God, please." Bronte squeezed her legs tight and dug her fingers into the shoulders that she had lusted after. "Jesus, yes, come hard, baby."

"Fuck." Griffin pumped her hips a few more times and shouted, "Jesus."

She collapsed on Bronte and kissed her hard. "I want to be inside you."

Griffin slipped two fingers inside Bronte's opening, and she gasped.

"Faster, it's not going to take—" Bronte came and grasped Griffin's hand to still it.

"More," Griffin begged. "I need to touch you."

Bronte lay with her head on Griffin's chest as Griffin stroked her fingers up and down her arm.

"I love your tattoos. They're so feminine and say so much about who you are."

Bronte leaned up on her elbow. She trailed her fingers over the tribal tattoo she'd discovered on Griffin's chest. Just above her breast was a compass.

"I love yours too. I saw the one on your arm, but I never knew this one was here. It's gorgeous." Bronte let out a breath. "That was the most intense feeling of my life, Griff."

"I just didn't have the words. My head was a mess. I've never tried to explain before."

"You can do it now." Bronte put her hand on Griffin's chest. "Because I care about you, and you are safe."

Griffin nodded. "I know I'm safe with you."

"What did you do when you found the cards?"

"When I got to the hospital, my aunt was there. I threw them on the bed and had a huge argument with my mum. She said she wanted to hurt him the way he hurt her."

Bronte cupped her cheek. "But by hurting him she hurt you."

"I know. My aunt was there and got the nursing staff to put me out. I went out that night and didn't come back for days. When I got home there was a lot of screaming at me. She couldn't understand how hurt I was. I said I was going back to Rosebrook, and Mum said she and my aunt were going on a cruise for Christmas."

"Then you came here?"

Griffin nodded. "I came here, and I met you. Honestly, I wanted to just walk and walk, travel all over the world to make sense of what I'm feeling."

"Tell me exactly how you feel, and maybe I can help. If nothing else, talking about it helps," Bronte said.

"It's the guilt. It makes me feel sick. Gyles obviously had his own demons, coping with alcohol and drug addiction, but I hated him for nothing. I never even met him."

Bronte rubbed Griffin's breastbone in circles trying to relax and soothe her lover. "The cards give the impression he was happy to have a child."

"Yeah, one of the things Mum said was that I would've only gotten hurt. I shouldn't have been around an addict, but maybe when I was older I could have helped him."

"It's the not knowing that's upsetting you?" Bronte asked.

"It's killing me."

"You said he left land as well as the money."

"Yeah, there's a land agent up in Hampshire that looks after it for me. He deals with my lawyer mostly," Griffin said.

"Is there a house on the estate?"

"Yeah, Marchbourgh Castle. It's sounds bigger than it is. When I read up about it, it said it was a tower house with extensions added on later. You'd know more about these things than me."

"A lot of the very old estates started as just a tower house," Bronte explained. "Have you never gone to see it?"

"No, I wanted to sell it when I inherited, but my lawyer said I had a great-uncle living in a gatehouse. Apparently my dad was fond of him and covered his expenses, didn't charge any rent and stuff. The land was earning money, so I just thought, leave it. No need to punish the man."

"He's your only relative on your dad's side that's alive?"

"He had a sister that tried to claim the inheritance, but once the DNA was confirmed, then she disappeared."

The answer was clear to Bronte. "I think you have to go to the house and, more importantly, to your uncle."

"No, I can't." Griffin got up and quickly pulled on her jockey shorts. She crouched by the fire and put another log in.

Damn it. Bronte had been so careful not to push too far, but she certainly had now. She pulled on Griffin's T-shirt, which was huge on her, and went to her lover. She placed a comforting hand on Griffin's back and tried to soothe her.

"I'm sorry. I didn't mean to push you."

Griffin hung her head low. "It's not your fault. It's even more guilt piled on top of what I'm already feeling."

"How so? You've continued to let him live there. You didn't turf him out, even though you had animosity towards the Beauforts at that time."

Griffin wiped her wet eyes and closed the stove door. "My uncle's named Gyles too—Dad must have been named after him. I never started charging any rent. I didn't need it, and my uncle obviously needed a rent-free house, so why be cruel."

"You did a good thing."

Griffin turned around and sat cross-legged on the ground sheet. Lucky they were really warm in here with what little clothes they were wearing.

"Over the years my uncle asked, through the lawyers, to meet me. Of course I never wanted to. The last time he asked was when I went to pick up your gifts from Fox. My lawyer called me before she went on Christmas holidays."

"What did you say?"

"I said I'd need to think about it." Griffin's shaggy hair hung down her face.

Bronte wasn't going to push Griffin and make the same mistake again. "That's a good answer. Not saying never but not committing yourself."

"I wanted to tell you so many times, but I was frightened if I let the feelings out that I couldn't cope."

Bronte took Griffin's hands and kissed them. "That's okay. Thank you for trusting me."

Griffin managed to give her a lopsided grin. "You're not mad that I've got a lot of money?"

"Not a bit. You are the most humble person I've ever met. Just don't tell my mother, or she'll have you down the aisle with me before you can say fortune."

Bronte realized how that sounded. "I didn't mean—ah, it was just a joke."

"I know. I mean who'd want to marry me? I'm an emotional mess."

She doesn't even have the first clue how lovable she is. Maybe I need to show her.

"Let's go back to bed. We can worry about the rest another day. You've got to freeze yourself to death first, and I'll be your biggest supporter on that beach."

"Thanks, Bron. Thanks for listening and not judging. I can't tell you how much I care about you."

Bronte was sure she could. Griffin just needed time.

Chapter Nineteen

Rosebrook had never seen a Christmas morning like this. The beach was busy with participants and supporters there to take part in the Big Dip event.

Clementine stood with Lucy and Fox's parents, watching Fox talk to the local television news. She had to admit Fox's hare-brained idea did tick a lot of boxes.

The extreme nature of the event appealed to Fox's need to challenge herself, but the challenge brought out the news outlets and allowed Fox to explain to a wider public that this weather was abnormal for the climate, and we had to change quickly.

Fox's event manager had everything running perfectly. There was a large inflatable marquee near the boat shop side of the beach. It was climate-controlled to give the participants warmth as they got changed to start, and after they got out of the water and med-checked.

"It seems like a fair few people have decided the dip is not for them," Cassia said.

There were meant to be one hundred participants, but around seventy turned up to register. The rest had failed the medical questions.

"Dr. Blake's medical team have turned quite a few away. It's better to have fewer people who can experience the event more safely, than more do it and get into difficulties."

Fox's dad Donny said, "It's been set up well."

Ash made her way towards them with a big jacket on but still looking freezing. "Merry Christmas, everyone."

"Merry Christmas. Everything okay, Ash?" Clementine asked.

"Yeah, I just left Archie with Fox having their med checks and signing consent forms. Archie said I was annoying her by worrying so much."

"Tell me about it," Cassia said. "You won't convince me it's not a foolish thing to do. I mean, look at the sand. It's white and frosty."

Clementine agreed, but she had learned that to hold Fox back from a challenge was nigh on impossible. So as long as Dr. Blake okayed her, what could she do? One minute with shoulders below the surface would get the money for charity, and hopefully Fox would work this out of her system.

"Is your dad watching, Ash?"

"Yeah, he's up on the pier keeping an eye on things. He thinks it's reckless too."

"I didn't see Griffin in the marquee," Ash said.

"Ah, no. She's running late. I think she and Bronte slept in." Clementine winked at Ash.

"Oh, got you." Ash smiled.

Lucy looked up at them quizzically. Clementine put her arm around Lucy and squeezed her tightly.

"I wish I could do this with Fox," Lucy said sadly.

Clementine shook her head. "Fox is lucky I'm letting her do it, so you have no chance."

Donny gave her a kiss on the head and said, "You're too precious."

Clementine heard her name called.

It was Bronte, as she and Griffin ran down the beach. "Merry Christmas. Sorry we're late."

Both Ash and Clementine had big grins on their faces. "Did you have a nice Christmas morning?"

"Yes, thanks," Griffin said.

They both stood awkwardly until Griffin said, "I better get going. Wish me luck?"

Bronte pulled Griffin into a hug. "Good luck. I'll be waiting for you."

Griffin kissed her cheek. "Thank you."

Clementine had to stop herself from cheering. She hadn't thought herself a romantic soul before she met Fox, but now she wanted everyone to experience what she did.

❖

Griffin quickly got signed up and med checked, then put on her waterproof boots and gloves that were handed out to everyone.

She heard her name called. It was Fox, next to the door of the marquee. She ran over to meet her and Archie.

"Too caught up in your romantic camping, eh?"

Archie sighed. "Fox, maybe she wouldn't like to talk about it."

"Nonsense. You two make a lovely couple."

With one sentence, Fox had coupled her up with Bronte without a moment's thought. Was that what she wanted? Was that what Bronte wanted?

Fox continued, "I've kept a place for you on the first line with us, Jonah, and Christian."

"Very kind of her to ask you, wasn't it?" Archie joked.

The medics and safety team were only letting five swimmers go in at a time. That way they could watch out for everyone, and deal with anyone in difficulty a lot more easily.

Griffin's head was still a mush of emotions, after telling Bronte her story, not being rejected, making love to her, whilst trying to make sense of what would come next.

She followed Fox as she led the swimmers from the warm medical tent into the throng of the beach noise. An MC had been entertaining the onlookers and now was commentating for the crowd.

Griffin could only hear noise, not words. The noise of her mind cancelled out the words.

The only thing that had brought calm to her mind since coming to Rosebrook was Bronte. How could she run away from that? But what if she couldn't handle a relationship—she had only ever disappointed women before.

They stopped just at the edge of where the waves were breaking. They all clenched each other's hands, and then the MC started to count down from ten.

Griffin's guilty thoughts then made more noise. There was an elderly man, her great-uncle, who just wanted to meet her, and she was letting him down, just as she'd let her dad down. Should he die alone like her dad? Without any family around him, just because she was scared?

Bronte said she maybe she should meet him. Should she?

Griffin heard Fox say, "Let's go, guys. Remember, slow your breathing down when you feel the shock of the cold, and not too much swearing. Remember, there's kids about."

Griffin gasped when she placed her feet in the water up to her ankles, but she didn't panic. She remembered what Fox had said and slowed her breathing down.

By contrast, Fox beside her was saying, "Fuck! Fuck! Fuck!" on repeat, despite her warnings.

Griffin's mind had jarred to a halt with the cold rising up her legs. Her vision narrowed to what was in front of her, and she just kept putting one foot in front of the other, each step taking her deeper into the icy cold. But far from hating or forcing every step, Griffin was finding the intensity of the cold both exhilarating and calming.

She didn't look to either side, just kept walking, but it came the time when she needed to duck under up to her neck. Griffin didn't think about the seconds they were meant to stay under, or that she was only required to go up to her neck—when she dunked, Griffin went right under the water.

It was so calm, so still, a stillness Griffin hadn't felt for a long time. As she broke the surface, gasping for air and treading water, things became so much clearer. She looked up at the sky and saw flakes of snow starting to fall. Why walk around with the burden of hate or guilt? Griffin could only deal with life in the now and moving forward.

That meant she should stop running away and travelling all over the world, deal with her father's legacy, and stay with the woman she could see waving from the shore.

The world came back to her in a rush. Griffin gasped and heard the swearing from her friends on both sides.

"What a rush," Griffin shouted.

"How are you fucking doing this?" Archie said.

Both she and Fox were up to their necks but really struggling.

Griffin swam around Fox and laughed. "I thought you trained for this, my friend."

A claxon sounded, and Archie, Fox, and Jonah jumped up so they were above water and heading to shore as quickly as they could. Griffin followed them, and it was only upon coming out of the water that she started to feel the excruciating pain of the cold.

Despite that pain or maybe because of that pain, Griffin never felt so alive. Bronte met her as she stumbled out of the water to the cheers of the crowds.

"Are you okay, Griff?"

A medic came over with a foil blanket and put it around her. "Are you okay?"

Griffin nodded as she tried to get her breath back.

"Go straight to the medic tent to be checked over."

"I was so scared when you went under. Why did you do that?"

To Bronte's obvious surprise Griffin started laughing. She wrapped the foil blanket around them both, picked Bronte up, and swung her around.

"Griff!"

"That was the most exhilarating moment of my life. Apart from kissing you."

Griffin did just that and kissed Bronte deeply. They both turned around when they heard clapping from some of their friends.

She cupped Bronte's cheeks and said, "I want to stay here, with you. No more running. I've found my safe haven."

Bronte sat on the edge of the bath, keeping an eye on Griffin as she took a steaming hot shower. Griffin had been high as a kite since she came out of that water. She went in weighed down by worries, pain, guilt, and confusion over what was happening between them and came out without those heavy weights and a mind that was calm.

Griffin turned off the shower, and Bronte walked over with a towel. She opened the door and said, "Woo, that was the best shower I've ever had."

Bronte couldn't help but be mesmerized by her. Floppy, wet, and sexy hair, a tall, strong body, and now a mind so full of some sort of purpose.

"You seem better than you did."

Griffin dried herself off and wrapped the towel around her bottom half, making her look even sexier somehow.

"I feel amazing. I would love to do that again."

Bronte took her hand and said, "Come with me."

"Okay."

Bronte began to pace backwards and forwards, the emotion of the last few days surging to the surface.

"What happened to you out there? I have been so careful, trying not to spook you, make you run, with all of these terrible emotions you've been dealing with. At the same time I'm trying as hard as I can not to fall for you, because any day, you could be gone. Then last night you tell me everything. Again, I'm trying not to push you, trying to keep my heart safe—then we make love, and I know my heart is going to break when you leave."

"Bron…" Griffin tried to stop her, but Bronte wasn't for stopping.

"You pop into the freezing cold water, I'm terrified about your safety, everyone thinks you've gone mad because you start swimming underwater. After my heart has sprung from my chest with worry, you come out and everything has changed. You don't want to leave, you want to stay, to stay with me, and all your fears are over."

Bronte only stopped because she ran out of breath. Griffin took the opportunity to pull her down onto the bed to sit beside her.

"Listen to me. Let me speak."

Bronte was fit to burst but nodded.

Griffin took her hand. "When I was standing at the shore, my mind was a mess. You know it's been a mess, but one thing I did know was that I didn't want to run any more. I wanted to stay with you, sort out my family, but I didn't know how to do it. When I was at the shoreline, I had so much baggage weighing me down. I took my first steps dragging it behind me, but when I stepped into that frigid cold, the shock was so intense that my mind jarred to a stop, and I felt calm."

"From where I was standing, you were strangely silent. I was really worried. Everyone else was squealing and swearing, especially Fox."

"I got this tunnel vision, and I wanted more of the calm, and the cold was giving it to me," Griffin said.

"But then you dived under. Everyone was worried at that stage. The MC was counting down the time for everyone else, who were barely coping, and you're swimming under like a water baby."

"I experienced such exhilaration—I can't put it into words, but when I came back to the surface those bags of baggage had floated away," Griffin said.

"And what was left?" Bronte asked.

Griffin kissed Bronte's hand. "That I don't want to leave, I want to build a life here, with you, that I'm falling in love with you."

Bronte's heart started to race out of control. She covered her face with her hands for a moment. "You are? I've been preparing myself for you to break my heart." Bronte's emotions started to overcome her. "I'm falling in love with you too."

Griffin took her hand and walked her over to the bed. "Help me warm up?"

Bronte smiled and took off her clothes quickly, then jumped in.

They both groaned when they were skin on skin. Bronte pushed Griffin back when she tried to take control.

"No, you've exerted yourself enough this morning."

Bronte kissed Griffin, taking her time to give her soft licks around her lips. Then she went on to kiss every part of her.

Before she kissed Griffin's sex, Bronte looked up and asked, "Are you warming up now?"

"Yes," Griffin said breathily. "Suck it, baby. Make me come."

"Anything for you."

Bronte peppered Griffin's sex with kisses and licks, then circled her clit before sucking it into her mouth. She didn't stop until Griffin was grasping at her head and coming hard.

"You are so good at that, baby."

Bronte grasped Griffin's hand and put it to her sex. "I need you too."

Griffin pushed her onto her back and split her fingers around Bronte's clit. She kissed and sucked her nipple while her fingers drove Bronte into a frenzy.

"Like that, like that, I'm going to come, shit."

Bronte dug her nails into Griffin's shoulder as she went rigid. It was only when she'd come to her senses that she realized how hard she had dug in her nails.

"I'm sorry, did I hurt you?"

"No, and it just means I'm doing it right." Griffin winked at her.

❖

Griffin had found her happy place, her safe haven, and now it was time for her to make some more decisions.

"Bron, I've decided that I'm going to see my great-uncle. I want to know him, and through him my dad, and visit the house, of course."

Bronte gave her a hard kiss on the lips. "I'm so proud of you. When?"

"I was thinking tomorrow."

"Tomorrow? That's quick. I mean what if Gyles isn't prepared for you to come?"

"He's a pensioner, alone at Christmas. He wouldn't have asked his lawyer to contact mine if he didn't want me to visit soon," Griffin said. "I know it's short notice, but would you—"

"Yes, yes, I'll come." Bronte smiled. "Oh, wait. That was what you were going to ask, wasn't it?"

"Yes, because I need your Land Rover to get through the snow."

Bronte play-hit Griffin on the stomach.

"I'm only kidding, don't beat me up." Griffin laughed. "We'll go together as a couple?" Griffin tested the waters.

Bronte smiled and gave her a peck on the lips. "As a couple. But seriously, how bad was Fox at the cold swim?" Bronte said.

Griffin laughed. "She was jumping around like a big baby. She was the one that trained for it as well."

Bronte glanced at the clock. "Shit. We're going to be late for Christmas dinner. We need to get a shower quick."

"It fits two, you know," Griffin said with a cheeky smile on her face.

"Yes, let's do that."

Chapter Twenty

A h, I couldn't eat another bite," Fox said. "I'm stuffed."
Despite being rushed off her feet. Christmas dinner had been wonderful, Clementine thought. She couldn't have done it without Cassia, and Fox and Donny lifting and carrying the food and drink to the table. As well as the Tucker twins, they had Fergus, who would have been alone. There was a lot more food than she would normally have had to prepare.

Donny lifted his glass of champagne and proposed a toast. "To Clementine and Cassia. Thank you for a wonderful Christmas dinner."

"To Clementine and Cassia," they all responded.

"One more toast," Fox said, "to the ice woman herself...Griffin Harris."

Griffin got a round of applause.

"You won the day, young Griffin," Fergus said.

"Who was it who did the cold water training again?" Donny teased his daughter.

Fox walked around the table filling up glasses. "Very funny. There is nothing and no one who could train for that cold."

Clementine took Fox's hand as she passed. "Don't listen to them, Foxy. You completed it, and there's lots of charities who are that bit richer tonight because of your vision."

"Thank you, Your Graceship." Fox leaned down for a kiss.

Clementine then saw Griffin and Bronte whispering between them. Griffin nudged Bronte and she said, "Clem, we wondered if we could ask a favour of you and Lucy?"

"Anything."

Clementine was so pleased to see these two people come together. Griffin deserved some happiness, and Bronte too. From what she knew of her mum Matilda, it couldn't have been an easy upbringing.

"Could you and Lucy keep an eye on the woodland for me for the next few days? I know we have the cameras and security now, but I still like to check up on the animals."

"Yes, I'd love to do that," Lucy said.

"No problem," Clementine said. "Where are you off to?"

Bronte looked at Griffin and smiled. "To Hampshire. To meet Griffin's great-uncle and look around her land."

Wow. Fox had told her a little of Griffin's background, but she didn't know she had any family left.

"I didn't know you had an uncle," Fox said.

"Yeah, um, Gyles Beaufort. My dad's uncle, he lives on the estate."

"Beaufort?" Fergus said. "That's a fine historical name."

Cassia took a drink and narrowed her eyes. "Was he not an artist?"

"I think so," Griffin said. "I don't know a lot about him."

Clementine grinned. "Of course we'll cover for you." She looked at the clock, and it was ten to three. "Oops, nearly time for the Queen's speech, Aggie and Ada."

"Oh yes, we don't want to miss that."

Fox and Griffin helped them and Fergus through to the drawing room. Once the TV was on, Fox got the Tuckers and Fergus an after-dinner brandy. The two ladies certainly liked a drink.

As the Queen came on the TV, Clementine looked around the drawing room and sighed in contentment. It certainly hadn't been the Christmas she was expecting, but it couldn't have been happier.

It wasn't a long journey from Rosebrook to Marchbourgh Castle, about an hour and fifty minutes. But as they got closer, Griffin's nerves started to make her stomach churn.

"Are you okay, Griff?"

Griffin looked at Bronte in the driver's seat and gave as good a smile as she could. "Just nervous, you know."

"Remember the cold water," Bronte joked.

"Don't worry. I know I'm doing the right thing, doesn't make it any less nervy."

"What do you know about the house?"

"Uh, I looked at a picture on Google once. It had a round tower and a stone extension on the left hand side."

"Is it broken down? In need of repair?" Bronte asked.

"No, it's in pretty good nick I think. My lawyer, Trent, funnels money into basic upkeep of the building, and a security firm patrols a few times a day. There's some expensive artwork apparently, but I never wanted to know the details."

"Maybe when you take possession of it, you can put it to better use," Bronte suggested.

That thought panicked Griffin. "I want to take an interest in my dad and his uncle, but I don't want to move here. I want to stay in Rosebrook with you, brewing beer. That's my safe haven."

"I know. I don't mean move here. I mean put it to better use, like I'm always telling my mother to let the National Trust take over and use it like a proper historic site."

Griffin thought that over quietly.

Bronte continued, "It doesn't have to be anything, just so it could be useful instead of sitting there gathering dust."

"I know what you mean. We'll have to have a good think about it all."

"We?" Bronte smiled.

"Yeah, we are a team now."

Bronte couldn't help smile at that. "That's nice to hear."

She thought about how much her mum would be doing cartwheels at the thought of Bronte being in a relationship with a landed heiress, but no matter what, her mother wasn't getting her claws into Griffin.

"It's the next right, I think," Griffin said.

The area was rural, but there was no village attached to the estate. According to the map app they looked at before they set off, there was a small town, five miles away.

They came to a wrought-iron farm gate that led up a dirt road. "You can see the top of the turret from here," Bronte said.

"I'll get out and open it. Hang on."

Griffin pulled back the gate and jumped back in the car. "Some kind of alarm went off."

"Let's go before we're shot for trespassing."

As they drove up the dirt road, they saw something astonishing.

"Wow, look at the turret," Bronte said.

"I see it, but I don't believe it."

The castle turret was completely covered in bright fluorescent pinks, blues, yellows, and red graffiti paint, but it wasn't the graffiti that ruined town centres and abandoned buildings. It was like impressionist art.

"That is amazing," Griffin said.

"Astonishing. Do you think your dad did that?"

"It must be. He was an artist."

"And a free spirit," Bronte added.

Bronte pulled up the Land Rover on the red chip of the driveway. Griffin got out straight away and walked up to look at the turret in awe.

It was nice to see Griffin pleasantly surprised by her legacy this early in the visit.

She got out to join her and looped her arm through Griffin's. "He was an unconventional artist then."

"Looks like it. Unconventional, a man after my own heart."

Bronte heard the crunch on gravel and then a voice shout, "Hey, this is private property, not an art exhibition."

When Bronte and Griffin turned around, there were two men in security uniforms coming towards them.

"It's okay," Bronte said. "This is the owner, Griffin Harris."

The taller man who appeared to be in charge started to laugh. "She is? She's the owner? You look more like you've come from the nearest squat. Get going before I call the police."

Bronte's defences on Griffin's behalf went straight up. "Excuse me—"

Griffin stepped in front of her. "It's okay, Bron. These nice men are just doing the job *I* pay them to do. I'll get my ID out, and everything will be fine."

Griffin took out her wallet and pulled out her driving licence, then handed it over.

He took it and looked at it briefly. "Griffin Harris? I don't work for Griffin Harris. This property is managed by Trent, Trent, and Masters. That's who pays our company's wages."

Griffin sighed and got out her phone and showed them Trent,

Trent, and Masters in the contacts list. "Now, I can call up Trent and have her confirm who I am. I know she is very particular about her time off with her family, but if you want me to call her on Boxing Day—"

"Gerry, Gerry," a voice behind them said, "I'm expecting them, Gerry. It's young Gyles's girl."

There was a building across the other side of the parking area. The gatehouse, Bronte thought. At the door was an elderly man in tweed suit and bow tie.

"That's him, Griff."

❖

Griffin tried not to visibly shake as she walked over to see her great-uncle. This was as close as she'd be to the dad she had never known, and he was smiling warmly and held out his open arms to her.

"Don't mind Gerry, he's just looking after the place. Look at you. You've got your father's height."

"Do I?"

"Yes, a strapping young lad, he was."

Gyles held out his arms, and Griffin went into them. She held on to him and felt a warmth in her heart.

When they pulled apart, Gyles had tears in his eyes. "Come in, come in."

Griffin followed him into a sitting room. He had an armchair by the fire, and sitting by his chair was a brown and white border collie.

"Beautiful dog," Griffin said.

"That Millie. Say hello, Millie."

She was a well-trained dog. As soon as Gyles gave her the say so, Millie was over to them like a shot.

"Hey, good girl." Griffin ruffled her ears.

As often happened, the dog broke the tension and now it was smiles all around.

Bronte stood awkwardly at the living room door. "Come in, young lady."

"Oh, sorry." Griffin realized she hadn't even introduced Bronte. "This is my girlfriend, Bronte de Lacey."

"Very pleased to meet you, Bronte."

"You too, Mr. Beaufort."

"Gyles, please." He took out his hanky and dabbed at his eyes. He was a dapper country gent, tweed suit, bow tie—Griffin even saw a deerstalker on the way in.

"You'll have to forgive me. I've been dreaming of meeting you for some years."

Immediately Griffin felt the guilt return. "I'm sorry, I should have seen you before now, but I didn't know my dad's story. I didn't know he wanted to know me."

Gyles held up his hand. "Shh, that is for another day. Suffice it to say, young Gyles and your mother didn't have the best of relationships."

"What a gorgeous girl you are," Bronte said.

Griffin smiled. Millie was all over Bronte.

"My girl certainly loves you on sight," Gyles said.

"Bronte's great with animals. She is an animal rehabilitator and just opened an animal sanctuary in our village of Rosebrook."

"Ah yes, you mentioned Rosebrook when you called yesterday. Down in Dorset, you said. That's a lovely part of the world."

"Yeah, it's made me want to stay in one place for once in my life."

"Been travelling, have you?"

"Yeah, backpacking all over the world, but I've just recently realized that I was running away."

Bronte took her hand and squeezed it.

"We all do that at some time in our lives, Griffin. Not to worry."

Millie ran to the fireplace and brought back a stuffed duck to show to Griffin and Bronte. "Ah, that was Millie's present from Father Christmas. I asked my cleaner if she would pick me up a present in town."

It was then Griffin realized that Gyles only had two Christmas cards on the mantelpiece.

"You have a cleaner to look after the place?" Griffin asked.

"Yes, Sarah comes in two days a week. Cleans and launders my clothes and does the shopping for me."

"Have you got any friends nearby?" Bronte asked.

"Most of them have passed on now, or are in poor health themselves, but I've got nothing to complain about. Thanks to Griffin's generosity and her father's before hers, I have this lovely gatehouse to live in, and Griffin's father left me a generous bequest in his will, so life is made comfortable."

Comfortable but lonely, Griffin thought.

"I should get you some tea."

Bronte stood up. "I'll get the tea. You two have a talk. I'm sure I'll find everything."

"Thank you, Bronte. There's a plate of turkey sandwiches I made up for you both. There was lots of it left after Millie and I had our Christmas dinner."

Griffin rubbed her face with her hands. He was alone for Christmas too.

"That's a good girl you've got there, Griffin."

"I know. I nearly ran away from her too, but I came to my senses. She's the eldest daughter of Baroness Lawton."

Gyles furrowed his eyebrows. "I met her once. Bronte is nothing like her mother."

Griffin laughed. "You met her? I think Bronte would be glad for you to think she's different."

"After we've had tea, shall I take you over to the house?"

Griffin nodded. "I'd like that. Uncle Gyles?"

He beamed when she used the title *uncle*. "Yes?"

"I only found out a few months ago that my dad wanted to know me and always tried to provide for me. I found hand-drawn cards in the back of my mum's wardrobe. It destroyed me."

"He used to show me what he'd drawn for you. It hurt him deeply that he couldn't see you. He thought about going to a lawyer quite a few times, but no court in the land would take him seriously with a drink and drug problem."

Griffin said, "I just wish he knew I found out who he was."

"He wasn't a bad boy, Griffin. My brother was a hard man, and an artistic soul like Gyles took his disappointment to heart. I understood him, because like him, I was the black sheep of the family."

"Why?"

He leaned forward and smiled as Bronte came in with the tea tray. "I liked the company of men and not ladies."

"You're gay?" Bronte said.

"Something else we have in common." Griffin smiled.

❖

They walked over the driveway towards the castle. Bronte looped arms with Gyles. Bronte loved him already. He was such a gentleman.

"Did my dad do this?" Griffin asked.

"Yes, about a year before he died. He was constantly trying to find ways, through art, to express himself. Others may think it's loud and garish, but I like it."

Griffin smiled. "Me too, Uncle Gyles."

He took them inside the castle's front door and into a small reception room. The inside of the castle was all dark wood walls and floors. To the left was a staircase, with paintings all the way up.

"That's some of your ancestors. A few rogues among that motley crew," Gyles said.

"I bet." Bronte grinned.

"You said my father's ashes were in the house?" Griffin asked.

"Yes, follow me." Gyles took them through to a drawing room. "Just over here." He pointed to a funeral urn on the mantelpiece. "I wish I could have done more for him."

Griffin shook her head. "It sounds like you were the only one who cared."

"I'll give you and Bronte a few minutes on your own."

Once he was away, Griffin walked up and touched the urn.

"How are you feeling?"

"Like I've failed my dad because I should have been taking care of Uncle Gyles," Griffin said. "I've wandered about the whole world, and I had family here the whole time. I want him with me in Rosebrook."

Bronte kissed Griffin. "You're doing a good thing."

"If he wants to come," Griffin said.

"He will. Come on, wanderer."

Epilogue

Five months later…

Griffin practically skipped home these days. Home was at Bronte's, and not her cottage. When she came out into the back garden, she saw Bronte and Lucy feeding the fox in the pen. He had been found at the side of the road and brought to the rescue. Bronte and Lucy nursed him back from death's door.

Bronte had another fox, but she was in the fox yard at the back. She was also taking care of a badger and an owl. The rescue centre was in full swing.

She looked into the summer house and saw Uncle Gyles sitting chatting with his new friend Fergus. They'd got on like a house on fire since Gyles moved to Rosebrook.

Her uncle had his own cottage, but he liked to come up most days to see Bronte and read his paper in the summer house. Luckily his dog Millie was very good with the animals.

Griffin waved to the two older gentlemen and walked over to Bronte just as Lucy was on her way to check on the other animals.

"How was your day, baby?" Griffin asked.

"Good, Little Nicky here is doing very well. I hope he can go in the fox yard soon."

"Have you thought about what I asked you yet?" Griffin said.

"Yes, about the house?"

"You let me pay off the debt of your house, and when it comes to you, we'll allow the National Trust to run it, without giving over ownership, and we'll do the same with my house."

"It's a lot of money. I swore I would never take money to save that house," Bronte said.

"If you don't, then a private owner will get it, and the National Trust will have lost access to the oldest house in London."

Bronte sighed. "I suppose it would be better to keep it, so that I can do the right thing when I inherit."

"Exactly."

"But I have a condition. I want us to go and visit your mum."

Bronte had persuaded Griffin to contact her mum again. They had shared a few phone calls but hadn't met up yet. Bronte was certain that her partner needed to rebuild that relationship that had once been so strong.

Griffin nodded. "I will do that. I need to build bridges with her, and I want to show her what a beautiful woman I have fallen in love with, but do you remember the catch?" Griffin smiled.

"That I have to marry you? That's no catch, Griff. I love you."

Griffin gave her a soft kiss. "I love you too, baby. Thank you for giving me my safe haven."

"Oh, I will marry you, but there's just one more question. Who is going to phone Mother about the money? You or me?"

"Oops, I think I hear Uncle Gyles shouting for me."

Griffin was off like a shot.

"It's me then, I guess."

She took out her phone and dialled her mum's number.

"Hello, Mother, I've got some news…"

About the Author

Jenny Frame is from the small town of Motherwell in Scotland, where she lives with her partner, Lou, and their well-loved and very spoiled dog.

She has a diverse range of qualifications, including a BA in public management and a diploma in acting and performance. Nowadays, she likes to put her creative energies into writing rather than treading the boards.

When not writing or reading, Jenny loves cheering on her local football team, cooking, and spending time with her family.

Jenny can be contacted at www.jennyframe.com.

Books Available From Bold Strokes Books

A Haven for the Wanderer by Jenny Frame. When Griffin Harris comes to Rosebrook village, the love she finds with Bronte de Lacey creates a safe haven and she finally finds her place in the world. But will she run again when their love is tested? (978-1-63679-291-0)

A Spark in the Air by Dena Blake. Internet executive Crystal Tucker is sure Wi-Fi could really help small-town residents, even if it means putting an internet café out of business, but her instant attraction to the owner's daughter, Janie Elliott, makes moving ahead with her plans complicated. (978-1-63679-293-4)

Between Takes by CJ Birch. Simone Lavoie is convinced her new job as an intimacy coordinator will give her a fresh perspective. Instead, problems on set and her growing attraction to actress Evelyn Harper only add to her worries. (978-1-63679-309-2)

Camp Lost and Found by Georgia Beers. Nobody knows better than Cassidy and Frankie that life doesn't always give you what you want. But sometimes, if you're lucky, life gives you exactly what you need. (978-1-63679-263-7)

Fire, Water, and Rock by Alaina Erdell. As Jess and Clare reveal more about themselves, and their hot summer fling tips over into true love, they must confront their pasts before they can contemplate a future together. (978-1-63679-274-3)

Lines of Love by Brey Willows. When even the Muse of Love doesn't believe in forever, we're all in trouble. (978-1-63555-458-8)

Only This Summer by Radclyffe. A fling with Lily promises to be exactly what Chase is looking for—short-term, hot as a forest fire, and one Chase can extinguish whenever she wants. After all, it's only one summer. (978-1-63679-390-0)

Picture-Perfect Christmas by Charlotte Greene. Two former rivals compete to capture the essence of their small mountain town at Christmas, all the while fighting old and new feelings. (978-1-63679-311-5)

Playing Love's Refrain by Lesley Davis. Drew Dawes had shied away from the world of music until Wren Banderas gave her a reason to play their love's refrain. (978-1-63679-286-6)

Profile by Jackie D. The scales of justice are weighted against FBI agents Cassidy Wolf and Alex Derby. Loyalty and love may be the only advantage they have. (978-1-63679-282-8)

Almost Perfect by Tagan Shepard. A shared love of queer TV brings Olivia and Riley together, but can they keep their real-life love as picture perfect as their on-screen counterparts? (978-1-63679-322-1)

The Amaranthine Law by Gun Brooke. Tristan Kelly is being hunted for who she is and her incomprehensible past, and despite her overwhelming feelings for Olivia Bryce, she has to reject her to keep her safe. (978-1-63679-235-4)

Craving Cassie by Skye Rowan. Siobhan Carney and Cassie Townsend share an instant attraction, but are they brave enough to give up everything they have ever known to be together? (978-1-63679-062-6)

Drifting by Lyn Hemphill. When Tess jumps into the ocean after Jet, she thinks she's saving her life. Of course, she can't possibly know Jet is actually a mermaid desperate to fix her mistake before she causes her clan's demise. (978-1-63679-242-2)

Enigma by Suzie Clarke. Polly has taken an oath to protect and serve her country, but when the spy she's tasked with hunting becomes the love of her life, will she be the one to betray her country? (978-1-63555-999-6)

Finding Fault by Annie McDonald. Can environmental activist Dr. Evie O'Halloran and government investigator Merritt Shepherd set aside their conflicting ideas about saving the planet and risk their hearts enough to save their love? (978-1-63679-257-6)

The Forever Factor by Melissa Brayden. When Bethany and Reid confront their past, they give new meaning to letting go, forgiveness, and a future worth fighting for. (978-1-63679-357-3)